USA TODAY BESTSELLING AUTHOR

DALE MAYER

A Psychic Visions Novel

STRING OF TEARS

STRING OF TEARS
Beverly Dale Mayer
Valley Publishing Ltd.

ISBN-13: 978-1-773367-15-6
Print Edition

Books in This Series:

Tuesday's Child
Hide 'n Go Seek
Maddy's Floor
Garden of Sorrow
Knock Knock…
Rare Find
Eyes to the Soul
Now You See Her
Shattered
Into the Abyss
Seeds of Malice
Eye of the Falcon
Itsy-Bitsy Spider
Unmasked
Deep Beneath
From the Ashes
Stroke of Death
Ice Maiden
Snap, Crackle…
What If…
Talking Bones
String of Tears
Inked Forever
Insanity
Soul Legacy
Coveted

Boxed Sets and Bundles
https://geni.us/Bundlepage

About This Book

Jewel wakes up in the hospital, with no memory of what happened to her or no reason why she was found on the highway—dead. As reawakening goes, this one is brutal, but even more confusing is her instinctive grasping for a missing necklace around her neck. Had she been robbed, beaten, and dumped? If so, why? She has few friends and even fewer family members left to care, but, unlike his name, Hurricane walks into her hospital room and becomes a safe harbor for a world gone nuts.

Hurricane had been asked by Stefan to help Jewel and to take possession of a necklace, if it was deemed dangerous. Hurricane has seen a lot of dangerous and crazy things in his life, but Jewel's current state is something new to him.

As the dangerous storm heightens around them, Hurricane's task—keeping Jewel safe, as she tries to regain her memories and her sanity—slips even further away …

Sign up to be notified of all Dale's releases here!
https://geni.us/DaleNews

CHAPTER 1

HURRICANE STEPPED OUT onto the deck of his Maine coastal home and watched as the Atlantic Ocean crashed over the beach. He loved it here; something about the storms electrified him. But then that was his specialty; it's what he did. That he was a climatologist was something else again. He hadn't fully utilized his education very much in the last ten years. He needed to help put out too many other electrical storms or energetic storms instead. And this last one had been a prime example—tarot cards that could kill. "What the hell?" he muttered. He shook his head.

He lifted his face into the wind and let it pour over him. When he heard Stefan's voice in the back of his head, he smiled. "That was a hell of a journey you sent me on."

But I knew you could handle it, he stated. *Besides, you were already in New Orleans.*

"Yep, and I was hoping to spend a couple days there," he muttered. "Not turn around and bolt."

You still can. I'm sure they would like to see you again.

"That Skylar is pretty amazing," he noted.

You have no idea, Stefan muttered. *The things she can do with the dead are something I've never seen before.*

"Okay, now you've got me fascinated."

I might have, he agreed, *but we have another problem.*

"What the hell is that?" he asked, with an eye roll. "You

know that I thought all this stuff would help, but instead it seems like the energy just keeps getting crazier and crazier."

You're right. It does, and I'm not sure what's going on with this one though.

"In what way?"

I think it concerns all your trips, collecting all these items and putting them in the museum.

"Yeah. What are you getting at?"

I have a jeweler, who has been putting a lot of emotions into the designs she makes, and, of course, that's making her products very attractive.

"That's smart of her. So what about it?"

She contacted me.

"About what?"

A string of pearls she's trying to repair.

"*Uh-oh.* Don't tell me. Teardrops?"

A whole string of them. Pearls are known to be the tears of the ocean.

"Sure, and?"

Every time she goes to repair this necklace, she gets visions of murders. One for every pearl.

He sucked in his breath. "Good God, are you serious?"

Yes, very serious, and I've done just enough surface digging to understand that an awful lot of energy is infused into these gems. The problem is, she seems to think that maybe whoever created this necklace had a matching bracelet, and he wasn't quite done with the job.

"Who is this person, the jeweler you're talking to?"

She lives in Maine, which is another reason for contacting you, since you're right there. … Her name is Jewel.

"Jewel. Jewel. Jewel. I don't think I know anybody by that name."

No, but you're likely to.

"Why is that?"

Because she just resurrected from the dead.

JEWEL OPENED HER eyes, the same panic choking her, as she bolted upright, swinging her arm against a bed rail. Machines beeped at her side, and a nurse came running.

"You're fine. You're fine," she reassured her, "and we're more than happy to have you awake."

Jewel stared at the nurse in shock. "What happened?" she murmured.

"We don't know everything," she began, "but basically you died and came back."

"I died?" Jewel asked in shock.

The nurse smiled. "Yes, but it's fine. You'll be just fine." The nurse stared at her with a big grin and added, "You've been very, very lucky."

Jewel nodded slowly, waited while the nurse checked everything, and then withdrew. Jewel wanted to ask a million questions, but, at the same time, she didn't want to ask any. She had no idea what had happened. Whatever had put her in the hospital was a complete blank. Did she have an accident? Was she having surgery? She didn't know.

She heard a man's voice in the background, somewhere in the dark recesses of her brain, telling her, *You better not say anything. You* better *not say anything. Or else.*

She didn't know what the "or else" meant, but she knew it was something important. Her fingers went to her throat, reaching for something that belonged there, something that was always there, a necklace. But not now. She looked around for it, but, of course, no personal belongings were allowed in the hospital. She kept clawing at her throat, prodding her memory to return. When the nurse returned, Jewel asked her, "My necklace, do you know where it is?"

The woman frowned. "Sorry, you didn't have on a necklace." She stopped and then calmly explained, "Honestly you didn't have a stitch on. We don't have ID for you. You didn't have any clothing, nothing. Nobody knows what happened or how you came to be found at the front of the hospital, completely nude but not a mark on you."

She stared at the nurse in shock. "My name is Jewel," she stated. "And I really need to get back that necklace."

The woman shrugged. "The doctor is on his way," she said gently. "You can talk to him about it." She held out a glass of water. "Here. Take a sip."

Jewel immediately took one swallow of water, and then, as if her body suddenly realized what water was, she sucked back the entire glass.

The woman raised her eyebrows. "Well, that's a good sign."

Jewel nodded. "Did you say I didn't have any clothes on?"

"You didn't have anything on, but, at the same time," she repeated, "you also didn't have a mark on you, so we don't know what happened."

"Good God," she murmured. She stared down at the hospital gown that covered her, and then she looked at her arms and the bruises all over her wrists and higher up. "If I didn't have a mark on me," she asked, "where did these come from?"

"Well, that's just it," the nurse added. "Bruises show up after any trauma but later on. We're still trying to figure out what happened though. So, if you remember anything at all, it would be a really good thing," she noted.

But Jewel just stared at her, shook her head, and said, "I can't remember anything."

CHAPTER 2

J EWEL STARED AROUND the pristine white hospital room, wondering how she could push past the clouds in her brain and get answers for the doctor, who stood here staring at her. Once again, she shook her head very gently and repeated, "I have no idea what happened." Her voice was no more than a murmur. Even that was hard to do.

His lips twitched, and the creases between his eyebrows deepened. He looked down at the tablet in his hand thoughtfully. "I don't see any physical issues. You don't appear to have any internal damage. Outside of the amnesia that you're experiencing …"

He let his voice trail off, and she knew he would say something about it being time to release her.

She pointed to her arms and asked, "What about the bruising?"

His frown deepened yet again. He almost gave a quick headshake, as if to say he had no clue. She'd already gotten that message loud and clear but figured it was worth a shot to ask him.

He sighed. "They all showed up after you were brought back to life. Bruises can take anywhere from an hour, mind you, to quite a few hours to show up," he admitted. "But not usually forty-eight hours."

She stared down at the bruises, wondering what possibly

could have happened to cause this damage.

The doctor asked once again, "And you don't remember, do you?"

No criticism tinged his tone, just exasperation, as if he wanted the answers and he wanted them now. This man was used to getting what he wanted and was stymied by the current situation.

Once again, she looked up at him and gave an almost imperceptible shake of her head. Just enough for him to acknowledge her lack of recall.

He sighed. "I'll arrange for the paperwork to let you go then." He smiled. "You may want to check in with your doctor in a little while."

"Now, if only you could tell me who that doctor is," she replied, with a humorous note.

Again he looked at his tablet. "Without a full name for you, we don't have one in your file, don't have much in your file."

"No, of course not, but an address, right?"

Startled, he frowned at her. "You don't know where you live?"

"I have some memories of it, and I think whatever happened to me happened there," she replied. "I gather no next of kin is noted in my file either, right?" She looked like a deer caught in headlights, just waiting to be run over.

Once again, he slowly shook his head, clearly feeling sympathetic to her plight. "No, nothing," he admitted. "I can release you into extra care, where we can have somebody look after you until you regain your memories, but that's expensive. It's a specialized program and not covered by insurance."

She raised her hand to cut him off. "I'll be fine," she

replied briskly. "I'll head home, as soon as the nurse has the paperwork ready."

"It'll be ready as soon as I say you're dismissed. Just go to the front desk," he shared. "We're a relatively small hospital, and people do multiple jobs here when needed." Then he gave her an encouraging smile.

She hesitated, and his sharp gaze searched her face again. "What? Are you remembering something?"

Her lips twisted. "No, I'm not, except I was told I came in with no clothes on, and now that you're releasing me, I still have no clue what happened, and I can't leave here naked."

He stared at her. "And again we're back to the fact that you have nobody to help you, right?"

"I don't think so." She pondered the issue and then asked him, "I don't suppose a Lost and Found is here, is there?"

A smile flashed on his face. "Absolutely there is. I'll have the nurse take you there and help you with everything." And, with that, he was gone.

If he took a certain amount of joy in being able to run as far and as fast as he could, she could hardly blame him. This wasn't exactly your standard accident case, involving a victim with very obvious injuries. Instead Jewel was a complete anomaly to him, and she had no idea what had happened to her. She reached up once again, her hand at her neck, trying to figure out what had happened to the necklace, a necklace she couldn't remember enough to describe.

Everything seemed plucked out of her brain in regard to it, except the one haunting memory. Vague and haunting. *Important*, she knew that much. She just didn't know why.

When a nurse bustled in a little while later, she wore a

bright smile. "So, the good news is you're leaving."

At that, Jewel just nodded and waited.

"More good news," she added, as she held up a couple pieces of clothing. "Now these are definitely not high fashion, but I think they might work. Leggings are amazing, and somehow anybody can fit in them, especially when the material is stretchable," She looked at her critically. "You're pretty slim, but you are tall," she noted, giving Jewel a once-over. "So these will probably work, but they might not come to your ankles, being short a little bit."

Jewel smiled at that. "I appreciate anything. Going out nude didn't seem like a great idea, but, hey, whatever it takes, right?"

The nurse gave a startled laugh. "No. We wouldn't let that happen. Absolutely not."

"If no other way, that's just the way it would be," she murmured.

The nurse looked at her, puzzled. "Are you sure that I can't call someone to help you?"

At that, Jewel stared and shook her head. "Nobody I can remember."

The other woman sighed. "I really hate to see you go out into the world like that, with only part of your memories and nobody to help you."

"I don't think I've had anybody to help for quite a while," she shared, frowning, looking off in the distance. "But it's all a distant memory, so I don't know what memories I can trust and what I can't."

"That's another problem," the nurse agreed. "For a while your memories will seem suspect. You won't know whether things are true or not. Something will trigger what seems like a perfect memory, and then something else will happen that seems to contradict it, and you won't know what to think. I just want you to know that is normal."

At that, she chuckled. "*Great.* That'll be a fun experience."

"You do need to see a doctor fairly soon and make sure those bruises heal."

At that, Jewel slowly sat up and asked, "Did you happen to find any other clothing?"

The nurse winced. "No underclothes, but I do have a sweatshirt. It's a men's medium but not too big."

"It's fine." Jewel gave a wave of her hand. "It covers the basics, so I sure won't complain. I had no purse or anything, right?"

"No, nothing at all," she confirmed. "No personal identifying marks either. If you didn't know your name, we would have been hard-pressed to find your records."

"But I do remember my name," she stated. She smiled her thanks at the nurse, who quickly disappeared. Something about Jewel made everybody uncomfortable here, whether the lack of answers or her oddly calm demeanor throughout the whole ordeal, she didn't know. But it seemed foolish to panic about something she couldn't even understand. Besides, what good would it do?

Maybe the panic would hit when she got to a house she didn't know or items in the house she didn't recognize. Not knowing where to find anything would be frustrating. She knew something important happened here, and she figured the memories were just sitting in the back of her head, almost welling up, just waiting for something to make it overflow into her consciousness.

She grabbed the clothing and headed into the bathroom, where she quickly changed from the hospital gown into the leggings and sweatshirt the nurse had found for her. Such an odd thing to not wear underwear. She'd gone without a bra many times, or so she thought, but to not have underwear made for a very strange sensation of something being very off in her world. She wasn't against the feeling; it just felt odd, the skin more sensitive, the bruising more painful, the fabric exacerbating everything. Yet her feet seemed happy to be shoeless.

But the sooner she could get to her home, the sooner she could start getting answers … and maybe her own clothing. Of course getting home would be her next issue, and it wasn't the hospital's problem. Jewel understood that, but how was she supposed to pay for a cab to get there? She had no phone, nothing. When she stepped out of the bathroom, she froze.

A man almost filled the doorway, both from side to side and from bottom to top.

She stared at him, wondering at the weird sensations circulating around her, almost analyzing and assessing. Something weird was definitely happening. She stared at him and bluntly asked, "Who are you?"

His lips crooked upward. "My name is Hurricane."

Her eyebrows shot up. "That's not a name. That's more like a nickname."

"In my case, it's also my legal first name," he stated, with a half smile. "My parents were both climatologists. Apparently my arrival in this world was very much like a hurricane and occurred during a hurricane, so they thought it an appropriate moniker."

"That must have been hell going through school," she stated bluntly.

"It had a certain cachet to it. Some kids thought it really

cool, and others pretty much just pitied me."

"Who has time for pity?" She waved her hand. She took a step forward and dropped the dirty hospital gown onto the bed. "But more to the point, what are you doing here?"

"Somebody sent me."

At that, she stilled and then turned and looked at him directly. A name slid through her mind. Going on instincts, she asked, "Stefan?" Hurricane's eyebrows shot up, and he slowly nodded. Relief washed through her. *Thank God.*

"How did you know he'd sent me?" Hurricane asked curiously.

"I didn't. But he collects people, strange people." What a weird thing to say. Yet it felt right. Memories stirred within those feelings, with shadows of conversations coming to the forefront.

"So, would that be me, or is it you?" he asked, matching her bluntness.

She stared at him for a moment and then smiled. "I would think that both of us are strange to the rest of the 'normal' world."

At that, he burst out laughing.

She asked shrewdly, "Did you ever have the feeling that nobody understood who you were and that people looked at you sideways and avoided you?"

"All the time," he confirmed, nodding. "You?"

"Sure. We're in that weird world, where we try to fit in and where we try to appear normal, but we aren't. So we can't fit in, and sometimes we just don't want that either."

"Agreed," he murmured. "Are you ready to go?" He looked at her attire, and a tiny smile played at the corner of his lips.

"I know, but this is all that the Lost and Found had to

offer." She looked down at the leggings that crept up her ankles and the sweatshirt that slid down her hips. "But I'm covered at least, so I really don't care."

"What happened to your clothes?" he asked curiously.

She stared at him and then answered honestly. "I have no idea. Apparently when I arrived, I didn't have any on." At that, his gaze narrowed, and something cold crept onto his features. She shrugged. "Now don't ask any more questions because I don't have any answers myself."

"Oh, I'll be asking lots of questions," he countered cheerfully. "Let's hope at some point in time in the next twenty-four hours that you'll have some answers."

"Oh, I have to follow that time frame? Why?"

He replied, "I don't know yet, but it has to do with the energy flowing through this town."

She sucked in a breath. "Something is almost familiar about that statement."

He looked at her curiously. "You really don't remember anything, do you?"

"No," she murmured, "and, if you keep commenting about that, it'll just make me angry. And I'm already irritable, in case you didn't notice."

"Why is that?" he asked casually.

"Because obviously I want to know what's going on, and obviously I need to know," she declared, trying to still the angry passion rising in her voice. "To not know anything beyond my first name is just … almost poisonous."

"It's hurtful," Hurricane confirmed. "It's frustrating, and it allows you to slide back into victim mode a little too easily. So I can understand."

"I am not a victim," she replied, her tone sharp.

"Glad to hear that," he murmured, but his gaze intensified, as he stared at her.

She groaned. "I don't suppose you're here to take me home, are you?"

"Are you ready to go home?"

"I am very much ready to go home." She brushed past him into the hallway. She stilled as the onslaught from the hospital hit her. Energy slammed into her—both alive and dead. She immediately shut down everything inside her.

He murmured, "That's interesting."

She hesitated, then turned and looked at him. "What?"

"You didn't do that before."

She nodded. "You're right, and again I don't have an answer as to why I didn't."

"You didn't because you didn't notice that you needed to," he offered, his voice soft and gentle. "For whatever reason, that room was a haven for you."

She looked back at the room and then the hallway that she was only one step into and admitted, "A part of me wants to run right back inside again."

"Why is that?"

"Because, as much as I hate to admit it, you're right. That room is a safe place—a haven, as you called it—and now that I'm out of it, I'm no longer safe."

HURRICANE FOLLOWED JEWEL, who chose to leave her safe hospital room. He was intrigued, as she walked as if she were a model, having absolutely zero care about the mismatched and ill-fitting clothes she wore, making them look like they were designer's editions and were fully intended to be exactly as they were. It took a lot of self-confidence to pull off something like that. He was quite delighted to see that aspect of her personality. What was coming up ahead could be pretty tough, depending on what she'd already been through. She would need every ounce of confidence she could muster.

That self-confidence was also likely how she'd ended up in this predicament too. But Hurricane may be jumping the gun on that. When they stepped outside of the hospital, she took several slow deep breaths, her eyes closing, her arms opening wide. He watched in surprise.

She looked over at him and shrugged. "Qigong."

He grinned at her. "That should help."

"It should." She looked down at her discolored arms. "I should have been doing it for the last day apparently."

"Yet do you remember?"

"No. Only when I stepped outside and felt the fresh air and smelled Mother Nature, it was a reflex," she replied. She stopped, tilted her head, then frowned at him. "I think I used to do this outside every morning."

He nodded. "That would make sense too. Of course, energy systems always prefer to be outside in the fresh air, when you're working them."

"Do you know Qigong?" she asked.

"Tai Chi. I've certainly seen and understood some of the Qigong movements," he replied. "That doesn't mean that I can do it better."

She took another slow deep breath, and he could almost visibly see the energy and stress start to dissipate from her tense shoulders.

"Feel better?" he asked.

"I do," she murmured. "Now where to?" she asked, looking at him specifically.

He smiled. "I have a Jeep Cherokee in the parking lot."

"Of course you have a Jeep in the parking lot," she noted

in a dry tone, repeating his words sarcastically.

He raised an eyebrow. "What's wrong with a Jeep?"

"Nothing at all." She chuckled. "You definitely look like a Jeep kind of guy."

He wasn't sure what to say to that, so he said nothing, just pointed out the Jeep a couple vehicles ahead of them in the parking lot. A few moments later, he stated, "I need your address."

"No, you don't." When he stopped and stared, she shook her head. "You already have it."

"You're right. I do," he confirmed. "What made you so sure?"

"Stefan."

He nodded. "What is your relationship?" He reached for the fob in his hand and unlocked the Jeep, then opened the passenger side for her. She stared at him for a moment and then accepted his assistance into the front passenger seat. Closing the door quietly, he walked around and hopped into the driver's seat, turned on the engine, and looked at her. "You didn't answer."

"No, I didn't." She shrugged. "We're both energy workers … and obviously you are too."

He gave a clipped nod in response. "At least we got that out of the way. It makes life a little easier."

"Sometimes, not always. I don't do very much with it, never have," she admitted. "I just try to infuse my art pieces with love and positive energy for the people buying them." She gave him a flat stare. "Some of the stuff that I've heard Stefan can do is pretty out there."

Hurricane chuckled. "Yeah, it sure is. I just came from a case where what one woman could do was very out there."

"Tell me about her," Jewel said.

He looked at her, hesitated, then shrugged. "I'm not sure that's my story to tell."

At the silence that followed, he glanced over at her. "Sorry."

"No, that's fine," she replied, her voice soft. "It's nice to know that you will keep a confidence, if needed."

"It's part of my job."

"Maybe so, but I think there's a whole lot more to it."

"I'm glad you remember that much of your life."

"I wish I remembered what happened to me."

He nodded, as he pulled away from the hospital parking lot and out onto the main road. He watched the scenery flash by and yet kept half an eye on her the whole time. She appeared to be completely unaffected by any of the surroundings. She stared straight ahead, looking calm and relaxed, until his gaze landed on her hands and saw how her fingers were clenched tightly to the point that her nails were digging into her palms. He reached over with his right hand and gently covered her hands. "Easy," he muttered. "I don't know what we'll find at your house, but I won't walk away until I know you're safe."

Her laugh was bitter, harsh. "That could be, but, if I don't know what happened in the first place, how will I know what's coming my way?"

"You have zero memories of the event?"

"Zero," she confirmed.

"How about on an energy level?"

She looked at him, frowning. "Remember when I told you that I infuse my pieces with joy and love? How is it even possible for that to put me in this position?"

"Stefan mentioned something about you repairing a necklace."

Her hand immediately went to her neck. His gaze went back to the traffic, and he quickly changed lanes and put on a signal to take the left-hand turn at the next intersection. "You don't remember a necklace?"

"The necklace is important," she noted, "but I don't know why. I don't know where it came from or what it is, … but I feel like it was around my neck and should be there."

Hurricane added, "According to Stefan, you were given a piece to repair, and you felt like every pearl in the necklace was a soul."

She gave a harsh laugh. "Seriously?"

"Yes, seriously. Feel free to contact Stefan yourself."

"I will because I have absolutely no memory of that."

Under his breath he couldn't help swearing. He glanced at her but saw absolutely no guile in her face. "That complicates things."

"You think?" she quipped, staring at him, her gaze huge wells of pain.

"You don't remember the necklace, and you don't remember what you told him?"

"No, I don't know who gave me the necklace or anything about it. I do know that it is important." She reached for possibly her phone, only to realize she didn't have one. "I need a phone and fast."

He pulled a spare that he kept for emergencies from his pocket and handed it to her.

"I can't use your phone," she said. "I need one of my own."

"It's a spare, something I would call a burner phone. Something I can throw away, if I needed to hide my tracks."

She snatched it from his hand, and her fingers immediately brought up the keypad to make a call, dialing Stefan's number, without even stopping to think about it. Instinctively she put it on speakerphone.

When Stefan's voice filled the front of the cab, she said, "Stefan, it's Jewel."

"Oh, thank God. How are you?"

"Empty," she murmured.

Shocked silence filled the other end. "In what way?" Stefan asked, caution in his tone.

"I don't know anything about the necklace, but my hand keeps going to my neck, and I know it's important. I know that … it was around my neck and should still be there."

"Interesting."

"Hurricane just told me something about souls in the pearls?"

Hurricane noted her anxious tone. He felt her tension take over the vehicle.

"And you don't remember anything about it?" Stefan asked.

"No, I don't remember anything about the necklace nor about what happened to me."

"Okay, don't panic. Obviously we need to figure this out. So you didn't have the necklace when you were found?"

"I had nothing on me, not a mark, not a stitch of clothing, let alone a piece of jewelry," she stated, her free hand going to her ear, frowning, as she realized no earrings were there either.

Hurricane kept an eye on the traffic, while trying to keep an eye on her to see her reactions. Once he took the next corner, he cut several more corners and then pulled up in front of a small bungalow.

He shut off the engine and said, "Stefan, we just arrived at her house."

"Call me back when you've been through the house," Stefan ordered. "Let me know how it feels." And, with that, he hung up.

Hurricane looked over at her. "You ready?"

She stared down at the phone, looked over at the house, and then he realized. "You don't recognize the house, do you?"

She stared at it. "Is that my address?"

"It is."

"Then it must be my house." She opened the vehicle door, hopped out, and determinedly walked up to the front door.

Not at all sure what was going on, he raced behind her. When they got to the front door, she stopped, looked down at her bare hands. "I don't have a key."

He reached forward and turned the handle. The door opened. As she stepped inside, she gave a soundless whistle. He stepped in behind her and looked around. "Barely any furniture."

"What there is, isn't really of value," she noted. "Am I broke?" Her tone was now curious, analytical, than horrified. She walked through the room swiftly, headed straight to her bedroom. The bedroom closet held a few women's clothes, mostly outerwear, and not really a substantial amount, with little personality reflected in this apparel. Nothing revealed a whole lot about who she was or what she did for a living.

Waiting, he couldn't quite decipher the look on her face. "What's the matter?"

"What's the matter?" she asked, her voice rising. "Are you sure this is my house?"

"It's registered to your name."

She stared at him blankly.

"You don't remember it?"

She shook her head. "No, but it's more than that. This is not where I worked. I suspect this was a house but not my home."

"It's got furniture and coats, jackets."

She nodded slowly, looking at him. "I don't know what to say." She threw out her arms wide, as she spun around, looking at everything there. "Except to say that this is not where I was recently."

"So where was that?"

She turned back, and that same flat look came into her eyes. She shrugged. "I have no idea."

He let out his breath slowly. "Okay. So, why would you have left this place? Is there anything you feel?"

She shook her head. "No, I don't know."

He took a stab in the dark. "Were you hiding from somebody?"

She gave him an odd look. "If I don't remember living here, how do you think I'll remember whether I was hiding from somebody?"

"I really don't have a clue. It's your place. You may have a feeling or an intuitive sense."

"Maybe I do." Only her face twisted in confusion, and then she shrugged. "Something is here, but I don't know what."

"Okay, we'll just give it time," he said. "But, if this is not your home, then you aren't staying here."

"And yet it is my home." Then she stopped, shook her head, and stated, "No, this is my house. But it's not my home."

"And, of course, you made a fine distinction that I apparently missed."

She walked into the kitchen, opened the fridge, and he peered in behind her.

"Absolutely no food here."

"Exactly. So I wasn't living here. So where was I living, and why was I not here?"

CHAPTER 3

J EWEL STUDIED THE interior of a kitchen cupboard. The basics were here to put on coffee. As she did that, she asked him, "Why would I have left coffee behind?"

He laughed. "Maybe you made a vow to get off caffeine."

"Nope, I would not have done without it," she noted, with a crooked grin. "I do love herbal teas, but I love my coffee too."

"That's good to know," he stated. "So, let's have a coffee, sit down, and relax. Do you think any paperwork is here?"

"No, I don't," she replied.

He pulled out his phone and dialed Stefan. "The house is in her name, but she wasn't living here."

An odd exclamation came from Stefan on the other side. "I suppose she has no idea where she was living either."

"Nope, she doesn't." Hurricane stared at her.

She raised her hands. "You don't believe me?"

"Oh, I believe that you weren't living here," he agreed. "Did the hospital tell you where you were found?"

She stared at him blankly. "Delivered naked and unconscious to the front of the hospital, from what I heard from one nurse. I was just dropped off at the hospital without a mark on me, only to have massive bruising that showed up after a few days."

He nodded at that.

"What we need to do is find out just what the circumstances were, whether you were taken to the hospital or found along a highway."

She nodded. "That would be good to know." She gave him an odd look. "Why didn't I even think to ask that?"

He smiled at her gently. "You had enough to adjust to."

Through the phone Stefan offered, "I'll phone the police department. Give me just a minute."

And, with that, Hurricane's phone went blank. He pocketed it and turned to her, saying, "Stefan will look into it."

She walked over to a cupboard, opened it up, and pulled out two cups. "Why would there only be two regular cups here?"

"I don't know," he replied, looking at her oddly. "Why was there just enough coffee for a single pot?"

"I know. It's almost like I preplanned this."

He sucked in his breath. She whirled, stared at him, and asked, "I couldn't have done that, right?"

But he didn't give her the answer she was looking for. He just stared back at her, then spoke. "Could you have? Yes, you could have. Did you? Now that's what we don't know. Not yet anyway."

She blew out her breath slowly, handed him a cup of coffee, and stated, "I'll go see if a proper change of clothes is to be found."

He followed her into the bedroom.

She pulled open the drawers and noted one pair of underwear and one bra. She lifted them up and turned and looked at him.

He asked, "Only one of each?"

She nodded slowly, and, in the same drawer, she found a pair of socks, a pair of jeans, and a T-shirt. One of everything. "Oh, my God."

"What?"

"Exactly one change of clothing here," she declared, her breath coming out in a rush. She shuddered. "I do not know what to think about this at all. Did I leave it …"

"Or did somebody else leave it for you?" he interrupted.

At that, everything inside her sank deep down into a pit of despair. "You mean, whoever did this to me?"

"Possibly, yes. But we don't know that for sure, so let's not jump to any conclusions."

She gave a bitter laugh. "A little hard not to, considering all that's gone on." She turned her back to him and pulled the man's sweatshirt off over her head.

He sucked in his breath.

She twisted, looked at him, and frowned. "What's the matter?"

"Just hold it a minute," he said, pulling out his phone. "I need to take a picture of your back."

She froze, and he took several photos while her back was turned, and then she quickly put on her bra and pulled the T-shirt over her head. Turning back around to face him, he held up the latest photo, and she stared at the pattern on her back.

"Good God. … What is that?"

"I have no idea," Hurricane admitted.

They both stared down at what looked like odd rope-shaped marks on her back. "Is that a bruise or a tattoo?" she asked hesitantly.

He glanced at her and asked, "Do you mind?" She immediately pulled the shirt off her back and turned. He gently stroked across the skin. "It looks like bruising. … Besides, a tattoo like that, they should have seen at the hospital."

"They should have," she murmured. "So why didn't they?" She watched, as Hurricane sent the photos to Stefan. "I don't understand what's going on," she cried out, looking at him.

"I don't know either," he admitted, "but we'll get to the bottom of it."

With a wordless exclamation, she snatched up the rest of the clothing and walked into the bathroom. She stared into the mirror in shock. Her skin, which was normally peaches and cream, was now alabaster white. And her hair, normally strawberry blonde, was now the darkest it had ever been, not quite black but almost. In a way blacker than black though, almost jet-black, and it seemed to be getting darker all the time. She dressed quickly, opened up the door and looked at him. "Do you have a photo of me from before?"

"No, I don't. Why?" he asked.

"Because everything is changing," she whispered. "My skin is pure white. My hair is much darker."

He looked at her more intently and nodded. "I thought it was the light. But I think it's gotten darker even since leaving the hospital."

"How can that be?" she whispered, staring at him, her eyes huge. "How is anything like this even possible? How can it even make sense?"

He shook his head. "I don't know, and I realize that seems completely inadequate, but I really don't."

HURRICANE ASKED HER for the umpteenth time as they

refilled their coffee, "So you're sure you didn't just dye your hair?"

"No, of course I'm not sure." She glared at him in exasperation. "Obviously I'm not sure about anything. But my skin is pale too. Between here and hospital, I noticed it now."

He nodded.

"Maybe we could focus on what we'll do right now," she muttered. "Or will you just leave, and I must deal with my world myself?"

"What would you do if I did leave?" he asked.

"You will leave eventually," she snapped, glaring at him. "I'm not even sure why you're here right now."

"Because I was told by Stefan to come and to assess the necklace. He wanted me to talk to you about what you'd found."

"Ah." She paused for a moment and then nodded. "How is it I can remember Stefan so clearly?"

"That would be another one of those questions that I would ask you, but, of course, you can't answer."

She groaned. "Look. I'm not trying to be snappy, but I don't know what I'm supposed to tell you."

"You tell me only what is the truth."

"Unfortunately the truth appears to be completely movable, changeable, mutable," she murmured. "So I don't know what to say."

"We better just stick with what we know to be true, which at the moment is that you woke up in the hospital, having apparently died and come back to life, and, since you've come back to life, things have changed."

She stared and then nodded slowly. "I guess that's as good a starting point as any."

"According to what you've told me, you have no idea how you came to be at the hospital. You have no idea what happened to put you in this condition, and yet you remember something about a necklace, that you use love in your work and you definitely remember Stefan."

She gave a half laugh at that. "I asked how it's possible that I could remember Stefan, but the real question is how would it even be possible to forget him."

"Have you ever met him?"

"In real life, or whatever that means, no."

Again Hurricane just studied her face carefully.

"And, if you're looking for truth in that statement, that's all I can give you," she murmured. "I don't believe I've ever seen him face-to-face."

"Good enough," Hurricane replied cheerfully.

She looked at him, puzzled. "Have you?"

"Yeah, a couple times. He is pretty hard to forget."

"Even for those of us who haven't met him," she murmured. She groaned, as she slowly lifted her arms over her head and rotated her neck and shoulders, letting her arms stretch as high as they would go and then back down again.

"Sore?" he asked.

"The bruises," she noted, "they're sore."

He nodded, his gaze going to her bare arms. "They are fascinating, as bruises go."

"I don't know that I like that term." She followed the direction of his gaze. She held out her arms, twisting them slightly to get a better look at them. "I mean, they're sore, but, if I've been beaten to within an inch of my life, which is what these bruises appear to indicate, they aren't that sore."

"Maybe that's a good thing at the moment," he suggested. "The mind has a tendency to only remember what it can cope with."

She stared at him and then nodded. "Meaning, it's a self-defense mechanism, and maybe what happened was so horrific that I'm not ready to face it."

"That would be one guess, yes."

She looked around the kitchen. "Where to from here?"

"You tell me," he replied, a note of humor in his voice. "I brought you to what I thought was your home."

"It's apparently the house, but it's not home, and that's a pretty important distinction at this point."

"So, you tell me," he prodded. "What I've come to understand about you in this short time is that you really care about and were obsessed with your work." She pondered that and nodded. "So, in that case, why don't we go to where your work is."

"Oh, well, that's a completely different story." Puzzled, he watched as she got up, pulled a travel mug out of a different cupboard, filled it with coffee, and then walked to the front door. When he didn't move, she called back, "Are you coming?"

"Sure. Why not?" With that and a disgusted sigh, he got up and headed toward her. "You want to tell me where we're going?"

"I'm not sure," she began. "But, if you drive, I'll give you directions."

His eyebrows shot up at that, but he didn't say another word, hopped into the vehicle outside, and asked, "Are you okay to leave the house unlocked?"

She nodded. "Nothing for anybody to find."

"Glad to hear that," he noted. "So now we need to know where everything you care about really is."

"I think it's in my head," she shared. "But that doesn't

explain where the rest of it is."

He turned on the engine and waited for her to speak. She hesitated a moment, and he watched as she appeared to almost meditate, looking for some answer. Then she stated, "Drive up to the next corner and take a left."

Following that vague statement was hard. The rest of the instructions came a little clearer each and every time, though sometimes right on top of each other. By the time he pulled up in front of what looked like a warehouse, he was staring at her, then back at the warehouse. "Does this make sense? You remember this place?"

"I'm not sure," she murmured. "But it's all we have to go on." She hopped out, still sipping the coffee in her hand, and waited for him to come around. When he did so, she smiled and pointed. "The left one."

"How is it that you're getting here? What are you following for a trail?"

She hesitated and then just shrugged, and he knew that whatever came out of her mouth wouldn't be the truth.

He immediately called out, "Stop."

She froze, looked at him, and asked, "What?"

"I only want the truth. If you don't have the truth to give me, or you're not ready to give it to me, then don't, but do not insult me with lies."

She slowly closed her mouth and shrugged. "Fine," she agreed. And, with that, she cut in front of him, her steps smart, clipped, and she was clearly irritated.

He grinned and followed. At least she hadn't followed through with the lie. He wasn't getting any information at all now, and maybe the lies would have told him something. However, for the moment, it looked like they had a truce. He just didn't know what the fight had been about.

CHAPTER 4

HOW DID JEWEL explain that she didn't really understand where any of this information was coming from, yet something inside her was following something, yet all just too nebulous to tell Hurricane? That was bound to trigger more of his questions, and, if their positions were reversed, she would have done the exact same thing. But that necklace? Just something about it. She also didn't fully understand what energy work entailed with anybody else.

As she walked, she pulled out her borrowed phone, and, when Stefan answered, she asked, "What did I tell you about that necklace?"

"Where are you?" Stefan asked curiously. She hesitated. "The truth is always a good way to deal with this," he replied, his tone mild but very aware.

She groaned. "The truth would be nice, but I'm not exactly sure what the truth is in this instance."

"Yet to me, it feels like you know more than you're telling."

"If I am, it's because I don't know how to tell it or I don't really know what part of it is real and what isn't."

"Okay, that makes sense," he noted carefully. "I can get behind that. Just remember that Hurricane is there to help."

"Is he?" she asked curiously. "I got the impression he was here because of the necklace."

"That's why I sent him initially, yes," Stefan agreed, "but we never walk away from somebody in need. Particularly when that somebody is like us."

"Am I though?" she whispered, hating the doubt rippling through her. She didn't know who she was right now.

"You are," he declared, his voice strong with conviction.

"What if it turns out that this is all something I manufactured? What if it's not the truth?"

"If you did, you must have a reason for it," Stefan offered. "So why don't we assume that, even if you did, you needed to do something. We still need to find out the what and the why. Now, to your predicament, I can tell you exactly what that necklace conversation was about." Then he told her the details from when she'd phoned him.

"Had I talked to you before that?"

"About this, no," he murmured.

"About anything?" He hesitated. "Now it's your turn to tell the truth," she snapped. She glared at Hurricane, who was standing beside her, one eyebrow raised. "It's really frustrating when everybody else knows things that I don't know."

"It goes along with that *how much do you want to know* thing," Stefan explained, with a note of amusement in his voice. "We've never spoken on the phone before this."

"You're making a distinction there."

"Yes, because we have spoken on the ether."

She frowned at that. "Recently?" At that, she watched as Hurricane's eyebrows shot way up and realized he'd heard Stefan's conversation. "I think we've shocked Hurricane."

At that, Stefan laughed. "It takes a lot to shock Hurricane, and, if you need to tell either one of us anything, Hurricane can absolutely be trusted."

"Maybe," she murmured, studying the man in front of her. "He's awfully big."

At that, Hurricane glared at her. "So my size is against me now?" He leaned forward and spoke into the phone. "Stefan, her hair and her skin has changed color."

"In what way?" Stefan asked, his voice calm but curious. She quickly explained the little bit she knew. "And you don't think you dyed it beforehand?"

"Since I don't know what I did beforehand, I have no idea," she admitted.

"Right, well, that's an interesting twist," he murmured quietly but giving nothing away–if there was anything there to give.

"I'm not sure *interesting* is quite the word I would use, but, when I look in the mirror, I don't see what I expected to see."

"*Uh-huh*. … Just keep in mind that sometimes we do things that make total sense at the time, but ever after we wonder why."

"That won't be very helpful," she argued.

"Nothing is, until we get to the bottom of this. Where are you now?"

"I'm outside a series of warehouses," she replied, "and they look to be mostly empty."

"Do you have an address?" At that, Hurricane piped up with that info. Stefan replied, "Ah, that's a newly renovated area. They were turned mostly into artists' lofts. Maybe you own one there."

"It would certainly be appealing," she murmured, as she studied the area. "Huge bright windows, a completely different look to them. On the up-and-up, I can see myself working here."

"So, as an artist, I can see that might suit you very well," Stefan stated. "Go in, take a look, and see where you're directed in your mind to go."

"I managed to find my way here already, so certainly no point in *not* going inside. I'll call you in a bit." And, with that, she hung up. She stood here in front of the building, staring up.

Hurricane faced her and asked, "You ready to go in?"

She winced and exhaled. "I feel like the answer to that is a yes but, at the same time, a very strong no."

He chuckled. "I can go in and take a look around, if you want."

"What good would that do?" she asked, frowning at him.

"I can assess any danger that might be there."

"I'm tempted," she admitted, "very tempted, particularly since I don't know what happened to me. But it has to be me."

CHAPTER 5

JEWEL TOOK A deep breath, looked over at Hurricane, and asked, "You ready?"

His lips twitched. "Always." When he reached out a hand, she stared at it. "You're really not used to having anybody around, are you?"

She frowned at that question and immediately placed her hand in his. "I don't know, but this doesn't feel like a natural move."

"No, I would say it isn't," he replied. "Let's go."

He moved forward at a steady pace, and she wasn't hard-pressed to keep up, but, at the same time, the pace wasn't allowing her to look around. "Are we in a hurry?" she asked.

"Maybe," he said, as he looked down at her. "Do you sense the energy?"

"I sense something, but I'm not sure what."

"Yeah, and it's that 'not sure what' part that bothers me. I sense something too."

Frowning at that, she picked up the pace, until she was almost running. He smiled at her. "Are we in a hurry?"

She groaned at his attempt at humor, especially since they both were uncomfortable. "I don't know. Everything's just weird."

As they got to the front exterior stairwell to avoid the working warehouses and to access the artists' lofts above, she started up, and he followed, their hands still entwined. She looked down at their hands. "It feels very much like I am wrong to use you as a crutch."

"Are you against having support?"

"No, it feels good but off in a way."

"Off?" He looked down at their hands. "Can you see the energy?"

She glanced down, frowned, and then shrugged. "I see something, but I don't know what it is."

"Interesting."

"Why? What am I looking at?" Even as they talked, she kept plowing up the stairs, as if using the conversation to keep her from thinking about what was ahead. When she got to the top of the stairs, she sighed. "I'm sorry. I'm not being very easy to get along with."

"But you're not being difficult," he murmured, looking at her intently. "Obviously something about this is very hard for you."

"But I don't know why. I don't know whether what I'll find is good, bad, or indifferent," she shared, "and, for all I know, this is just a space that I rented for work."

"If it is, then it should be interesting," he replied. "Come on. Let's go see."

Then he pulled open the main door and held it for her to walk through.

Even in this public hallway, the space felt momentous, there was just something about it. She took a deep breath and strode through, trying for that same confidence she had had when she had walked out of the hospital earlier today. Almost immediately, she got hit with a blast of cold air. She shivered.

He looked at her in concern.

She shook her head. "I'm not sure where the cold is coming from."

"No, but I can feel it too," he agreed. "So it could be anything, from air-conditioning left on to something much more, maybe energy-oriented."

Casting him a startled glance, she raised her eyebrows. "I'll ignore that last part for the moment."

"Good, but you've already acknowledged being an energy worker. We're all energy wielders, and we know when not to ignore the signs. You would do well to remember that."

"Sure, but I'm not sure that I know exactly what that means, what all that entails."

"We can sit down and work on a definition of it later," he suggested. "First, let's deal with this."

She kept walking down the hallway; clearly her feet knew where to go, even if her mind wasn't sure. They came to sudden halt in front of a door. It looked like a steel door. She motioned at it. "Whatever it is, it's here."

He reached out a hand, but the door was locked. He looked around and saw no cameras or anything like that to be accessed. "It's an interesting space, so far," he stated.

"Maybe, but I don't really know what it is. It just feels like maybe a shop or something."

"I'd really like it to be your workshop." He hesitated, looked at her, and asked, "Security?"

"I don't think so, but I don't know for sure."

He nodded. "So, if I go in, and the alarm goes off?"

"First you'd have to get in," she pointed out, with a note of laughter. "And that looks like something we'll have to call security or something for."

"Not necessarily. Turn your back."

"Why?"

"I want you to keep an eye out, in case anybody happens upon us and sees what we're doing."

She slowly turned, not at all sure that was the wise thing to do. Almost immediately she heard a *click* behind her. She spun and looked at him, only to find the door wide open.

"What is the point of security," she stated bluntly, "if guys like you are out there?"

He gave her a ghost of a smile. "It's because of those bad guys out there that I do this."

A twisted way of saying he was needed to help people like her, but she wasn't even sure what that meant right now. She stepped through the door and gasped.

He came in behind her, nudging her a little bit forward, and closed the door behind them. "Oh, this is interesting," he murmured.

It looked like an apartment and art studio combined. At least that's what it used to be. Currently the whole of it was in ruins.

"I would say that this is where you spend your time."

"It's where I *used* to spend my time," she stated and shuddered.

He wrapped an arm around her and pulled her against him. "Just stand here and get a feel for what it is that happened here," he said.

"Whatever it is, my space has been destroyed." She stared in horror at the ripped bedding that had been tossed to the floor, the chairs that were dumped, the cushions that had been cut, her tools that were flung far and wide. Canvas pieces and brackets were scattered everywhere. "What did anybody want from here?" she cried out. It was all she could do to keep the tears out of her voice, forcing them back, before they were running down her cheeks.

"The question is, did they find it?" he murmured.

She shuddered at the thought. "I hope not," she wailed, pain in her voice. "Anybody who could do this doesn't deserve to have found it." Even as she spoke, she registered the odd phrasing and knew that he would pick up on it as well.

"It?"

She nodded slowly. "But I don't know what *it* is."

"The necklace," he declared, with that note of surety in his voice.

"Is it though?" she asked, twisting to look up at him. "How do we know that?"

"We don't. So we keep all thoughts open and check this out."

She took a step forward and whispered, "It feels very …" And then she fell silent.

He reached out a hand, gently squeezed her shoulder, and replied, "I know. It's like a violation that you could never have imagined would hurt so much. It is a violation, as a space that was precious to you has been invaded and destroyed in many ways. But it's not all in vain, and we won't let them destroy everything that you worked so hard for."

She gave a broken laugh. "I'm not sure that I have a choice. I don't even know what work I was in the midst of here." Then she paused, gasped, and whispered, "Oh my God, the safe." She raced to a landing, halfway up the internal stairs. He followed, and she pointed to a small area of paneling. "It's behind there."

"What is?"

She shrugged. "I don't know," she cried out. "Just open it and see."

"Do you know how it opens?"

She frowned. "Can't you see the door?"

He studied the wall and looked at her, then shook his head. "No door is there."

She glared at him. "Of course there's a door."

"No, there's no door," he repeated. "It's just wall paneling." He ran his hands up and down the wall to show her.

"No, no, no," she cried out in frustration. "A door is here." She bent down in front of it, her hands pushing against the wall, trying to open up what, as far as she was concerned, was a door.

When she started to pound on the wall, he bent down beside her and whispered, "Easy, take it easy."

She stared at him. "I am not crazy."

"I know you're not crazy, and we will get to the bottom of this."

She took a slow deep breath. "Yeah, and when will that be? This is not normal and is not my life. Why is this happening to me?" At that, she stared up at him, her eyes going wide. "Oh, good God."

"Oh, good God what?" he asked, but his gaze revealed that he knew.

Something in that look of his confirmed that he already knew. "You knew, didn't you?"

"No, I didn't know anything," he argued, frowning. "You need to be a little clearer than that."

"Yeah, you did know," she whispered.

"I don't know anything," he cried out. "Please, talk to me, tell me what's going on."

She shook her head, slowly straightening. "It can't be."

"What can't be?" he asked, throwing up his hands in frustration. "You need to give me a little bit more to go on."

She reached out, gripped his hand, looked at him carefully, and stated, "That's exactly what's wrong."

"Good, I'm glad you figured it out," he noted. "Now enlighten me."

"I just said it," she snapped. "It's not my life. It's literally not my life."

He looked at her in shock and then slowly nodded. "But, if it isn't your life, whose life is it?"

AFTER MAKING THAT statement, Jewel fell silent and headed to the workshop area, as if everything was so normal, and started picking up pieces. He waited, quietly watching her for any sign of possession or something else that he couldn't quite understand. He texted Stefan with a couple warnings that this would not go anywhere and was not getting any better, or so it appeared. He got back a question mark from Stefan, but Hurricane couldn't explain, at least not yet.

He knew that pushing Jewel wouldn't help and that whatever revelations she was getting were coming in bits and pieces and straining her own belief system as well. Something was obviously wrong, and it wouldn't be easy to get to the bottom of it. He walked over to the little kitchenette area and saw that nothing here had been touched. He opened the cupboard and found dozens of cups, glasses, and, yes, packets of coffee.

He watched as she slowly, methodically, picked up various bits and pieces. Then he turned to put on some coffee but heard an odd sound, so focused on her again. Jewel was standing in the middle of the place. He walked over and asked, "Are you all right?" She looked up at him, and he saw the tears in her eyes. He winced. "I'm sorry, sweetheart. I know this is a really difficult time."

She stared. "*Difficult time*," she repeated, but her tone was flat, almost disassociated. "Is that what people say during times like this?"

"I don't know," he admitted. "I've never really been involved in anything like this."

"Neither have I," she replied, staring, as she looked around. "How could I have said it wasn't my place? I know where everything is. I recognize everything here."

"I know. The only thing I wonder is ..." And then he hesitated.

She gave him that look. "You wonder if I'm crazy, wonder if I'm being possessed by somebody, wonder if I'm absolutely losing it."

"No, no, and no," he stated immediately. "I mean, possession is always something that we must consider, particularly when you seem adamant that it's not your place."

"Yet I know where everything is. I know where everything belongs."

He nodded. "So we'll just go with the assumption that it's yours anyway."

"I feel disassociated from it."

"I'm not sure that isn't somehow related to whoever attacked you," he explained.

"But how could they have done that?" she asked, looking at him. "It didn't even occur to me that somebody else might have engineered these feelings."

"I don't know, and that is just more of what we have to get to the bottom of."

"But you're not staying, are you?" she asked, looking at him, one raised eyebrow. "I don't know where the necklace is. I can't give you any details about it right now. I'm not even sure that what I told Stefan applies because I don't have any memory of it."

He nodded and didn't say anything more.

"I'll just keep cleaning up. For some reason it seems to make me feel at peace."

"Then you go ahead and do that," he agreed immediately. "Anything that helps you right now is golden. You want me to put on some more coffee?"

She gave a strangled laugh. "I suppose coffee is here, isn't there?"

"Coffee and cups," he replied. "Have you checked your personal belongings? Is this where your clothes are?"

She looked at him, startled, and then turned and headed up the stairs to the small loft, where they had stopped partway before. She got up there, and he raced up behind her.

"Yes," she answered, her voice faint. "It looks like these are my clothes."

"Good. That helps."

She nodded. "It helps, but it's certainly not the answer."

"Maybe not, but we'll take whatever answers are coming right now."

She nodded, then turned and headed back downstairs. He stayed on the stairs and watched her cleaning up.

Stefan phoned Hurricane and announced, "We have to go into the ethers." He hung up his phone and turned around to find Stefan standing here.

Hey, I don't know what's going on. Hurricane quickly relayed the little bit that had happened so far, and it was hard to even explain to him.

Stefan frowned at that. *Did you check for a safe?*

No, the space has been boarded over or walled over, he shared, *so I'm not even sure how there could even be one. I swear, it's just a wall.*

That doesn't mean that there isn't one though, Stefan argued. *Show it to me.*

Although not a whole lot of space to turn and maneuver, he pointed out the spot on the wall where she had been so sure that a safe would be.

Why did she mention a safe? Stefan asked. *What was she looking for?*

I think the necklace, but I can't be sure.

Ah. The note in Stefan's voice made Hurricane stop and look at him.

What does that mean? Hurricane asked.

I don't know about you, but I'm seeing energy where the safe is or was.

Hurricane turned, looked, and nodded. *Not only that but, from this perspective, I can see other energy signatures around it.*

Exactly, Stefan agreed. *So I vote you take a closer look.* And, with that, he was gone.

Hurricane turned to see her standing there, staring at him. "Hey." He gave her a lopsided grin.

"What did you do, just zone out?"

He hesitated, not sure what to tell her, and then shrugged. "Maybe." He walked to where the safe was, and she laughed. "What? You'll return to see if I'm crazy?"

"I don't think you're crazy at all," he stated. "Do you know how long you were in the hospital?"

"Just a couple days maybe. I'm not sure. Why? Again that's something I should have asked about, wasn't it?"

"Not necessarily, I think you were more concerned

about getting out of the hospital than how long you'd been there."

"That's very true, but still it seems like something I should know."

"Maybe it's something we should all know," Hurricane declared. "Depending on what's going on here, that's something we'll need to find out."

"Did Stefan ever come up with any answers from the police station?"

"Why don't you ask him?" he suggested, turning to look at her. "Send him a text and see if he has any updates."

She hesitated and then looked around at her place. "Maybe I'll just fix this stuff first."

He nodded and watched as she deliberately turned away. He wasn't sure whether she feared what Stefan would say or feared not having any answers, but definitely fear was coming off her.

He asked, "Don't suppose you'd mind if I ruin a wall, *huh?*"

She turned and shrugged and asked, "Can you do more damage than has already been done?"

He smiled at her. "I can at least fix the damage I do."

"Good for you," she quipped and pointed around the room. "Have at it. I don't know what's going on anymore, so, if you think you can find answers, go for it."

And, with that, she deliberately turned away and went back to sorting through the mess. He walked into the kitchen and found a hammer in one of the drawers. With that in hand, he headed back up the stairs to where the safe supposedly was and gently pried apart the drywall. With a hard *snap*, it came away in his hand.

She came up and looked to see what he was doing. Her

eyebrows shot up. "Good Lord, are you just checking to see if I'm crazy, or are you really crazy?"

"Neither, but an energy signature was around this that didn't make any sense."

"An energy signature?" she repeated, staring at him, not comprehending at all.

He hesitated and then nodded. "We really need to see how much energy work you are acquainted with."

"Not enough apparently," she murmured. She watched as he cut off a piece of drywall, exposing the wall behind it.

"Oh my God," she gasped in shock, staring at it.

"Yep, your safe."

She reached over and quickly turned the dials on the safe. Within seconds, the tumblers clicked into place, and she turned the handle but stopped there. She let out a slow sigh. "Good God. Why and how?"

"Why and how what?" he asked, waiting for her to open it.

"Why and how would somebody do this?"

He held his own counsel on that but looked at her curiously. "Why are you waiting to open it?"

She winced. "Because I don't want to be wrong. I don't want to find out that it's gone."

"Then open it and see," he invited.

She took a deep breath, focused on him, and then pulled open the safe door. Inside were black velvet cases.

She reached for the foremost one, leaving the other cases behind it.

"It should be in here."

"Let's find out," he murmured and waited.

Again she hesitated, and that same fear was evidenced in her aura.

"Go on," he urged. "We can't deal with the truth if we don't know what it is."

She gave him an odd look, then nodded and pulled the case toward her. When she opened it, an absolutely incredible pearl necklace was revealed.

Almost instantly the hairs on the back of his neck rose. He reached out and immediately snapped shut the hard case.

She looked at him, frowning.

"That energy. It's a vortex, by the appearance of it."

"A vortex? What does that mean?"

"It means that we aren't opening that right now. So I presume that's the necklace you were talking about?"

She nodded. "Does that mean this necklace is of interest to you?"

"Oh, you could say so," he teased, his eyes gleaming in the light.

She stared at him. "It's scary. Something's very different about you right now."

He took a slow deep breath and eased back some of his energy.

"It's … It's this thing, isn't it?" she asked.

"It is, and it isn't," he replied. "I'm very attuned to artifacts like this."

"*Great*," she muttered, "meaning this is something that's possibly … dangerous?"

"Oh, it's very dangerous. Particularly in the wrong hands." She frowned at that. "How did you get ahold of the necklace in the first place?"

"I was contacted on my website," she replied.

His eyebrows shot up. "You have a website?"

"Sure. Doesn't every business?"

He shook his head. "It would have been nice to have

known that ahead of time."

"And here I thought you would have already figured that out," she said.

"What's the name of your business?"

"Jewel's Box." Her smile turned reminiscing. "A play on words." Her words came out naturally without hesitation, she was almost speaking from heart and not memories.

He nodded, his hand still resting on the case as he studied her gaze intently. "I'll take a look at your website later."

"You won't let me open that again, will you?"

"Not right now," he stated. "It's been triggered."

She frowned, looked down at the case, back at him, and said, "And again that's supposed to mean something to me, and it doesn't."

"Not to you, but it sure does to me, and it certainly does to Stefan."

CHAPTER 6

J EWEL RETURNED TO her workshop area, trying hard to sort through the bits and pieces of information that were coming both from the cloudy areas in her brain and from Hurricane's words. She knew there had to be some sense to be made of all this, yet it was just out of reach. Yet there must be something, something that she knew ahead of time. Unable to forget about it, she walked back over to the stairs by the safe and sat down in front of it.

As she studied where the drywall had been cut, Hurricane sat down beside her. "What are you thinking?"

She shrugged. "It's not a professional job."

"No, it isn't," he agreed, his voice calm.

She looked over at him. "Did I do this?"

His gaze was steady, as if the idea had already occurred to him. "I don't know. You tell me."

"I can't." She showed her palms. She went back to the safe, pulled open the door, and studied the contents. "I knew it was here. I knew everything was here, yet hidden."

"But not hidden from you."

"Sure it was," she disagreed, looking back at him. "I knew it, but I couldn't see it."

"No, so somebody hid it on purpose, but, because you already knew it was here, it wasn't hard for you to see through that deception."

"Yet you're the one who saw through it," she stated, a hint of accusation in her tone.

"That was mostly Stefan, seeing energy around it. So I followed his lead and took out the drywall."

She nodded, as she stared at it. "I guess drywall isn't hard to put in, is it?"

"No, it sure isn't, and it's not a very big safe," he noted. "This isn't more than one foot square, and they used what's known as a Texas drywall patch to cover it up."

She nodded. "And that's not all that hard to do either?" she murmured.

"No, there would be plenty of DIY videos online that would show you how to patch this fairly quickly," he replied. "So somebody who wanted to hide it could do so fairly easily."

She nodded. "I don't know that I could do any drywall work," she murmured.

"Do you know anybody who does this work?"

She shrugged at that too. "I mean, it's fairly smooth, it's simple, but this whole piece juts out."

He nodded. "Yet you wouldn't think anything of it, if nobody had shown you the safe was here. It would have just been a strange design, and you would have gone from there thinking that's all it was."

She nodded, but, as she looked down, she noticed several other juts. "Do you think other things are hidden behind these other jutted spots?"

Startled, he studied it, then frowned. "You tell me."

"Well, I can't," she snapped and glared at him. "I can't tell you anything."

He knocked on the other panels in question and got a hollow echo back. "I think they are just part of the architecture here." Just then his phone rang. She half listened as he frowned into the phone and then his face cleared. "Hello, Detective, thanks for contacting me. … Yes, I know Stefan can be very insistent when he needs something," he added, with a chuckle. "In this case we appreciate it very much, as we're a little skimpy on details for her accident. … No, she's right here with me."

He looked over at her and put his phone on Speaker and placed it midway between them. "It's the detective on your case."

She called out, "Hello, Detective." At least if he knew she was here and consenting, it would allow him to pass on information.

The detective, his voice calm and almost ponderous, asked, "How are you doing?"

"I'm fine, except for a lack of memories."

"Amnesia?" he asked, his voice sharp.

"Maybe, selective amnesia for sure," she replied, trying to hold back the bitterness. "It's pretty rough when I don't know what's going on or if I was attacked. And, if I was, then who the hell did the deed."

"If you weren't attacked, how could you possibly explain what happened?" the detective asked her.

"I can't explain a thing because I don't even know all of what happened. The hospital didn't give me much information, which is why Stefan reached out."

A moment of silence came on the other end. "I intended to meet with you before you were released," he explained. "Can I come by now?"

"Ah …" She hesitated and looked back at Hurricane.

He just shrugged and replied, "Sure, why not? The sooner we find out what's going on, the better."

"Okay, good," he said, and then he shuffled some paperwork. "I have one address on file, but I was there a couple days ago, and nobody answered. Is that where you are?"

"Nobody answered? Did it look like anybody was there?" she asked curiously.

"No, it looked deserted, and mail was piled up outside. I left it in a cardboard box that was just off to the side."

"Interesting," she replied. "Okay, well, I guess you should come to my studio. That's where I am right now." She gave him the address, ended the call, and then sat back, looking at Hurricane. "Did you see a cardboard box with mail?"

He shook his head. "I didn't, but that doesn't mean a whole lot."

She just nodded and asked, "What the hell is going on?"

"The sooner he gets here, the sooner we can ask him some questions and maybe get a few more answers," Hurricane offered.

She hopped to her feet and stated, "Let's not tell him about the safe."

"Yeah, and how do you want to hide it?"

Startled, she turned and looked back and winced. "Can you at least put the drywall back into place and try and just hold it there?"

"You want me to just sit here on the stairs and hold it?" he asked, his eyebrow shooting up.

She glared at him. "That's not what I meant."

He nodded. "Okay, let me see if I can fix something up." And, with that, he got to work, and she headed downstairs to her workshop area again.

Hers was one open workspace loft, with the bedroom on a half space, half a floor up. In her mind, it felt like a good place for her to be, like home or something. Yet it didn't feel quite right, as if unfamiliar to her or simply because it had been violated. Something was not sitting right with her.

She didn't know what to say about it. Obviously it had been violated. She found it hard to refocus though, and just knowing that the detective was coming for some reason made her extremely nervous. She shifted anxiously around the workshop, picking up tools and replacing them, but her mind wasn't on it at all.

Finally a gentle hand came down on her shoulder, and Hurricane suggested, "Why don't you sit down?"

Startled, she looked at him. "Why?"

He pointed to where she had arranged all of the tools in a row. "It's the third time you've arranged them."

Her shoulders sagged. "I'm just worried about what he'll say."

"Another reason to sit down and to try to relax. I'll put on some fresh coffee, and you can spend a minute just calming down. Then we'll see what he has to say. It doesn't have to be bad news. Remember that."

"Maybe not bad news, but it sure doesn't feel as if it's good news either."

He smiled. "Let's not judge the news before we get it." He chuckled. "Any information that we learn will be to our benefit."

"Our benefit?" she challenged, glaring at him. "You can get up and walk out of this at any time. I can't."

"No, you can't," he agreed, his gaze searching. "But I wasn't planning on getting up and walking out. You remember that."

"Oh." She frowned at him. "Why not?"

At that, he stated, "It's not who I am."

"Maybe not, but maybe it's who you should be." And, with that, she turned and walked over to one of the kitchen stools at the island and sat down. "I'm not trying to be difficult. … At least I don't think I am. I don't even know what I'm really like as a person."

"I am certain that you are very creative, independent, and outspoken, and it's quite likely that you don't take anything new into your world very easily."

At that, she slowly raised her head and stared at him. "Where would you get that assessment from?" she asked. "I didn't think you knew me. To me, it just looks like I am being difficult."

"It not that you're being difficult, but I think this whole scenario is difficult for you."

She waved her hand. "I think it would be for anybody."

"Exactly, I agree with you. And, for some people, it would be even more unnerving. In your case I think it's a situation where you're trying hard to stay afloat, and I think you're doing a damn fine job. We found the necklace, though I'm not sure what you're supposed to do with it. We don't know if it belongs to somebody and what your job was with it."

"To repair it," she stated baldly and shook her head. "But something else is in there, and I don't know what it is."

"Of course. That's the part that we still need to understand."

She nodded. "I get that. I just don't know quite what I'm supposed to do with all this."

"Nothing at the moment," he reassured her.

Just then the doorbell rang. She froze and looked up at him in shock. He reached out a gentle hand. "Easy. That will be the detective."

She let out her breath slowly. "Wow, I didn't realize just how unnerved I am by this whole thing."

"That's why you need to just sit back and relax a little bit. We don't want to set the detective off, thinking something wrong is going on here, when there isn't."

"But isn't there?" she asked, looking at him.

"We don't really know what's wrong and what isn't yet. And we don't really want …" Then he stopped and shook his head. "Or maybe I'm wrong. Maybe you do want the police involved. Do you? If you do, that's a different story."

The doorbell rang again, and he turned and walked to the front door. He opened it, and she heard conversation in the background. When she turned around, Hurricane accompanied an older man, a little rotund and maybe in his early fifties, with an eagle-sharp look in his eyes.

"What happened here?" he immediately asked, looking at the disarray around him.

"A break-in," Hurricane noted. "We've cleaned it up a bit, but I have photos of the original mess, when we first entered the property. We presume it is related to the attack on Jewel. I'll send those pictures to you, and we'll sign any statement you need."

The detective nodded. "Not per procedure but I'll take it." He studied her for a moment and stated, "You're looking a bit better than when I saw you in the hospital."

She gave him a half smile. "Yeah, a little bit. Now, if only I knew what had put me in the hospital."

"And that's what I'm here for," he replied, his voice serious. "I'm not sure what happened to you, but whatever it was had a pretty strong impact on everyone around you."

"What did happen?" she asked.

"All I can tell you is what I have in the report." He

handed the paper copy to Hurricane and asked, "Did you want to read about it or be told?"

"I want to be told," she stated, "but I'll take the copy to try and get my brain wrapped around it afterward, when I get over the shock."

He smiled. "I guess that's not a bad way to look at it," he agreed. "The fact of the matter is, your body was found on the side of the highway. We have the location per the GPS of the caller who found you. It's in the file. You weren't wearing anything, not a mark on you, but your body was cold, and it appeared that you had possibly been dead for one to two days," he shared intently. "As I gathered, whoever found you then called 9-1-1, and the caller remained anonymous, just saying that he would take your body to the nearest hospital. Once you arrived at the hospital, you were determined to be deceased, placed in a body bag, and taken to the morgue. While you were awaiting autopsy, you woke up."

She just stared at him. "I was in a body bag in the morgue," she repeated, her voice faint. "Good God."

He nodded. "I would like to think that the morgue would have realized you were, in fact, alive before they started an autopsy, but I really don't know how that works."

"Has that ever happened before?" she asked him in shock.

He gave a half laugh. "Not in my experience, no. I guess my question is, has that ever happened to you before?"

And again, hard for her to understand.

"I researched and found a couple diseases where people can appear to be dead. It's like a sleeping disease, and I ... Given your case was so unique, and I have come across Lazarus syndrome, it's a possible explanation for you. People appear dead but, … but they do come back to life."

"Are you asking if I have a disease like that?" she asked curiously.

"You tell me."

"I have no idea. If I do, it's the first I've ever heard about it," she stated bluntly. "Presumably, at least I would hope, the hospital ran a few tests to find out for sure."

"All the tests came back negative," he noted.

Her breath came out in a sudden gust of relief. "I know I shouldn't be relieved at that, but I am because that sounds terrible. To think of it happening once is bad enough, but to think that this could be repeated is terrifying."

He turned and looked at Hurricane. "What's your relationship to her?"

"A friend," he replied, as if he had expected the question.

And, of course he probably had, whereas she had been staring at Hurricane, hoping he could give some coherent answer because she didn't have one.

The detective just nodded, then turned back to her. "Now that you are awake and conscious, what do you remember?"

She shrugged. "I woke up in the hospital, and that's where I have the first comprehensive awareness. Other than that, I don't know. I don't know how I ended up on a highway. I don't know what happened to my clothing. I don't know anything at all," she stated, "and it's fairly traumatizing to think that so much could have gone on, and I wouldn't have any clue."

"The mind does a lot of wondrous things," the detective shared. "Really, its job is to protect you right now, and that's what it's doing. The problem is, that makes it very difficult to get any answers."

She swallowed hard and then slowly nodded.

"Can you tell me anything about your life before this?" the detective asked.

"Yes. I've made some progress there. I'm a jeweler, and I do repairs. This is my workspace. I have a house, as you saw. I was there earlier, but it didn't feel like home at all. I think I must have been in the process of either moving here or just deciding that I should stay here all the time. I really don't know for sure. I'm just going by how it feels. Maybe I was trying this out, and I would sell the house afterward." She shrugged. "I really don't have an answer for you there."

"That's fine," he murmured, as he looked around and nodded. "This does look very much like a place that you've spent a lot of time in. That's also important to know."

"So, nobody saw what happened to me?" she asked the detective.

He shook his head. "Not that we know of, at this point, no. The doctors have run as many tests as they can, and forensics ran over your body at the same time, and no forensic evidence was found."

She took a deep breath. "Sexual assault?"

He looked at her and shook his head. "No visible signs there."

She nodded, feeling a certain amount of relief, and a tension inside her eased back. Realizing how much that had been a concern, she murmured and gave Hurricane a smile. "At least that's good news."

He nodded, but his gaze was watchful, as he studied her. "Do you have any memories along that line?"

"No. … But then I have no memories at all," she noted, with that same flat tone that she used every time he asked a question about memories for which she had no answer.

He didn't say anything but looked back at the detective. "Any hypotheses?"

"No, none, outside of the fact that she was attacked and left for dead."

"The attack, that was for sure? How?" Hurricane asked him.

"No, I don't know for sure," he admitted. "The fact that you're still alive could mean that you were meeting some-body, you died—or they thought you died—so they panicked, took off in hurry, and just dumped you on the side of the highway, hoping you'd be found."

"I was found, and now the question is, who was this per-son and why wouldn't they have called for help?"

"Most people don't call for help if they're more afraid of what could result from the problem in front of them," he explained succinctly. "So, if getting rid of a body was easier than trying to answer questions, they would have taken that route in a heartbeat."

"Right." She stared at the detective. "I don't think I have very much if any connection to that world because every-thing you're saying sounds so foreign to me."

"That's a good thing," he said cheerfully. "I'd hate to have to come back and to imagine that you were a part of all this shit."

She winced. "I don't know how I could have been, and it certainly doesn't make any sense that I would have been, since I don't know anything and don't have any answers for you. Plus I was dead for two days. Who does that willingly?" Then she stopped and asked, "How long was I in the hospital?"

"Four days. You were in the morgue for the first one. Then in a coma for two days and fully woke up on the next day, released that same day."

"Oh good God," she wailed. "I was lying in a cold body bag for all that time?"

He nodded slowly, his gaze intent. "That's one of the reasons everybody was so shocked. They'd figured you'd already been dead for a day, if not longer, before you ever got to the hospital."

She swallowed at that. "That's a long time to be out of circulation in my own life."

"Which is why I was concerned, and why I'm here now, to see if you have any idea who you hung out with, who might have known something, who might have seen something, who might have known who you were dating, or any questions like that."

"That makes sense," she admitted, frowning, "but, since I've been here, I haven't come up with any names or any connections for you."

"Of course not." He gave a hard sigh.

"Why is nothing like this ever easy?"

He shook his head. "A case like this shouldn't be easy because we need to make sure we get it right."

She shrugged. "It just seems that there could be so many things wrong with this entire scenario. I just want to make sure that we get it right, whatever the answer ends up being."

"I agree with you there." The detective nodded, looking at her intently. "Still, without something to go on, not a whole lot to say. The good news is that you appear to be fine, and, if a little memory loss is the result, that's still pretty minor compared to what it could have been."

"Considering that I was thought to be dead, yes," she murmured. "Absolutely."

He looked over at Hurricane. "I presume you have an

alibi for all this time."

"I was out of state, New Orleans, in fact. But feel free to contact my boss," he added cheerfully, presenting his business card.

"We'll get to it," the detective confirmed, then stood. "A certain number of cases we never ever get any answers to," he shared, "and I'm not saying that this will be one of them, but honestly I've never seen a case like this before."

She nodded. "I do prefer the idea of somebody coming upon me or having been out with me, when I suddenly collapsed. It does bother me to think that I would be with anybody who wouldn't have my care or my health in mind and would have just dumped me on the side of a highway though," she shared bluntly. "If we could find out who that was, I'd be happy to never see them again."

He gave a bark of laughter. "Yeah, you and me both."

With nothing else to discuss, the detective left soon afterward, leaving things murkier than ever.

AS HURRICANE CAME back from letting out the detective, he saw Jewel sitting there, on a kitchen stool, twisting a cup of coffee in her hands. "What are you thinking?"

Startled, she looked up at him. "What? Oh, it's not as if that was helpful."

"It gave us a timeline at least," he corrected.

"No, that's true," she agreed, "and that just makes it all even more bizarre."

He smiled. "It does, indeed, but I always like a challenge." At her inquiring look, he shrugged. "So, unless you're against the idea, I'd like to stick around, until we get more answers."

He watched the skin under her eyes tighten, and he wondered just what reaction he was seeing. Then she relaxed and nodded. "Thank you, that would be nice." And then she added, "You'll also have to keep in mind that we may never get any answers."

"I am an optimist," he stated, "so I'll assume that we will. This case is way too intriguing not to."

She gave a bark of laughter. "Maybe so, but it's not exactly the easiest to think that somebody could have done that to me."

"No, and I'm quite fascinated at the concept of somebody having done that. Those aren't the people in my circle, so I wouldn't have thought they were in yours either."

She frowned at him. "I get that people have circles of friends, but why would you think that our circles would overlap with the same kind of people?"

He gave her a ghost of a smile. "Generally, anybody who can see energy and be a part of the ether can see trouble coming at them."

"Is that always the case?"

"Not always. We have certainly seen a number of criminals, with energy abilities, who have fooled even the best of us."

"Even Stefan?" she challenged.

"Yes, even Stefan." He hesitated and then said, "Now you contacted Stefan about these pearls, but did you by any chance contact anyone else?"

She stared at him. "I don't imagine that I would have," she replied, "but I don't know that for sure."

"Right. Because that would really be my number one suspect, if you had."

"I don't know about that," she disagreed. "It seems like

we would be judging them ahead of time."

"I'm okay to judge them ahead of time," he declared, deliberately hardening his tone. "Something happened to you. I don't know whether you knew or it was done with your permission," he said, ignoring the look of shock on her face. "However, something happened, and somebody knows something. The problem is, we'll have to find out who that someone is." He hesitated, looked at her directly, and shared, "And the fact is, you may not like the answers."

"I'm already not liking the questions, let alone the answers." she said. "So what else is new."

"Good, so, in that case, are you okay to stay here, or do you want to go somewhere else for the night?"

She looked around and sighed. "I think we can stay here."

"Interesting phrase. Why *I think*?"

"I don't know." She shrugged, turning to swivel on the stool and to look at the space around her. "I really don't know. Yet still I have a sense of uncertainly, so very much a case of *I think*."

"Okay, we'll go with that for now," he murmured. "I guess we'll have to see what comes up after this. I don't know about you, but I'll need some food."

"Of course you do." She winced and added, "My stomach is not terribly thrilled at the idea of food at all."

"No, but then you've been eating hospital food for days."

"I didn't," she murmured, shaking her head. "I don't think I ate any of it."

At that, he slowly turned and looked at her. "Were they feeding you intravenously?"

"I have no idea," she replied. "Why?"

"Because your body needs sustenance," he stated, looking at her intently. "Unless you have some magic trick I don't know about."

"If I did, it's probably a magic trick that I wouldn't want to share with everybody because then it's not magic anymore, is it?"

Her tone was light, but her movements were jerky, as she got up and walked around to the other side of the counter. She picked up the coffeepot and dumped the last of the coffee into her cup. Looking over her shoulder, she asked, "Did you want more? I can put on another pot."

"No, I'll need food first."

She just nodded and continued to stare out the window.

"Do you have any food allergies? Any preferences?"

Startled, she looked back at him and then shrugged. "I don't think so. I guess that's one of those things we'll have to find out the hard way."

At that, he allowed a ghost of a smile to escape. "I'd just as soon not though. We've already had enough excitement, and anything that might trigger another repeat—with you dropping to the floor, looking dead—isn't something I want to experience."

"No," she murmured. "Can you imagine whoever would have been here and what they would have thought?"

"I can almost see why they would have run."

She nodded. "Almost, yes. But somehow it does feel like a betrayal, and, no matter what, they should have stuck around and at least gotten me some help."

"Maybe they couldn't. Maybe they had no internet service out there on the highway. Maybe they were a jogger with no cell phone at all," he suggested, his tone gentle. "Maybe some poor kid found you, as he or she tramped through the forest nearby, and they had no idea how to deal with you. So let's not judge them too harshly just yet."

With a shrug, she replied, "Whatever. I'll go back to cleaning this up. No food is here that's really edible, but you're welcome to take a look around."

"That's okay. I'll order something in."

She frowned. "I feel like some of the most common things are missing from my brain. Like it never occurred to me that you could order in."

"I don't think your brain is firing on all cylinders right now," he noted. "So maybe just give it a break too."

"Right, I'm not exactly doing any heavy in-depth brain-work right now," she muttered.

"No? But you are because you're still trying to figure out what happened to you."

"Of course I am," she cried out passionately. "How does one end up on the side of the road in the condition I was in, supposedly dead, and then wake up again?"

"I know of a couple people with this disease that the detective was talking about, the Lazarus syndrome, but I'm not sure the symptoms are the same. In this case, the heartbeat and breathing drops to awfully low levels, so mistakes can be made in declaring a death."

"Nothing would ever be exactly the same anyway because apparently everybody is different," she added, with just enough bitterness to have his eyes narrow.

"Stay strong," he ordered. "We will get to the bottom of this."

She gave a jerky head nod, got up from her stool, and told him, "I'll go lie down." She stopped, turned to him. "Unless you have any reason why I shouldn't."

"Absolutely no reason why you shouldn't. In fact, I

think it's a great idea."

As she went to the stairs, she passed by the safe. "The detective didn't notice the safe."

"No, I don't think he did," Hurricane agreed.

"Why not?" she asked, pointing at it. "It's pretty obvious."

"Is it?" He gave a ghost of a smile. "Maybe it wasn't obvious to him."

She looked at him in confusion, then headed up to the bedroom. At the top of the stairs, she stopped and looked back at him. His gaze had followed her all the way up, making sure she went up to bed, a little worried about her physical condition but more about her mental state.

She hesitated at the top. "What's the matter?" She stared at him, wordless.

He got up and walked to the bottom of the stairs and asked, "Do you want me to come up?"

She shook her head. "No. … Yes." And then she shook her head. "No, at least not right now."

And then he understood. "I'll come up in an hour," he offered. "To make sure that you're alive."

She grimaced. "Thanks, because, yes, that's what I want. Somebody who checks on me and who doesn't just dump me on a highway," she stated bitterly. "But, at the same time, how will you know?"

His smile was deep and genuine. "Hey, I'm an energy worker," he reminded her. "If your cord is attached, I'll know."

She gazed at him, startled, then gave him a dawning smile that hit him like a punch to the gut. She nodded. "Thank you. That's the first bit of sense I've heard yet." And, with that, she disappeared at the top of the stairs.

A moment later he heard her flop down onto the bed.

He thought about her words and realized just how much pain and fear was sitting so close to her energy. He called up, "If you have the means, you should work at clearing some of that fear out of your energy."

When no response came, he wasn't sure whether it meant she didn't have the means or if she was just too tired to do anything. He'd remind her when she woke up again. Then he winced because it really was a case of *if* she woke up again, and that worried him above all. He had no idea if she *would* wake up.

CHAPTER 7

J EWEL WOKE SUDDENLY, half out of bed, her eyes flashing open to stare up into the darkness of the room around her, then directly into Hurricane's blinding light-blue eyes, staring at him in shock.

He smiled down at her. "Hey, it's all right. Calm down."

She relaxed slightly. "Is there a problem?"

"No, I was just checking that you were okay."

She stared up at him, the conversation before she'd gone to sleep barely in her brain. "Looks like I got to wake up another day," she noted lightly.

He nodded, but his gaze was watchful. Something was almost reassuring about the intensity of it too. She sighed. "It'll take a bit to get used to."

He laughed. "I would think so. Not everybody has a chance to be dead for as long as you were and come back."

"And yet why?" she murmured. "I was afraid I wouldn't fall asleep at all, and yet I went out without any trouble. How does that even happen?"

"You were exhausted. Remember? A lot of things transpired in the time you were awake and while you were in the hospital. Yet even you didn't have any trouble sleeping."

"Right, and how does all that work?"

He smiled. "Maybe just accept that some things we won't know the full answers to."

But inside something twinged at her heart, almost as if she had expected to wake up. And, of course, she had because, in her mind, she always had. She didn't know whether the morgue was completely incompetent or if something else was at play. "Could somebody have faked my death? Or maybe they thought I would just die slowly in the body bag?" she murmured.

"It's not a small town," Hurricane noted. "The coroner has degrees, credentials. Could somebody have mistaken you for being dead? Yes, I've heard of that happening," he noted. "But, in this case, for as long as you were supposedly dead, I don't know how that would work with competent medical personnel. And deliberately? Well, we have a word for that."

"Yeah, it's called murder," she declared, her tone turning harsh. "But, in that case, why wouldn't they have done something to have completed the job?"

He gave a clipped nod. "Exactly."

She pushed back the light blanket she'd tugged over her shoulders and sat up. Almost instantly a yawn split her face wide. She groaned when her jaw came back together again. "Wow, even that yawn hurt."

"It looked like it was coming from a long way away," he murmured lightly. Holding out his hand, he added, "Come on. Get up, and let's see if you can walk."

Without question she put her hand in his and slowly stood. "Was there any reason to suspect I couldn't walk?" she asked curiously.

"Not really, but nothing about this makes any sense, so I just want to ensure that you're alive and well and fully functioning."

She cracked a smile at that. "The *fully functioning* part was in doubt from the beginning," she murmured.

He gave her another ghost of a smile. "If you're feeling better, maybe you should go to the bathroom and then come on downstairs."

"What will downstairs do for me?"

"Food," he stated. She frowned at that. "No, I don't want to hear it," he ordered, his gaze ever watchful. "I need to know that you're eating."

"Why?" she groused. "Especially if I'm not even hungry."

He didn't say anything, but something stirred deep beneath the surface.

"What's the matter?" she asked.

"I'm not sure yet," he admitted, "but I want you to come downstairs, and I want to see you eat."

She frowned at that, not liking anything about his tone of voice, but more so about the oddness in the tone than the words setting her off. She shrugged. "Fine, I'll be down in a few minutes."

She walked into the bathroom, washed her face, and used the facilities, then slowly made her way downstairs. She was feeling better, but nothing about this entire scenario was geared to make her feel good, and *good versus better* were two very different things. As she walked into the little kitchen area, she saw him sitting there, with a big mug of something. "What, more coffee?"

He shook his head. "No, it's tea. You had some herbal teas, so I'm trying them."

"Herb tea?" she repeated. "You really don't look like the herb tea type."

He didn't respond but lifted it and took a sip from his mug. He pointed to the pizza in front of them. "I also had pizza delivered."

"Here?" she asked, startled, as she looked around.

"Yes, here. Although I met him outside at another door."

"Why would you do that?" she asked, twirling to face him.

"To keep our location secret."

"But how secret is it if we're sitting here the whole time?"

"That's what I don't know," he replied. "It's just one more of those questions that I don't have answers for."

She nodded, put on the teakettle, and added, "I'll have a cup of tea too."

"Good," he said, and he waited.

She glanced down at the pizza and winced. "Can't say I like pizza much."

"Maybe not, but have you looked at yourself in the mirror?"

"No, not really," she stated. "Why? What's the problem?"

"Do you see how skinny you are?"

"I've been in the hospital," she noted in exasperation. "Of course I lost a pound or two." He nodded and once again left it very open-ended. She added, "Okay, so obviously food and eating appears to be something that's really bothering you."

"What's bothering me is whether you *can* eat or not."

Exasperated, but not sure where the odd tone to his voice was coming from, she picked up a piece of pizza and chomped down on the end of it. Almost immediately she winced. "God, why did you have to put anchovies on it?"

He looked at her. "Why not? It makes for a great pizza."

"No, it does not," she argued, with an eye roll. "I suppose you love pineapple on your pizza too."

He shook his head. "Can't say I've ever tried it."

"I picked it up in Canada, when I was up there before, but it's not exactly my style."

"I don't think anybody I know puts pineapple on pizza." Then he frowned and noted, "Yet it doesn't sound that bad."

"There, now that I've had a bite, will you lay off?"

"Nope, not yet," he stated.

She slowly turned and asked, "Okay, so what am I missing?"

"Not yet." He looked at his watch. "Have another bite, make it two more, then we'll wait thirty minutes, and I'll explain."

Not sure why she was even following his instructions, but knowing it was important, at least to him, she had two more bites, choking down the anchovies that she really hated. Then she walked over to the sink, grabbed some water, took a drink, and never said another word. She made tea, sat down across from him, then used her phone to check up on a few things going on in the world.

And finally he said, "Look at me."

She glanced over at him, and finally he nodded, with a satisfied air. "Do you want to explain that to me?" she asked.

He gave her that ghost of a smile *again*, which seemed to be the only one he used lately. "There's actually a type of energy worker who doesn't need to eat and can fool almost everybody into thinking they're human."

"And they aren't?" she asked in amazement.

"They were, but they aren't any longer," he murmured.

"You thought I might be one?"

"I don't know. But it was one possible explanation."

Goose bumps rose on the back of her neck. She showed him her arms. "Just you saying that has got my whole body in chills." He nodded, his gaze still watchful. "And that was supposed to be a test?"

"Generally they can't keep food down, so, if you race for the bathroom and start upchucking those few bites, believe me. I'll be a little more suspicious."

"If I am somebody like that," she asked, staring at him, "then what?"

He gave her a glance that revealed nothing and yet so much. "Let's just hope you're not." And, with that, he got up and said, "I'll go lie down for a moment."

"Where will you do that?"

He pointed to a couple blankets stretched out on the floor.

"Does this have something to do with that little test you gave me? You'll go check in on my energy or something?" She was trying hard to keep the bitterness from her tone, then gave it up and let it show. "Because I really don't know what's going on."

"Right now, that's a good thing because I believe that you don't know what's going on," he agreed. "Still that doesn't mean something isn't happening with you."

She gave him a few minutes to relax, and then, with her tea at her side, she sat down on one of the dining table benches, more comfortable for her and at least close to her work, and started researching what he was talking about. However, nothing showed up. She frowned at that, wondering whether it was something super secret or if it was something very few people ever came across—which would be why the internet didn't have anything other than ghost stories about it. Either way, she didn't like the sound of it. As she sat here, pondering what had happened, her phone rang.

When she answered, a woman's voice on the other end

introduced herself. "Hello, I'm Dr. Maddy. I'm a friend of Stefan's."

"Hello, Dr. Maddy," Jewel replied. "I've heard of you, but I certainly didn't expect to ever hear from you."

"Apparently some strange things are going on in your system."

"You could say that," she agreed cautiously. "Did Stefan contact you?"

"Stefan and Hurricane," she replied. "So I took the initiative of calling you myself. I gather you don't ask for help easily."

Startled, she stated, "I've never really been in a position where I needed to."

"We all do sometimes," Dr. Maddy noted. "I can already confirm some very strange things are going on in your energy, and I would like to run a scan."

"I don't think I'm in any shape to travel right now," Jewel told her apologetically. "As interesting as that might sound, it will have to wait."

"I don't need you to travel. I can do it right where you are."

"So you want to come over?" she asked, puzzled. "Are you in town?"

At that, Dr. Maddy laughed. "I don't need to come over, and I'm not in town," she replied. "I try not to travel as much anymore, if I don't have to. I can do the scan over the internet or over distance."

"*Okay,*" Jewel said, completely confused. "What do you need me to do?"

"I'd like you to go back upstairs to your bedroom, lie down on the bed, and try to be as calm as you can. Keep an open mind, while I run some tests. You might hear a voice in your head, and, if you do, please respond, as if we were talking normally, as we are now."

"In my head?" she asked, startled.

"In your head," Dr. Maddy murmured. "Maybe not. Maybe it'll be easier without that."

"I think I can do that," she began, "but …"

"It will be noninvasive. I won't hurt you, and, no, I won't tell anybody of the results, if you don't want me to."

"I don't even know what you're looking for," Jewel cried out.

After a moment of hesitation, Maddy shared, "I'm looking for evidence of another person lurking around with you."

At that, Jewel's throat tightened down hard. "You mean, like a possession?" she asked in a strangled voice.

"That's one word for it, but it's not the only word that applies in this case. We're barely keeping up with people who have extraordinary skills in terms of just cataloging what they can do. So that would be one word for it, but there could be a lot of other explanations."

"Such as?"

"Split personality for one. Also somebody from the other side who's got hooks into you who won't let go, and they're influencing who you are and what you're doing. And those are just a couple things," she noted, giving Jewel a few other options.

However, she was sure Maddy probably had kept others to herself.

"So, is that a yes or a no?" Dr. Maddy asked.

Jewel found it hard to formulate an answer, but she definitely understood that Dr. Maddy's impatience was coming through the phone. "If I say no, that's the end of it, and you're gone, right?"

Dr. Maddy hesitated. "Look. I'm sorry. I understand that probably nothing about this makes any sense to you," she noted. "I guess I was hoping that you would take it on trust, as I'm really busy, but, if this isn't something you want to do, you certainly don't have to do it," she stated firmly.

"But then I won't get answers, will I?"

"I'm not guaranteeing you answers regardless. I'm just hoping that maybe I can help."

"Fine." She got up, and, carrying her cell phone, made her way upstairs. "I'm heading to my bed right now."

"I know," Maddy stated. "I can see you."

"Oh God," she murmured.

At that, Dr. Maddy laughed. "It's not nearly as scary as it sounds."

"That's because you're used to it."

"Yes, that's true," she agreed. "Very good point, and I tend to forget that. I am so accustomed to what I do that I tend to struggle with the fact that, for some people, it's all very new."

"Maybe you could remember that, in my case, this *is* all very new."

"Yet you are an energy worker."

"My impression of being an energy worker and the conversation I had with Stefan in the past did not include anything quite like this."

"Nope, and I guess I needed to realize that you may not be consciously aware of anything going on."

"Not only *may not be* but most likely am not. Did Stefan fill you in?"

"He did, which is one of the reasons I'm contacting you. Obviously something is going on, and the sooner we can sort it out, the better."

No way to argue with that, and Jewel really did want to figure out what was going on, so the best answer was for her to do this. "If this is like hypnosis, I don't think I hypnotize well."

"That's good," Dr. Maddy replied, "because I don't do hypnosis. Now"—her tone turned more businesslike—"lie down on the bed and just rest."

"Will I feel anything?"

"I don't know. I guess it depends on how much of an energy worker you are." And with that cryptic comment, Dr. Maddy hung up the phone.

Jewel slowly lay down on the bed, trying hard to figure out just who and what this was, dredging up the bits and pieces she had read about Dr. Maddy on the internet. When Jewel had been studying, researching who best to contact about the necklace, Stefan's name had come up time and time again. Jewel remembered sending out a mental message, wondering if she should contact Stefan, and got a response, incredibly harsh and forceful with a yes, so she'd picked up the phone immediately and had called Stefan.

He'd been the right person to call about the necklace, but, after that, everything seemed to spiral out of control. She didn't even know how and in what way. She didn't know what had even happened, yet everybody wanted to know the details. As she lay here, she wondered if she should send Stefan a text, asking about this.

A voice in her head replied, *Feel free to do it afterward.*

Jewel froze.

Relax, Jewel! You freezing up on me won't help, Dr. Maddy explained. *I need you to relax.*

Jewel took a deep breath. "Easy for you to say."

Once again that lovely peal of Dr. Maddy's laughter

rolled through her mind. *It's not only not that easy,* she shared, *but it is something that's very precious, and, if it works, … very valuable. Now I need to work. So just relax, lie there, think happy thoughts. I don't care what that means to you, if it's puppy dog tails and kitten pictures, then do it. I'm just here running scans of the energy in your system.* And, with that, the voice was gone again.

Jewel lay here, completely befuddled as to what was going on, but it didn't take long to note an odd hum, almost a buzz running through her body. She felt it in her toes, her hands, up and down her spinal cord. At that, her eyes widened because since when did anybody ever feel their spinal cord? But she could, and, in a weirdly odd way, she felt energy sliding up and down her body. Fascinated, she followed the energy as it moved from body part to body part. When it slowed, she asked in her mind, *Did that tell you anything?*

Maddy spoke up in her mind immediately. *Some things, not everything.*

Is it possession?

No, you are you, Maddy stated.

"Oh, thank heavens for that," Jewel murmured.

Maddy laughed. *I didn't expect it to be because you sounded so much more like yourself.*

"How would you know?" she asked bluntly.

I would have heard it in the energy within your voice, she murmured. *However, right now something else is going on, and I'm not sure what it is.*

"That just means we're back to square one then."

No, not quite, she countered cheerfully. *I definitely found some blocks, definitely some energy that you're not letting me see, and I won't force it because everybody has reasons for that,* she explained. *We're allowed to keep our private business private, but those blocks could be hurting you.*

"*Great,* but is everything else okay? The detective implied that I might have some disease where I appear dead."

That may or may not be, but you wouldn't appear dead to an energy worker because we don't look at physical signs. We look at energy.

"That's what Hurricane said."

Trust Hurricane, Maddy ordered. *He's a hell of an energy worker. If anybody can control foreign energies or strange out-of-control energies, it's him.*

"Strange out-of-control energy?" she repeated, trying the words on, but struggling with how Maddy meant them.

Maddy smiled in her head, a movement that seemed to make the space in her mind softer, gentler. *He's a good man. You can trust him.*

"That solves one of the problems," she murmured, "but that's only if I trust you."

I'm really happy to hear that you're a little bit reticent on some of this, Dr. Maddy replied. *Because blind belief isn't helpful either.*

"Maybe not, but right now it would be nice to trust something."

You contacted Stefan. Do you trust him?

She hesitated and then said, "I contacted Stefan because I had a very strange scenario going on that I thought maybe somebody like him would help me out with."

Did he?

"I don't know. Whatever happened to me happened not long after that," she replied.

Then Dr. Maddy murmured, *It's all those other energies.*

"What are those other energies?"

I don't know, Dr. Maddy admitted, *but I need to step out now. I will take a look at this in a little bit and get back to you, if I can help with anything.* And, with that, she was gone.

Almost immediately Jewel felt the energy from this weird scan withdrawing from her body. She wanted to reach out and tell her to leave it, that it felt good, that it was warm and cozy and felt secure. After a hesitation, Jewel wondered if Maddy took a layer out but left a layer in. Such a weird feeling and yet at the same time almost gratifying. She whispered, "Thank you."

Instead of a voice, Jewel felt almost energy, like a warm hug, and then leaving that bit behind, she sensed that Dr. Maddy was gone.

STEFAN? MADDY WHISPERED gently in her mind.

A stirring on the ethers and then Stefan slowly appeared in energy form in front of her. *What's up?*

That scan that I did on Jewel.

What about it? he asked, his voice coming fully awake. *What did you find?*

I'm not sure, but … definitely an anomaly.

What kind of an anomaly? he asked warily. *Every time you say something like that it makes my back go up.*

She chuckled. *And with good reason, considering the crap we've seen over the years, it's definitely something to be wary of.*

Now, is this something to be wary of?

Yes, but I don't know what it is.

He groaned. *If you don't know what it is, then how can you be sure it's of any consequence?*

I can't, but I'm very concerned. All I can tell you is that something very strange is going on in her energy, and it appears that she's completely unaware.

Possession? His tone was sharp, almost too sharp.

I won't say yes to that, she replied slowly, *because I don't really understand what this is, but something is there.*

Great, he replied snidely.

Because we don't know what it is, we have to assume a certain amount of danger, but I think the danger is more to her than anyone else.

Which goes along with possession. What is it you're seeing that doesn't fit with everything else?

The entire matter of it, she stated immediately. *A calmness to it, a surety to it.*

It?

The energy.

Inside?

Yes, and hidden all too well.

Of course it's hidden. So, … what then? We have somebody here with the ability to take over or lockdown into her mental space somewhere, into her energy, so that he can rise again when he wants to?

That's possibly what it is, she agreed cautiously. *And I know you're not enjoying this lack of answers when normally we have them, but definitely something is very strange about it.*

Okay, is she doing it to herself?

It's possible because I can't tell anything about it.

Possible, but then, considering what she's going through, it's not all that likely.

No, but, over the years, we've also seen some pretty strange things, strange and wonderful things, she added with a sigh, *so I can't say no for sure, but it doesn't make sense that it would be her.*

Can you tell me something, anything?

Yes, I can tell you that it's recent, some connection between it and her.

So, like family, friends?

Yes, but, according to her, she has no family that she knows of, and that may be something we want to track down.

Right. I don't remember much about her history, so that's something we'll have to follow up on. Do you think it's the killer?

I'm not getting a killer energy, but that's like saying no serial killers are out there because I haven't met them.

Which, in your case, you absolutely have. Stefan chuckled.

More than I would like to, yes, she murmured. *However, that doesn't necessarily make this any easier.*

No, of course not. Fine, so I'll talk to Hurricane and see if he can get some more information for you.

Okay. Maddy hesitated and then added, *Stefan, I also can't be sure that Hurricane's not in danger.*

A heavy pause ensued on the other end. *Not what I want to hear. I sent him there, so I'm responsible for him too.*

You also know that, if he knew what this was, he still would have gone anyway to protect Jewel.

Which still doesn't matter, considering I'll feel horrible if something happens to him. Stefan sighed. *I presume we need to put a watch on her then.*

Yeah, Maddy agreed. She hesitated and then added, *If I had a little more confidence in that energy, I would have put a hook in there,* she noted. *But I definitely sensed resistance, as if any hooks I put in would have caused some reaction, and it wouldn't be a reaction we would have liked.*

We never like any of these reactions, he muttered. *And now you're just worrying me about what else is going on, whether Jewel herself has been targeted by a serial killer or if there's something even more bizarre. Which, considering all we've gone through, it's pretty hard to imagine anything more bizarre. And yet …*

I know, she agreed immediately. *Anyway, I'll let you get back to sleep,* she said, with a note of laughter, *presuming that you can, of course, and I will follow up in a little bit.*

Only with her permission though, right?

Yes, she confirmed immediately. *For some reason that's the only way this will work.*

It's for the best. We have to keep her under watch and more. So, having her permission to go into her space will go a long way toward building trust, but, at the same time, nothing is really easy about this, if we are thinking something is going on.

Definitely something is going on, but—

I know. I know. We don't know what. We don't know who. We don't know why. We don't know anything. The usual.

Maybe contact Grant, she suggested suddenly.

He froze. *Why would your husband need to be brought into this?* Stefan asked curiously.

I'll fill him in on the case, but it feels as if he needs to be a part of this.

Oh, I won't argue that. All hands are welcome.

He won't be terribly happy, period, she said, with a chuckle.

That's because his hands are always full, Stefan murmured. *I'm not sure you're ever doing him a favor by bringing him into these things.*

No, no favors at all, she confirmed, *but, at some point in time, we have a choice to make, and, in this case, I don't feel that we have a choice at all.*

Long after Stefan had disconnected, Maddy sat here in the quiet of her bedroom alcove, a little space she had created just for herself. It wasn't much, just one of those comfy round chairs, a tiny little coffee table, and a warm glowing light above, but the massive window that looked to the sky made this space truly hers. Sensing a presence, she turned slowly to watch Drew approach.

"You okay?" he asked.

"As okay as I can be."

"Another one?"

She chuckled. "Always another one."

"Yes, but some of them really bother you and yet others? Not so much."

"I know," she murmured. "This one'll bother me, mostly because I've never seen whatever this is that I am looking at. Now, as soon as I can figure that out, then I think we can relax."

"But, if it's something you have to figure out," he noted, his voice rising in alarm, "then it's not good news."

"I did tell Stefan that he needed to contact you," she admitted. "I'm sorry."

He stared at her in the darkness. "That bad?"

"Yes," she murmured. "And I don't know if this woman even has a clue."

"Well, if she has you by her side, chances are she will be all right. Is her life in danger?"

Maddy paused for a moment and then replied, "It's worse than that. Her soul is in danger."

CHAPTER 8

J EWEL LAY THERE, dry-eyed, for a long moment, trying to figure out just what the heck had gone on. Who was this person, and how powerful could somebody be to do something like that from afar? When she heard footsteps coming up the stairs, she frowned. They were heavier than normal, and she immediately rolled over and dropped to the floor on the other side of the bed.

"That's encouraging," Hurricane noted, as he stepped forward into her bedroom. "At least you have the natural instinct to run and hide if something's wrong." He leaned over the bed to see her on the floor. "But you do realize that's really not a very good hiding spot, right?"

"I heard you coming up," she replied, "but you didn't sound right."

He stared at her for a moment. "In what way did I not sound right?"

She hesitated, shrugged, and added, "Heavy, uncoordinated, not all there, like you were lumbering instead of the coordinated person that I have seen up until now."

"Interesting, maybe because I just woke up," he murmured. "It is me, and I see you met Dr. Maddy."

At that, she stared at him for a moment and then bolted onto the bed. "That really was her, wasn't it?"

"It absolutely was her," he confirmed, with a smile. "She

told me that she scanned you."

"Yeah, and what does that even mean? She was looking to see whether somebody's energy was in there or if anything odd was going on. She couldn't figure out some of the stuff though."

"I heard that."

"What do you mean, you *heard* that?" she asked, her eyes going wide.

"Stefan told me."

"Whoa, whoa, whoa, whoa." She held up her hand. "How do these people talk without me hearing anything?"

He looked at her. "Ever hear of a telephone?" She glared at him. "Also both Stefan and Maddy can communicate telepathically."

Her breath came out in a *whoosh*, and she sat down on the bed beside him. "Seriously?"

"Oh, very seriously," he said. "The way they do it and the reason they do it is also very serious."

"You don't want to explain what that is, do you?" When he shook his head, she sighed. "You guys have secrets, and that's not fair."

At that, he gave a bark of laughter and added, "Look who's talking."

"But I don't know what my secrets are," she argued. "I don't know what's going on here."

"I hear you," he murmured. "The good news is, Maddy doesn't know either."

"How on earth is that good news?" Jewel cried out. "If you guys have all these kinds of skills, surely that's not good news."

"Oh, it depends. She could at least say that you weren't doing something or weren't being held hostage energy-wise."

"Great, so she ruled out something that I didn't even know needed to be ruled out."

His lips twisted. "Maybe, but the bottom line is, Maddy's not done. She's done what she could for the moment, and she'll check back in on your energy in a little bit."

"Okay, but that didn't sound terribly much like what I thought. Although she did mention that she would do that earlier."

"It's all right," Hurricane reassured her. "They're good people, and they're there to help."

"Maybe."

Just then her doorbell rang. She bolted to her feet, racing toward the closet.

He caught her halfway across the loft, pulled her into his arms, and whispered, "Easy, take it easy."

But she was shivering, staring up at him. "Dear God, I don't even know why I'm reacting like this."

He looked at her and nodded. "What you've been through would make anybody react like this. I'll go answer the door because I want to know who's there. If you don't want to know, you can stay up here, while I talk to them. Then I'll come up and talk to you. Or you can come down with me, and we'll open the door together. I'm right here."

She took a deep breath and exhaled. "The latter. I need to know. I need to stop reacting and instead take charge of this."

"Yeah, that sounds perfect in theory," he agreed, "but you need to go a little easier on yourself. This isn't something that you can just naturally hand over control and expect to be perfect at right off the bat."

"Maybe not." She gave him a blunt stare. "But I remember just enough that whatever is going on is confusing me."

"CONFUSING IS AN interesting term," he noted, as he looked at her. "Come on. Let's go down and answer the door."

The doorbell rang again and then a third time.

He called out, "Hang on. I'm coming."

When he got to the door and opened it, two men stood there, glaring at Hurricane. When they caught sight of Jewel, their faces cleared.

"Dear God." They stepped into the living room, throwing their arms around her.

She submitted to their hugs, but Hurricane could see from the confusion on her face that she had no idea who they were. He studied them both energy-wise as much as he could, and, of course, their energy was locked down and not open to being shared. He wondered if it was because the two of them were partners in a community where maybe being homosexual wasn't welcome.

When they stepped back, with big grins on their faces, one of the men asked Hurricane, "Excuse me, do you want to identify who you are?"

At that, the bigger of the two turned on him and added, "Who are you? She never told us anything about a guy being with her."

"What did she say to you?" Hurricane asked.

He shrugged. "She left us a weird message, but we ignored it at first because it wasn't something she would normally do."

At that, Hurricane looked at him and frowned. "Okay, I need a bit more of an explanation."

"You're not getting any explanation," the other man declared, "until we get one."

Hurricane looked over at Jewel and asked, "Do you want

to explain it or shall I?"

"I think you need to," she said. She looked at the two men, then apologetically added, "I'm sorry. I've been in an accident and have amnesia. So I don't know who you guys are."

Hurricane watched the shock and disbelief on both their faces. He immediately believed that they knew nothing about it. He closed the door. "Come on in. I'll try to explain as best I can."

Both of them immediately stepped in farther, their gazes going from her to him and back again.

"How does she know you?" the first man asked.

"First off, my name is Hurricane," he shared. "I was part of a group she had already contacted over a problem she was having," he explained, without giving away too much information. "And since we were already friends, it seemed like a good idea to come. Unfortunately, when I got here, she was in the hospital."

"The hospital?" the smaller of the two men repeated, his hands going to his mouth, before turning to look at her.

She gave him a wan smile. "Yeah, apparently I was found dead on the highway," she replied, with a careless air. "They took me to the morgue, and … I woke up in a hospital bed a couple days later."

The men just stared at her, their gazes turning from shock to horror to disbelief.

She shrugged. "I would expect that look on your faces too. Yet Hurricane's here. He arrived in time to pick me up when I got discharged from the hospital. The detective was here earlier, and he's the one who filled me in on what happened—or at least what they know to this point."

At that, the larger man introduced himself. "I'm Charles.

So what on earth is going on?"

"I don't know," Hurricane admitted, "but what she told you right now is the truth. When I saw her in the hospital, she had just woken back up again. Her body is covered in bruises and nobody knows whether somebody tried to murder her or she suffered an attack that dropped her into a very deep coma. That theory would mean that the paramedics and others didn't check her vitals all that closely and pronounced her dead, where she was left in a body bag in the morgue."

At that, the other man started to shake. Charles wrapped his arms around him and said, "It's okay. She's okay now."

"Oh my God though," he replied, "what she must have suffered."

"The good news is," Jewel noted, "I don't remember a thing."

"Maybe that *is* good news," Charles agreed, studying her face. "You also look a little different," he said cautiously, "not a lot different, but a little bit."

"When you say a little bit, what do you mean?" she asked.

"Your skin is whiter than white," he stated, "but I guess maybe hanging out in a body bag will do that." He grimaced, an odd look on his face. "I really don't know."

"The hair?" she asked.

"You changed your hair just before whatever happened to you," he stated. "Maybe you don't remember that."

She shook her head. "No, I don't remember that."

"I asked you about it, and you got a little put off and didn't say anything."

"When did you see her last?" Hurricane asked Charles.

"Four days ago, probably right before whatever happened to her."

"Where did you see her?"

"Right here, at her place. She was working on some jewelry, and she told me that she was feeling off and just needed a break. I asked her if I could help her with anything. Jewel said she was fine, just really tired. So I left her alone, fairly early on that evening," he explained, frowning. "Now I'll feel terrible, thinking, if I'd stayed, I could have stopped whatever happened."

"Or maybe you would have been hurt too," Jewel stated, reaching out and gently patting him on the cheek. "We can't have that. What would Lucas do without you?"

At that, Lucas looked over at Charles, and his bottom lip trembled.

Hurricane held back saying anything, but she clearly remembered them both. Charles had introduced himself, but she had identified the other guy on her own.

Charles reached out a hand, gripped Lucas's hand, and stated, "I'm fine. Nothing happened."

Lucas nodded. "I get that, but still …"

They both turned and looked at Hurricane. "So now what?"

"We're here, trying to piece back together her life," he shared. "Did she tell you whether she was being followed, was worried about something, or anything along that line that would have made you suspicious?"

At that, Charles and Lucas both shook their heads. "No," Charles replied. "Honestly I would have stayed to help if I thought something was going on."

"And they would have," Jewel confirmed from the sidelines. "We've known each other for years."

At that, Lucas looked at her eagerly. "You remember that

much, right?"

She gave him a half smile. "I remember all kinds of things," she said, "and none of it is particularly useful. For instance, I clearly remember last Halloween, when you went as a hula girl and lost your skirt."

Immediately his face flushed. "Why, out of everything, do you remember that? So humiliating."

She burst out laughing, and even Charles groaned, then added, "Honestly, I thought it was terribly cute."

Lucas shot him a look and said, "Yeah, that's just because you were entranced with getting an eyeful."

"Didn't need an eyeful," Charles noted cheerfully. "I get an eyeful all the time. But the fact that you were so embarrassed was pretty damn cute."

"Humiliating," Lucas muttered. He turned and glared at Hurricane. "Why would she remember that?"

"I don't know," he replied, with a headshake. "What else do you remember?" he asked Jewel, turning to look at her.

She shrugged. "Lots of evenings with coffee and herb tea." She frowned, looked over at Charles. "You like peppermint."

"I do," he admitted, looking at her carefully. "Anything else?"

"Bits and pieces, events that we went to, musicals we've attended together." She hesitated, pondering it. "I mean, it seems like we were always busy and having fun."

"Exactly," Charles agreed, "always busy, having fun. We always promoted your jewelry designs, and you were always there for us, for our artwork." He turned and looked at Hurricane. "Both Lucas and I are artists. We've been together for many, many years, and we've known Jewel for almost as long."

"Good." Hurricane nodded. "She needs friends, and right now she'll need you even more."

At that, Lucas turned to him. "Do you think whoever attacked her will come back?"

"We don't even know whether she was attacked or, shall we say, spending an evening with somebody….and maybe it just went bad.

"But why wouldn't they have taken her to the hospital?" Charles pointed out.

But Lucas offered, "They wouldn't have, if they couldn't afford to have anybody question them. Then the question really is, do we know who she might have been dating in this last while?"

At that, Hurricane emphatically nodded. "Exactly, any information you can tell us about her previous days or weeks would be a big help."

The two men looked at each other, and then Lucas shrugged and replied, "Honestly I don't think she was dating anybody." He turned to look at her. "Ever since you broke it off with Darren, you've been reticent about hooking up again. We kept trying with lots of our friends, but nothing seemed to work out."

She nodded. "I kind of remember that. A bit of a running joke, wasn't it?"

"Yes," Charles agreed. "We wanted to see you happy, and you kept pushing us away, telling us that you were happy alone because being alone was better than being with somebody terrible."

She smiled. "That sounds very familiar."

"Good," Charles declared. "At least if you remember that much, we know you're still there with us."

"No, I'm definitely here," she stated. "I just don't know

what happened. However, the detective did suggest this weird coma disease thing, which might leave holes in your memory at the same time," she noted. "I haven't … I haven't figured out enough of it yet to understand all the implications."

"Whatever it is"—Charles shivered—"it sounds terrible." And, at that, Charles walked over and wrapped his arms around her. "I'm so sorry," he muttered. "We would never want anything bad to happen to you."

Hurricane watched as she wrapped her arms around him and held him close. "We've been friends for a long time. I'm so glad that you popped back into the loft right now," she said. "I was starting to wonder if anybody in my world was out there."

"So you didn't remember us until we came over?" Charles asked in horror.

She shook her head. "No, but, once I saw you, and we started talking, it jogged my memory, and you fell into place."

"Thank heavens for that," Lucas claimed, almost affronted. "How could she possibly forget us?" he asked Charles, a pained look on his face.

Charles shrugged. "I don't think anything was on purpose. Keep that in mind," he told Lucas.

"I know but …" he muttered, "it's not as if we're very forgettable."

Hurricane had to agree with that. They were both one of a kind, yet an obvious pair, and appeared to be extremely happy together. And he was happy for them, but what he really needed was answers as to what had happened to her. "So, as far as you know, she wasn't dating anybody. She wasn't seeing anybody casually, had no sweetheart on the internet, nothing like that at all? Do you know if she had signed up for online dating or something along that line?"

"Why don't you check her computer?"

"Because there isn't one here."

At that, she bolted to her feet and asked him, "There isn't, is there?"

He shook his head. "No, there isn't. I checked." He looked at the men. "She was also found without a stitch on and with no phone."

"Oh no," Charles gasped, staring at her in shock, "not your phone."

As far as Hurricane could tell, it appeared that, for Charles, losing your phone was the absolute worst thing that could happen to anybody. And Hurricane understood the frustration of losing a phone, but certainly a whole lot worse could happen to people. "Exactly. She's using a spare phone of mine right now." He looked over at her and suggested, "You may want to exchange numbers, so you can stay in contact."

"Right," she replied, pulling out her phone. "Give me your numbers, and I'll send you both a text." And, with that done, she nodded. "Now you have it. I don't know for how long I'll have this number because I don't know what happened to my other phone, nor do I have a clue what's happened with any other calls that may have come in."

At that, Charles gasped again. "Oh no. You were waiting for phone calls on a jewelry show."

She stared at him. "I don't remember that."

He looked at her in shock. "You don't? It was huge for you. Every morning you would get up and say that maybe today was the day."

She slowly shook her head. "I don't remember anything

about that," she cried out, frowning at him. "If so important, how could I possibly have forgotten?"

At that, he winced. "I don't know, but the real question is, if they were trying to get ahold of you, what are the chances that they've now given up trying?"

Hurricane interrupted. "That brings up a good point. We can track your phone number, Jewel, if somebody gives it to me." He pulled out his phone. "I'll see who all the calls came from."

At that, Charles looked at him. "How can you do that?"

"I have connections," he replied bluntly.

She looked over at Charles. "If you could, that would be very appreciated."

Hurricane nodded. "Your phone number?" he asked Jewel.

She stared at him blankly, turned to the men, and said, "I have no idea."

Immediately Charles recited the number. Hurricane put it into his phone and sent the number to Stefan, asking him to talk to the detective. "Stefan will talk to the detective," he stated, by way of explanation to her.

She nodded. "I just … wow," she murmured. She sagged onto the only couch. And then she looked around. "Did I always stay here?"

"Almost always. We heard that you had another place, but we've never been there," Charles stated candidly. "This is the place we know you from. This is your heart. Your soul is here," he said, with a wave of his hand. "So any other place really won't matter to us because this is so you."

She smiled at him. "I forgot how melodramatic you were."

He looked at her in horror. "I'm not," he cried out in

protest.

"Sure you're not," she said, with a teasing smile.

At that, Charles grinned. "I'm glad to see you are in there."

"I'm in here," she confirmed, "just a little bit beaten up."

"And did they?" he asked in a shocked tone. "Did they beat you up?"

"I don't know," she replied, with another wave of her hand. "That was just a phrase. I'm feeling bruised, let's put it that way, as if everything's gone chaotically wrong in my world."

"It has," Charles agreed. "Absolutely it has, and, if we can do anything to help, you just need to tell us. You know that, right?"

She smiled at him. "I do know that, thank you." She looked over at Hurricane. "We have been friends for a very long time."

He nodded. "And that's good to hear." He turned, looked at Charles, and asked, "So she's never mentioned anybody as a stalker? She's never had problems, not with any ex-boyfriend who was ugly?"

Charles pondered that. "She wouldn't ever tell us if it was *ugly*," he began, "but she certainly was not interested in going back into the dating scene."

"I could have had a lot of reasons for that," she protested. "Not necessarily because whoever my last boyfriend was could have been abusive."

"Exactly," Charles agreed.

But, as Hurricane considered her, he shared, "Somebody is involved in this. … Now, if your ex-boyfriend wanted to see you again, would you have gone back to him or at least had coffee with him?"

She frowned and shook her head. "I don't think so, but I don't know."

He looked at the two men. They both shrugged. "We don't know whether she would have or not. I would like to say emphatically no, but I can't."

And that honesty was something Hurricane really appreciated because so much more was going on here that it's obvious things wouldn't get cleared up anytime soon.

Charles added, "But I can tell you that she was always very cautious and that she wouldn't have gone unless it was somebody who she knew very well."

"That's not quite true," Lucas disagreed. "If anybody had wanted to meet her over this show, she would have definitely gone for that."

At that, Charles turned, looked at him, and nodded. "Yes, you're right. She really, really, really wanted that show to happen."

"What are the chances that whoever was working on this show used that as a means to get ahold of her?" Hurricane asked. "Do we even know if there was a show?"

"No, I don't know." The two men turned to look at her.

"Do you have any documentation?" Hurricane faced her.

She gave him a flat stare. "How would I know? Do you remember what this place looked like when we got here?" Turning to her friends, she explained, "It had been completely upended."

At that, their faces blanched. "Oh my," Charles exclaimed, "definitely somebody is after you then. You would not have done this to yourself, but why would anybody else do it?"

"Unless they were looking for something," Hurricane suggested. "The question is, did they find what they were looking for?"

CHAPTER 9

THE NEXT MORNING when Jewel woke up, the conversation with Charles and Lucas still rolled through her head. They'd talked for an hour, until Hurricane had finally ushered them out. She'd protested that they didn't need to leave, but everybody had apparently seen the fatigue in her face and had ignored her. Even as she lay here in her bed, she wondered at the odd feeling coursing through her right now.

The fact that she'd woken up was great, but still something was off. Waking up to an odd feeling was an even odder feeling. Waking up was now something Jewel had to be curious about, apparently after being dead for a while. And being dead-dead to the point that she had been in a body bag was enough to make her worried in that way. Thank God those memories weren't in her brain. She couldn't imagine waking up in a body bag, all zipped up, wondering what had happened to her. That would have been horrific.

Almost immediately after she thought about it, she determined that she needed to talk to someone in the morgue. She didn't know why. She didn't know what he could possibly tell her, but it just seemed to be one more piece of the puzzle that either she needed to know, or she was torturing herself about that could put her mind to rest. She slowly got up, realized that her body was more or less pain-free, and headed for a shower.

She steadied herself, as the water and soap bubbles ran over her body, and noted that some of the bruising was easing back. Seemed her body was on some delayed response, after whatever had happened, with the bruises showing up many hours later, and now were slowly going away again.

She didn't even know whether she was healing faster than normal or this was really just what *normal* looked like. She snorted at the word being applied to her. Dressed and somewhat ready to face the day, she headed downstairs, moving quietly, in case Hurricane was still sleeping, but instead she found him sitting at the kitchen island, sipping coffee.

Without looking up from his phone, he asked, "How are you feeling?"

"Better," she murmured. "At least I think so."

He turned and looked at her, then smiled and nodded. "I'd say you're looking better."

"Which just means that I was looking pretty horrific to begin with."

He chuckled. "The fact that you're even worried about your looks from back then says you're feeling better."

"I'm not a vain person," she stated, with a shrug. "So I can't say that I was particularly bothered about it at any point in time."

"Good, because, for a while there, you looked like death warmed over."

"That's not funny," she scolded him.

He again smiled at her. "There's coffee, if you want."

"Now that would be good." She walked around, snagged a cup, and asked, "I suppose you heard no new developments, *huh?*"

"What developments? If you mean on your case, no, absolutely nothing. And I'm not sure that the detective has gotten anywhere with your phone records."

"I suppose, if he's not allowed to, is that part of the problem?"

"I think there are some laws about checking someone's phone records. It's possible that it requires approval from a judge or something. I can't imagine the detective would be in a big hurry to stand in front of a judge, while trying to explain this mess."

"Right. What if I signed a form or paid something for it?"

"Maybe." He quickly sent off a message. "I just asked him about that."

As it turned out, there was a way to get it done, but she would have to send in a request. With that done and the paperwork digitally signed, she sat down with her coffee and noted, "It would be nice to know that I haven't missed a big chunk of my world because of this."

He nodded. "Do you remember anything about the art show?"

"I remember feeling like it was *very* important, and I would be devastated if I didn't get to participate in it. But now I don't even know what it was about and couldn't care less," she murmured.

"Until the memories come back, and then the art show will come back with all that emotion."

"Maybe I'd be better off if knowledge of the show doesn't come back," she said.

"You can't assume that you didn't get it, since you really haven't been available or able to get a phone call or even an email," he reminded her.

"No, but it does feel to me that maybe it's something that isn't or shouldn't be as important as it apparently was to me."

"Life is like that. Sometimes things are important, and then you get a paradigm shift, and you realize it really wasn't that important at all. And, right now, something else has happened to you that's put it into perspective."

"I guess. It's that necklace."

"I noticed that you didn't mention it to anybody."

"No, and I waited to see if they brought it up, but nobody did."

"Is there a chance that you didn't tell anybody you were working on it? Were you in the habit of telling people about jobs you were working on?"

"I don't think so," she replied. "It doesn't seem like something I would do. Especially repair jobs, you know? It's not like a new piece I'd created and wanted to share with my friends."

"So, we have to consider the possibility that nobody knew about the necklace."

"I don't know. Not for sure." She turned and looked at the wall safe. "From here it does look like it's closed off."

"It does," he agreed. "Of course the pearls are back in there again."

She looked at him, startled. He shrugged. "I removed them, and you put them back in. I don't know when you put them back in, but you did."

She let her breath out slowly. "I don't remember putting them back in," she cried out.

"I know, and I was afraid you would say that," he stated, his gaze ever watchful.

"Then you get that look in your eye, and it feels like you

think everything I say is a lie."

He shook his head. "I'm not calling you a liar at all, but something is obviously going on, and those pearls are at the heart of it. Do you have any history on them, any emails or anything?"

"If I had a computer, then I could let you know. Why would they take my laptop?" she asked.

"You tell me. What was on it?"

"My whole world." She stared blankly at him. "Everything. I mean, isn't everybody's life on their computers these days?"

"Their computers and phones, and, yes, they did take both of those. I, however, do have a laptop. I got it out of my vehicle last night." He pointed beside her. "Maybe that's when you put the necklace back in the safe."

She immediately snatched up Hurricane's laptop and then stopped, looked at him, and asked, "May I?"

"Absolutely. Do you know all your logins?"

"I think so," she murmured. "As long as I can remember my email." And, with that, it took her just a few clicks, and she had her email up. "Oh, thank heavens for that," she whispered.

She sat down on the bench beside him, with her hot coffee, and started going through everything. "Here it is! The communication with my client about the pearls," she said and pushed it over, so he could see it.

He leaned forward to read the email and then asked, "If you have a printer, can you print that off?"

"Sure." She quickly sent it to her printer, and, off to the side, he heard a printer whirring away, behind a bunch of canvases. "There's just a couple of them."

"How did you receive the pearls?" he asked.

"They came by courier, and that's how they were supposed to be sent back."

"Have you ever had any communications with this guy before?"

"No, not at all, but then I haven't really been doing very much online recently."

"Any idea why?"

"No reason, it's just that I've been busy with my own designs," she explained. "That whole art show thing again."

"Like pieces of jewelry? And yet, you didn't look for any of those here."

Startled, she looked at him. "No, I didn't."

"Why is that?"

She got up and raced up to the safe, had it open as he came behind her. "They're not here." She looked around the safe again. "I didn't even remember about the show."

"Wait. When is the show? Could it already be in progress?"

She stopped, then slowly nodded. "Yeah, setting up at least," she replied. "My God, could I have sent them out for the show?" Then she turned and looked back at her front door. "But, if the show was on, I would have told Charles and Lucas, wouldn't I?"

"Would you? Or are you the type to make it a surprise and take them there?"

She and Hurricane returned to their seats near his laptop. She slowly nodded in response to his question. "That is something I would do."

He smiled. "So let's not think everything is negative here," he stated. "Maybe this is all good news."

"Maybe," she murmured. She returned her attention to her emails, then let out a sigh. "The contract's right here.

The show is happening, but it doesn't start for another three days. I had to send in all the pieces, so they could set it up."

"There you go. So that's some good news. Having access to your emails is important, and you can recapture some of what has been lost. That's pretty important, and congratulations on the show."

"In a way it's groundbreaking for me—for my work, I mean. It's the first show I've ever had."

"Why is that? You're obviously very talented."

"I've deliberately avoided everything to do with shows," she said, with half a smile. "I'm not a very public-oriented person."

"And yet you seem to be quite excited about the show."

"It's because of who and what it is," she murmured. "It's huge for my name as an artist, so, of course, I'm excited. And I was invited to attend, to participate. I wasn't just submitting material, hoping they would think it was good enough. I was invited to show some of my work. The process was fairly complicated to get it to them."

"But you did it, right?"

"Yes, everything's ready to go. I remember now. I can't believe I didn't tell Charles and Lucas about it."

"It's interesting that you didn't," he agreed cautiously. "Does it say something about your relationship?"

"I don't know." She pondered that. "It seemed totally normal last night, like no reason to be at all upset or worried. I think you were right. I think I might have just planned on surprising them."

"They didn't mention anything about that last night though."

"No." She frowned. "I'm not sure whether I was leaving it until the show started or what." And then she sighed. "The show is running for two weeks, so I would probably wait until it was actually live and then send them the link and show them."

"Would they be happy for you?"

She looked up and smiled. "They would be ecstatic for me." She nodded. "I guess I was just … It just seemed so weird to see them yesterday and to feel so, I don't know, distant and separate from them."

"Understood," he replied. "I think with so much going on in your life right now that it'll feel that way for a little bit. Especially with your memory coming back in such a seemingly random way. So don't judge anything about it. Just be accepting right now."

"I'm working on it," she said, looking at him seriously. "Listen. When I woke up, I had this thought that I wanted to talk to the morgue attendant or whatever it's called. The one who found me alive inside the body bag."

"Why?" he asked, staring at her.

"I want to know the details. Like, was I sitting up inside a body bag? Did I get out of the body bag? Did he see the body bag moving around? What happened?"

He continued to stare at her. "Does it matter?"

She frowned. "I don't know. I guess it's all the missing pieces that bother me."

"I can ask the detective, if you want."

"Would you mind?" she asked hopefully.

He shook his head. "No, I wondered myself how that played out."

"It just seems off somehow."

He chuckled. "A lot about this is off, so we can't really blame anybody yet."

"No, I'm not trying to blame anybody. I just would like

to know what that was like, in my mind."

"Good enough." And he quickly sent off a couple text messages.

She sighed. "Thanks for being so helpful."

He shrugged. "Hey, nothing about this is normal. This isn't a situation where somebody else will go, 'Hey, that happened to me a while ago too.' I mean, right? It's unique. It's different, and, therefore, nobody really knows how to help you."

"Except you," she stated, looking at him steadily. Yet she saw absolutely no change in his expression, absolutely nothing that said he was bothered in any way.

"It's not even that," he added, looking at her. "That necklace is something that I really need to know more about."

"Right," she murmured. "I didn't tell anybody about it."

"Why is that?"

"Because it terrified me," she replied bluntly.

He nodded. "That is what I need to hear more about too. Specifics, like why, how, and in what way? How do you remember? Because I can't have you making it up or assuming you felt a certain way. Yet, if you have something concrete you remember about it, I need to know."

"What will you do when you find out?" she asked him curiously.

"I'll have to track down the information and figure out whether what you're feeling and saying are for real or not. We need that distinction."

She asked, "The … possessed necklace can't be for real, can it?" But that fear in her voice revealed that, deep down, she thought it was all too real.

"You want to tell me what you felt?"

She stared at him, took a long slow breath, then bluntly said, "Every pearl gave off a weird energy. I always try to infuse my work with love, joy, and peace," she explained. "I want the wearer of my pieces to feel that love when they have it on. But this necklace? I didn't notice anything odd at first. I don't know why, but the more I worked on it, the more I kept getting these creepy images, creepy feelings. Then I realized that it seemed like, with every pearl, I was getting images of a different woman who had died, and the woman somehow seemed to match a pearl," she shared. "I know that makes no sense, but I don't know what else to say."

"No, that's fine. Let's not worry about whether something makes sense or not. The more I work in this field, the more I realize that nothing really makes sense. You just go with the flow and accept the energy as is."

"I'm not sure how accepting I've been up until now."

"Maybe you haven't been, but nothing quite like this stuff to send your belief systems into a tailspin. So, back to the necklace. Were there any names that went with these images?"

She gave him an odd look. "Yes, but I'm not sure I remember them."

He pondered that. "If you held the pearls again, would you?"

"I don't know," she said, looking back at the safe. "I can tell you the necklace is dangerous."

He grimaced. "It absolutely is dangerous, and I'm doing my best to minimize the danger. What I don't know is why it's dangerous now and yet not when you first got it—except, from what I can understand, it's somehow been ... activated."

"You said something about that before. *Triggered* I think

was the word."

He nodded. "Something you did, something that happened to you while you had it, has charged the necklace in a way that I don't think it's been charged in a very long time. So, now that it's charged, a lot more energy is around it than was even there to begin with."

She stared at him. "I'm not sure I know what that means, but what could possibly have charged it?"

He hesitated and then replied, "You said you tried to put loving energy into it?"

"Yes, of course. I do that with everything I work on or create."

He nodded. "In that case, you would have opened up whatever energy lock was on it, and you are the one who charged it. The question now is, what happens next?"

HURRICANE COULD TELL that he'd shocked Jewel.

She sat back, such a confused, dismayed air about her that he immediately reached out with one hand and said, "It's not your fault."

But her glare immediately turned on him. "Really? Then whose fault do you think this is? Was anybody else playing with this necklace at the same time?" she argued. "Therefore, it is my fault."

He waited until some of her emotions had subsided, and then he murmured, "Were you aware ahead of time that it was a full-on negative-energy piece? I know you well enough to say that you did not," he declared. "So, let go of feeling that you're responsible, and let's get back to finding a solution."

At that, she looked at him, startled. "What solution? Is

there anything we can do about it?"

"There are always things we can do."

Her shock reminded him that she was relatively new to all of this energy work. She might have been working in the field, but she was working as somebody who came from the heart and was trying to do good things for the people around her. She wasn't somebody who had worked with or had even been around the energy workers he had worked with. She didn't see the negatives and was naturally drawn to that which was good. She really was an innocent in all this. He slowly ran his hand through his hair, trying to figure out how to explain it.

"I've never had any exposure to this stuff before," she murmured, then stared at him. "I mean, when I phoned Stefan, I had no idea what I was even getting into."

He smiled at that. "Honestly, unless you know Stefan, you really don't understand what you're getting into."

She gave a quiet, quick flash of a smile in his direction. "Most of this appears to be completely foreign to me."

And yet Hurricane had to wonder because she had the presence of mind to understand what the problem was and to contact somebody who was in a position to help her. That's the part that confounded him because that versus the person in front of him appeared to be very different and that brought it back to the fact that she didn't have the same memories.

When his phone rang a few minutes later, she waited expectantly for him to answer it.

"Stefan?" Hurricane greeted him. "You're on Speaker."

"Any change?" Stefan asked immediately.

"No, nothing yet. We met a few people from her world. We accessed her emails, and we're working on trying to get clearance to get a copy of her phone calls. The detective's been brought in on that," he added for clarity.

"Yes, and I heard from him too. He's working on it."

"It would be helpful if we could get that information," he murmured. "Health-wise, I think she's doing okay. She's had some sleep, and we've got some food down her."

At that, Jewel heard Stefan's relieved sigh, and that confused her.

"Did she eat well?" he asked, his tone almost noncommittal, as if he didn't care, but Hurricane knew just how important it was.

"She didn't eat a lot, but she did have a few bites. I'm hoping she'll have a better appetite today." He looked over at her, and she shrugged.

"Depends on what you'll offer me."

"What is it you want to eat?" Hurricane asked her.

She stared at him for a moment. "Bacon, eggs, and pancakes," she announced.

His eyebrows shot up. "That's interesting."

"Why? Last night you weren't happy when I wouldn't eat, and now you don't sound happy that I want to eat everything." Jewel now sighed.

He chuckled. "I'll take this over the other. We can go out for breakfast, if you want."

She looked around and nodded. "I guess we have to, unless you want to go shopping and bring it back and cook." And then she winced. "Honestly I don't even remember if I know how to make pancakes."

He burst out laughing and returned to his phone call. "Stefan, if you have nothing else now, I'll call you back. I guess I have an army to feed."

"Do that," he replied, "and be watchful." And with that

warning and no explanation to go with it, Stefan hung up.

Her next comment really surprised Hurricane.

"So, is Stefan concerned about me or about the necklace?"

"Both," Hurricane stated, choosing his words cautiously. "Stefan has an invested interest in any energy worker."

She snorted that. "If I was any kind of an energy worker, I would have understood what I'd done."

At that, he smiled. "Ninety-nine percent of energy workers wouldn't have had a clue what you did, not to mention how to do it. I'm also amazed that you recognized a problem, and that is another huge plus in your favor."

"But I didn't do it consciously," she murmured. "I didn't know anything about it. I don't understand," she said. "How does Stefan keep track of people like me?"

"That is a hard thing because how is he supposed to know you even exist, if you don't pop up to the surface somewhere?"

"The surface?" she asked, with an odd look in his direction.

"If you don't contact him, if something doesn't happen to put you on his radar, how is he supposed to know that you are even out there?"

"That's exactly what I meant," she murmured.

"You did contact him in this case, so that's an easy answer."

"Nothing about this is easy." Then she got up, walked over to the front door, turned to look back at him. "Are you coming?"

Startled, he hopped to his feet. "Sure. Where are we going?"

"I need food," she demanded, her tone defiant. "And I

need to get out of here."

Stepping up beside her, he nodded. "Good. We can also pick up some groceries while we're out."

"Are you staying that long?"

"Yes." And this time there was nothing unequivocal about his tone. He watched, as she let out a slow breath, then he nodded. "I told you that I wasn't deserting you."

"You can say all kinds of things, but I have come to realize that people are complicated. Words don't always match actions."

"No, they sure don't," he agreed, with a smile. "However, we're way past that. I won't desert you, so you can relax."

She shrugged at that. "Just because you say I can relax doesn't mean I'll turn around and immediately drop my guard."

"Oh, heavens no, don't drop your guard." His words held a sharper tone than he intended, and, when she froze in front of him and slowly turned to look at him, he winced. "I didn't mean that quite the way it came out."

"Somehow I suspect you meant it exactly that way," she stated, staring at him. "You want to explain?"

"Outside of the fact that you've quite likely been attacked and that you were left on the side of a road nude with absolutely nothing to identify who you were and what was going on in your life? Do you need more than that?" He felt her searching gaze, as if she was looking to see the validity of his words. Then he gave her the gentlest of smiles. "I meant it. Don't drop your guard. For all we know, somebody out there is still after you."

She winced. "That is not a thought I want to dwell on."

"Of course not, and it's not a thought I really want you reminded of, but, since the police have no leads, and nobody has any idea what happened, you are the best lead we have to find out what happened to you. And the best way to do that is to always be vigilant. Look around. See what's going on. See if anything, any people, any faces, anything at all triggers a reaction and causes you alarm. Anything at all."

Locking up the loft, they headed outside. He led the way to his truck and opened up the passenger door for her.

Jewel stopped to eye him. "Are you always this chivalrous?"

"Maybe. Definitely something about you makes me feel that way." Her frown was something he almost expected. He laughed. "It's all right. I'm not a threat to you in any way."

"I wouldn't let you be," she snapped. "And besides, after what I've been through, it'll take a lot for me to trust anyone."

"Yes, until you find the one person you're used to trusting, and then all bets are off."

"Considering the fact that I don't know anybody anymore, and I have no clue what happened, I'm not likely to trust easily, am I?"

"I hope not," he said, with as much sincerity as he could infuse into his voice. "Because it is important. It's important that you don't let somebody close enough to hurt you a second time."

And, with that, he hopped in, started the engine, and asked, "Where to?"

She had no idea what to make of him. Friend or foe? Time will tell.

STEFAN WAS IN the studio, studying his latest work in progress. He smiled at his wife, as she brought him a cup of tea, blew him a kiss, and disappeared out the door. "Thank you," he called out.

She just waved a hand in acknowledgment.

Something was so full and so refreshing and so joyous about his life right now that made it easier to dip into the dark side and to come up still intact, whole, and healthy when done. But he knew that he had to take a look at Jewel's energy. What he didn't know was what kind of reception he'd get. Maddy hadn't gone back in, neither had she talked to Jewel since, and honestly Stefan was just coming off a pretty ugly criminal case, and those often left him more than drained.

He needed time, respite, a chance to turn around and to cleanse his soul. Thankfully, being with his wife was a true joy for him. He sat down cross-legged in front of the empty canvas, which rested on the floor beside him. He didn't want the easel. He didn't want anything to do with it. He just wanted to have it nearby … in case.

As soon as he opened up his senses, he sensed why. Images flowed toward him, women's faces, most of the time in a horrible distortion of their regular features, as if screaming for help or even now crying out for somebody to talk to them, to reach them.

Taking a deep breath, he picked up his charcoal and let his senses open wider. Immediately his hand started an erratic pattern of chaotic movements on the canvas. He kept his eyes closed, having been through this process more than enough times to know that his mind would only interrupt the energy flow. He couldn't see anything except a kaleidoscope of faces emerging.

He hoped they were ones who would help, but he had no way at this point to be sure. All he knew was that he had to do something, whether his own psyche needed to be refreshed or something else needed to be released. Regardless this need within him pushed him to do this. He slowly shut down his consciousness and let his arm move at the speed it needed to.

Some hours later he finally slowed and stopped. He'd heard the door open once, twice perhaps, but never interrupting.

That was the thing about having a partner who knew and understood. She knew when things were something he could talk about and understood when he couldn't. Slowly he let his arm rest on his leg, and then, even slower, with careful movements, he stretched his bent knees out in front of him. He wasn't exactly sure what this was and what had just happened, but he knew that whatever it was had been incredibly powerful.

Opening his eyes, he stared down at the canvas and grimaced. Incredibly powerful did not always mean nice, particularly with his skill set. The faces that stared back at him were indescribable. He'd given an image to the voices, and yet the result on the canvas was not a kindness to anybody else. They were all screaming, their eyes open, some appearing to be tortured, others appearing to be in some hellish bondage.

Something evil had them in its grip. He released his breath, as he tried to pull back from the horror in his consciousness and to remind himself that this was only an image. He knew it represented the energy of souls, but he didn't know that they were in this condition at this time. That would be a little hard to recognize.

Still, a complex image, a set of images really, and he stared at them for a long moment, hoping that there would be recognition on some level of who these people were, offering some way to track them, to trace them. And when there wasn't, he sighed, took several photos of it, and immediately sent it off to Drew and to Maddy.

Maddy phoned him within minutes. "Did you just do that?"

"Yes," he replied, his voice soft and faint.

"Make sure you cleanse from this one," she stated. "That's what I was seeing before."

"*Great*," he murmured. "Is Jewel one of them? Or is she slated to become one of them?"

"I don't know. I just know that to have had this many victims, … it's been going on for a very long time."

He gave a broken laugh. "How is it that these guys continue to operate, and we only barely scratch the surface of who's out there and who's capable of doing this?"

"I don't know," she murmured, her voice equally soft, gentle. "We can only deal with the ones who we know about."

"Yes, but, as you mentioned earlier, with this one, it's very strange. Something's off about all of it."

"There always is," she agreed. "That's one of the things that I came to understand. Always something is off about these cases. We'll never solve them if we try to fit them into the boxes that we already know."

"How about new boxes?" he asked, a note of humor entering his voice.

"Wouldn't that be nice? At least that would mean something we had a box for. I don't think we do in this case."

Stefan sighed. "Are we really suggesting that some madman has killed these women and somehow captured their souls inside these artifacts?"

"That in itself isn't terribly new, unfortunately. Yet it's the energy tucked just behind the veil in Jewel that has me worried because I can't get any clarity on it."

"Right," he whispered.

"You need to rest," she said. "Disconnect and go spend time with Celina."

"That's the plan," he replied, his voice gaining in strength. "I just came out of this and wanted to show you right away."

"Thanks," she said, with a note of humor. "Now my nightmares are yours." Just before she hung up, she added, "You need to send that to Hurricane. We don't know, but it's possible that somehow those images might yet save her life."

"What about her soul?" Stefan asked softly.

"I'm not sure. I'm worried it has already been acquired in a way."

"Then he can damn well unacquire it," Stefan declared, his voice gaining in volume.

"I agree with you, but we have to figure out how." And, with that, she hung up.

CHAPTER 10

THE FACT THAT Jewel could give Hurricane the address and the name of her favorite breakfast spot revealed a lot. Yet it didn't say very much about her life, and the difference was just enough to keep her quiet the whole trip.

"Are you bothered by the holes in your memory?" he asked her.

"Wouldn't you be?"

"Yes. Absolutely. I would be making myself crazy, trying to figure out what happened. I know that's what you're doing, but still you have no guarantee that doing that will bring you the answers you're looking for."

"There aren't any guarantees here at all," she snapped, with a passion that went deeper than she was expecting. "I … just feel like something's very wrong."

He pulled into the restaurant parking lot, parked, and turned to look at her. "That's the first time you've said that."

Confused, she shrugged. "I don't know what I'm saying."

She hopped out, and, ignoring him, walked at a fast pace toward the front door of the restaurant. Inside, she knew there would be little privacy for the questions that were still on his tongue. Only so much she could handle right now, and she was quickly reaching her limit. Thankfully he didn't push, and, when they were inside, she grabbed a seat by a window and waited for the waitress.

When the waitress showed up, she beamed at Jewel. "There you are. I've missed you the last couple days."

Jewel looked at her, glanced over at Hurricane, and gave an almost imperceptible nod of her head. She hoped he would pick up on the meaning, and almost immediately it seemed that he did.

"She had an accident," he offered. "And now … she still has some partial amnesia."

The waitress stared at her, horrified. "Oh no, I am so sorry to hear that." She shook her head. "That's just terrible."

"Anything you can tell me about my life and routine would help. Such as how often I came here and things like that," she said, with a note of humor. "Obviously I remember this place, since I came here like a homing pigeon."

The waitress laughed. "Absolutely. You're here, I would say, three out of five weekday mornings, if not more, and usually you have a stack of flapjacks, with bacon and eggs on the side. And coffee, lots and lots of coffee. A couple times when we've spoken, you've mentioned that you tend to get caught up in your work, forgetting about food, and then, when you resurface, it's like you're starving and need to be topped up."

She nodded. "That's exactly how I feel right now too."

"Good. I will head into the kitchen and place your order." She turned toward Hurricane and asked, "What would you like?"

"I'll have exactly the same as Jewel here." When the waitress took off, Hurricane leaned forward and noted, "You've never told me that before."

"Told you what?" she asked in confusion.

"About how you end up here so often."

"No, and I didn't know that about the artist work either," she murmured. "Does it matter?"

He nodded slowly. "It matters."

She glared at him. "Now you have to tell me why."

"Maybe, but I don't know that I have an answer yet."

"If you don't have an answer, then it doesn't matter," she muttered, glaring at him even more. "Getting no answers is very irritating. So I will add still another item to my list of all the things I don't know."

He smiled at her. "But every moment we're picking up bits and pieces, and, no matter what, they are important. So keep them coming."

"What's so unusual about the fact that I would have been coming here for breakfast after a night of work?"

"Nothing," he replied.

She stared at him, shook her head, and asked, "Are you trying to make me crazy?"

He burst out laughing. "No, I'm not trying to."

"Well, that's … that's good. You obviously have a talent for doing it naturally then, because your answers just make no sense. They sound like more questions."

"I'm not trying to *not* make sense," he told her, as if speaking slowly and trying to pace his words. "Obviously we have a lot going on here, and the more information we get, the more I can find some clarity in this."

"Sounds like you're just looking for excuses," she muttered.

"For what though?" he asked, looking at her in astonishment. "No excuses needed. Something happened to you, and we need every little bit of information, so we can find something to explain what is happening. Let's keep it simple."

"Sounds normal, sounds rational, feels off."

Just then the waitress returned with coffee. When she went to put cream and sugar down in front of her, Jewel looked at her and frowned. "Do I really take cream and sugar in my coffee?"

She stared at her and nodded. "Yes."

"Oh. Okay, I wasn't going to add it this time."

"Maybe don't add it at all then."

As soon as the waitress left, Jewel leaned forward and asked in a harsh whisper, "Why would I no longer take cream and sugar in my coffee?"

He shrugged. "I don't want to say anything, and I certainly don't want you upset," he murmured. "However, it appears you're changing."

"But what am I changing into? Or better yet, ... who?"

"I DON'T HAVE an answer for that either," Hurricane replied, "but things are obviously different, so just go with it."

She glared at him but picked up her coffee, tasted it cautiously, shrugged. "It tastes good black, so why would I change it?"

"I don't know. I'm not sure how much you've changed either." He glanced back at the waitress, frowned, and added, "Before our food comes, I'll go to the bathroom."

He got up, headed to the washroom and used the facilities. On his way back, he waylaid the waitress. "Hey, I wanted to ask a couple questions without Jewel around, so she doesn't get upset."

The waitress immediately nodded in sympathy. "I can't

imagine what she's been through. She's been here so often, she's definitely somebody I know."

"You know *for sure* that she took milk and sugar in her coffee?"

"Absolutely," she replied, "but that's only been just recently. Before that she had it black, so it's almost as if she's just reverting back."

He stared at her cautiously. "How long has it been? The addition of the cream and sugar?"

She stared at him. "A little while ago. Weeks, I guess. She told me that she was tired and needed the extra sugar, which made perfect sense to me."

"It does make perfect sense," he agreed, with a nod.

She sighed with relief. "I'm really sorry that anything happened to her."

"Tell me if you notice any other changes."

"She's definitely looking more tired," she said instantly. "Which, that's saying something because she was always tired. She was always working hard, but she still had kind of a glow around her. Now she just looks really worn out, but then I imagine what she's been through has been pretty hard."

"It has been," he noted. He smiled, thanked her, and headed back to his table.

As soon as he sat down, Jewel looked at him. "Did she have anything else to add?"

"Only that the cream and sugar has been a recent addition."

She stared at him. "What?"

He nodded. "Apparently you mentioned something about always being tired and about you needed the extra *oomph* from the sugar."

"*Huh.*" She pondered that. "That almost makes sense."

"It does," he agreed. "Almost."

She glanced at him. "Do you really think something en-ergy-related is going on right now?"

He stared at her. "I'm not sure, but I certainly wouldn't rule it out."

She didn't say anything to that.

The waitress returned a few minutes later with two plates heaped high.

Immediately he sniffed and grinned. "Now this looks awesome."

"Good." The waitress wore a big smile, as she placed the food down in front of them. "Because a lot of food is here." She looked over at Jewel. "Now, if you want your usual doggie bag, just let me know."

"Do I take a doggie bag home?" she asked, as she looked down at the plateful.

"You do. Often you have a big appetite, then, all of a sudden, you don't have any appetite at all," she shared. "Of course that's a recent change too." At that, she bounced off again.

Jewel looked over at him, frowning.

He shrugged. "Let's not judge. Let's just go forward and see how many other changes there are."

"Any change like this is scary," she muttered.

He grinned at her. "Absolutely, but it's also fascinating, don't you think?"

She took a couple bites, closed her eyes, and muttered, "Why does the food taste so awesome?"

"I don't know," he replied. "In what way does it taste awesome?"

Fearing yet another trick question, she glared at him.

He shrugged. "I mean, a lot of your tastes have obviously changed, whether they're changing back or have just changed differently yet again, I can't say. However, the food is great here, so, if you're really enjoying it, that's even better."

"I am," she murmured. "I'm not sure why it feels like it's all different and new. Maybe I haven't had it like this before, which is kind of how it feels, but I have to admit it tastes really good today."

She dug in and didn't even surface until the plate was half gone. Then she sat back, looked down at the food, and muttered, "I can see why she mentioned the doggie bag."

"Maybe. Just let it sit in front of you for a bit, and, when you've had a chance to settle some of that food you scarfed down so fast, you might find you want a bit more."

She shrugged. "Maybe, but, at the same time, it is a lot of food."

"They certainly haven't spared any effort, and that's always nice to see in a restaurant because, too often, the portions are small."

"And then again," she said, with a laugh, "too often the portions are way too big, and we eat them anyway."

"That's the American way," he noted, with a grin.

He had absolutely no problem finishing his plate, she noted. And, by the time he put down his fork, she was tackling another pancake. Signaling the waitress for more coffee for both of them, he just sat here and waited for Jewel to work her way through more food.

When she put down her fork for the second time, she said, "This time I am done for sure."

"You didn't leave much," he noted, looking down at her plate. "Barely enough to pack up."

She stared down at the plate and nodded. "I'm really

surprised."

"I'm not. You didn't eat much beforehand, and yesterday's events were stressful for you. Seeing that you have a good appetite is something that makes me happy."

She laughed. "If I keep eating like this, I'll need to go home and have a nap again."

"You can do that," he agreed. "With everything you've been through, your body needs time to heal, and, in order to heal, it needs rest—and sustenance."

She shrugged. "That also feels like a cop-out."

"I don't know why it would," he said.

"Because I think I work all the time," she muttered, staring off in the distance. "I think my friends would call me a workaholic."

He nodded. "And that wouldn't surprise me because a lot of entrepreneurs with their own businesses, particularly artists, tend to be workaholics. You get caught up in your own joy of what you're creating, and you forget about everything else going on around you."

"Apparently that's happened here a time or two," she murmured, as she stared around her. "According to the waitress, at least."

"If you've come in hungry and looking for something to replenish yourself, that's a good thing. It's only a concern if you stay home and don't fill the void of food and even social connections," he stated.

"I don't think I have any problems that way. At least Charles and Lucas made it seem like I'm a social person."

"Absolutely." Hurricane smiled. "And that's good. We need balance in life."

"Yeah, so how much balance do you get?" she asked, challenging him.

He grinned. "Not as much as I should. I spend too much time traveling the world, dealing with some odd scenarios."

"Do you go wherever Stefan sends you?"

"I go wherever Stefan asks me to go, when and if I can," he corrected. "I'm not on his payroll, and I'm certainly not indebted to him, but we're both involved in this energy work. Realizing just how dangerous some of these artifacts are, I do what I can because there aren't that many options. If I say no, who else will do it?"

She stared at him, fascinated. "I'm not even exactly sure what you do, but it sounds fascinating."

"It's certainly taken me to some interesting corners of the world, and I've met some incredible people," he murmured. "In a way, that's an education you can't get anywhere else, and, once you get hooked into this field, you really don't ever want to leave."

"Says you," she quipped, with a laugh. "I'm not even into it, and I already want out."

"But do you really?" he asked, looking up at her. "Or is that just the answer you think I'm expecting to hear?"

She winced. "I don't know. I mean, if it got me into the situation I'm in right now, I want nothing to do with it."

Just then the waitress returned, checked their coffees, and left a bill. He picked it up, looked at the amount, and nodded. "That's reasonable too."

The waitress returned a moment later, having been just a few tables over, then lowered her voice and said, "Jewel gets a discount because she comes here so often."

"Oh, I'm glad to hear that," he replied, looking up at the waitress with a friendly smile. "The food was excellent and abundant, and the service was equally lovely. Thank you."

She flushed and, with a pleased smile, disappeared.

"Wow." Jewel stared at him. "You're quite the smooth talker, when you want to be."

"No, not at all. But it doesn't hurt to be friendly in this world, particularly in a service industry, where they have to deal with an awful lot of unhappy people and not many happy ones."

"True enough." She stood and pointed. "My turn in the washroom."

He nodded. "I'll pay the bill and meet you outside?" He raised an eyebrow in question.

She smiled and agreed.

Jewel headed to the bathroom, one she'd used many times she was sure, and, as she stood here in front of the mirror, she stared at the woman who even now was looking so foreign to her, what with the alabaster skin and the jet-black hair, wrinkles around her eyes, deepened by the focus of her attention. As she washed her hands, the door opened, and the waitress stepped inside.

"Hey. Are you all right?"

"Absolutely. At least I'm getting there," Jewel said, not at all sure what relationship she had with this woman.

"You're scaring me," the waitress replied, looking at her. She made no attempt to go to the bathroom or to wash her hands. "I just came in here because I guess I want to know if everything's all right."

"It's fine," Jewel replied, startled. "The accident shook me up, and obviously I need to fill in a few holes in my memory, but I'm getting there."

The waitress nodded slowly. "Good, okay then." But she remained, awkward, as if she didn't seem to know how to leave.

At that, Jewel added, "Thanks for breakfast."

The waitress just nodded and didn't say anything.

Finally Jewel stepped to the doorway, looked back at her, and asked, "Is there something you want to add?"

She hesitated. "It's just that, the last couple times you were here, you were different."

"Different how?"

The waitress hesitated.

"Look. I won't know if you don't tell me the truth. So please, just tell me the truth."

"Shorter tempered, not as nice, tired, obviously very stressed. It's not that you were mean or anything. It's just obvious that you were going through a bad patch."

"Did I say why?"

The waitress shook her head. "No, but you were really worried about something, and, if I'm being honest, I'd say you were scared about something." And, with that, she added, "But you're looking much better now." And she quickly disappeared out of the door.

Jewel was left behind to stare at her reflection, once again wondering what the hell had gone on in her life and why she didn't remember it.

HURRICANE WAITED OUTSIDE the restaurant for Jewel to come out and could tell immediately that something was wrong.

She hopped into his Jeep too quickly and then motioned at the steering wheel. "Can we just go, please?"

He nodded, and, as he pulled out of the parking lot, he said, "You want to explain what that was all about?" She told him, and he turned and stared at her. "She couldn't give you any specifics, I suppose."

She gave a broken laugh. "No, apparently people know me enough, but I don't share well."

"Unless you're friends with her? That would make sense."

"I know. I just … Obviously I was close enough with her that she felt that she should come into the restroom and talk to me to confirm I was okay."

"Which says a lot about her," he noted. Jewel gave a broken sob. He turned and looked at her again, then winced. "Hold it together. We're going home." And then he shook his head. "No, let's go get groceries, so we don't have to go out again for a while."

"You mean, just in case somebody else says something, and I go to pieces?"

"No, in case we don't want to deal with people."

"I don't think I dealt with people a lot. I think some of these visits out were more a case of trying to keep my sanity and not become totally antisocial."

"And that's probably what Charles and Lucas were for you as well," he murmured.

"Meaning that they weren't friends?"

"Oh no, clearly they are your friends. I just wonder how close you allowed them to get?"

She sighed. "I wish I knew what happened, what danger I thought I was in, and how I might have gotten into trouble. I mean, why don't I know?" she asked, her voice plaintive.

"I'm wondering if maybe, by chance, you did know something, and you were trying to keep yourself safe and didn't know who you could talk to."

"So what then? I called Stefan?"

"He does …" Then Hurricane hesitated.

"Oh, don't stop now," she said, looking at him. "Not when it's just getting interesting."

He smiled at her. "Stefan has a lot of skills, but one of the things that he does keep up, … I know this will sound weird, but what he is a transmitter, both the sending and receiving kind, to let people, like you, know that he's there to help."

She stared at him.

He shrugged, turned back to his driving, and added, "I know that sounds bizarre, but maybe just try to hold that thought."

"It doesn't sound bizarre. … It sounds absolutely crazy."

He smiled. "No, you're right. It does. On the other hand, that doesn't mean it's wrong."

"I'm not saying it's wrong at all, and maybe that is how I found him. I don't know. The fact that I don't know and that all these bizarre incidents are happening is what's getting me down."

"With good reason, but that's temporary," he reminded her.

"Do you think the doctor's right, and all my memories will come back?"

"I think we'll go on the assumption that he's right because what you focus on is what you create in your world."

She stared at him. "That sounds like some New Age mumbo-jumbo."

He grinned. "For some people it will be, but for others it definitely won't." And again she just stared at him. He laughed. "Oh, I get it. I really do. This sounds like it's very far-fetched and incredibly hard to deal with," he agreed. "So again have a little bit of faith."

"A little bit of faith is one thing, but it does start to tax after a while."

He pulled up to a grocery store and asked, "Is this place okay?"

"Sure." She shrugged. "I don't know that I've ever been here."

"Maybe that's a good thing. I was trying to avoid places you might have walked to, so we didn't have any more personal relationships to deal with."

"Yet, according to you, that is a good way to get information."

"It is, but we don't want you on overload." He turned off the engine and added, "Now, if you don't want to come in, I can go in alone."

"I'm not a coward," she said, and, pushing open the door, she hopped out. As she walked toward the front of the store, she looked around. "In a way I do feel like I have been here before. I'm not sure it's an issue either way, is it? I mean, it's not that far away."

He frowned and asked, "Do you have a vehicle?"

She blinked. "Yes, of course I have a vehicle." Then she frowned too. "I think I have a vehicle." She let her breath out slowly. "Let me put it this way. In my mind, I definitely have a vehicle."

"That's something we need to follow up on." He stopped and quickly sent the detective a message.

"Who are you contacting?" she asked, looking at him.

"The detective. He can find out if a vehicle is registered in your name, and we might track it down."

"Do you really think I was in it at the time?"

"I don't know, but we can't go wrong getting one more piece of information." He opened the door of the grocery store and held it for her to walk through.

She moved slowly, as if a little hesitant at what she'd find inside. So many things about her made perfect sense, and then she did something that made none at all.

He reached over, linked her arm with his, and said, "I've got a basket. I don't suppose we need to grab too much right now, but a couple of meals' worth would be good."

"Yeah? I … I'm not sure I cook."

"I do," he stated cheerfully, "so that's no big deal."

"Wow, a man who cooks."

"*Ah, ah, ah.* No sexist comments now."

She snorted at that. "Seriously? You'll cause a problem over that?"

He grinned at her. "I don't cause problems over much, so just keep an open mind, and we'll see what we can come up with for me to cook. I didn't say I cook well, just that I can cook."

"Good point," she muttered.

They moved through the aisles, with a surety that he projected, knowing what he needed for a couple meals, and, when he stopped at the pasta aisle, she immediately reached for spaghetti.

"You like spaghetti?"

She paused, looked at it, then shrugged. "That's what my hand is reaching for, so I guess I do."

"Good, because I love spaghetti."

"Do you know how to make a good sauce?"

"Yep, I sure do, but we'll have to go to the fresh produce aisle for that."

By the time they were done twenty minutes later, his basket was overfull, and she was carrying a gallon of milk. Looking down at it, she noted, "I'm not sure I've ever had this much milk."

"I'll drink it if you won't," he said.

"I'm not sure if I'm supposed to run in a panic at the thought of you being able to digest this much dairy all at once or if it's so normal that I'm the one who's odd at this point."

"Just because you haven't had a whole lot of exposure to somebody who eats and loves his groceries like me is no reason to run off in a panic or to insult me about it either," he teased in a mocking aggrieved tone.

She laughed. "Says you." As they got up to the cash counter, she froze.

He looked at her carefully and asked, "What's the matter?"

She shook her head, and her voice was faint. "I don't know." Yet a note of panic entered her tone.

He quickly looked around, but her gaze was staring outside. "Is somebody out there?"

She looked up at him. "Maybe."

His eyebrows shot up, and he nudged her closer to the counter, as the person in front of the aisle had cashed out and left already. "Stay close to me and stay focused on whatever it is that's bothering you, and we'll take it from there, when I'm done checking out."

He quickly unloaded the groceries onto the counter, and the checker moved the items through fairly quickly. By the time he was done, Jewel was barely moving at all. "Come on. Let's go."

She looked up at him and shook her head. "I don't think I can go outside."

He stopped and stared at her. "How about we go out another exit?"

The checker instantly told him, "There isn't one, only one way in and out of the store." The checker studied Jewel, as if something were wrong with her.

Hurricane smiled at her politely and replied, "No problem. We'll go out the front. She's just having a tough day."

The checker's eyebrows shot up, but she didn't say anything and turned to the customer behind them.

If they were trying to *not* make an impression or to stay on the down low, they'd just failed big-time, yet whatever was going on with Jewel right now was also seriously important.

Outside, he quickly stowed the groceries in the vehicle, but his gaze was on her. She was almost frozen. She did what he said, and she turned when he told her to turn. But, other than that, he got almost no expression out of her, and whatever this was, was starting to freak him out. He quickly got her into the vehicle, and just as she went to climb up, so he could shut the door, she froze.

"What's the matter?" he asked urgently.

She turned, looked back at him, and replied, "That man coming toward me." But her voice was struggling, as if an internal fight was going on inside.

He turned to watch a man, tall, dressed all in black. He looked at the guy, studied him carefully, and asked, "Do you know him?"

"No," she whispered, but again that struggle with a single word was too evident. Then suddenly, like somebody cut a string on her, she relaxed. "I don't know what that just was," she stated, her voice tight, "but can we leave now?"

"Yeah, you're not kidding," he muttered.

He took one last glance in the direction of where the man had been, but he was long gone. Swearing to himself,

Hurricane hopped up into the Jeep and took off from the parking lot. Rather than going straight home, he took several turns. When he was finally convinced that nobody had followed them, he pulled up in front of her place and turned off the engine.

She stared at him. "Did you lose him?" she asked.

"I don't know that he even saw us," he replied immediately. "I just wanted to make sure that *nobody* was following us."

She let out a slow breath. "I'd feel better if we were inside."

"Me too."

He hopped out and grabbed the groceries, came around to her side. Making sure to keep a hand on her, he gently maneuvered her up the stairs and toward the front entrance.

"Is there something wrong with me?" she whispered. "Something in my energy?"

"Yes."

"Was it from that guy?"

"I don't know, but I need you inside, where, whoever it is, hopefully can't extend the energy that far."

She shot him a look but kept walking toward the door. "It feels like I'm not even myself."

"I know. You're not acting like yourself, and you don't look like you," he stated, his voice harsh. "Again, another reason to get you in safely."

"Unless they already know where I live."

"Let's not consider that right now," he snapped.

Once inside, he threw the dead bolt home, putting the groceries down right here at the entrance, turned, and looked at her. Then he reached up with both hands on either side of her shoulders and said, "Now close your eyes."

She immediately closed her eyes.

Then he closed his, and, with a gentle breath of air, sent a warm cleansing energy over her. When he did it a second time, he began to feel some of the freezing around her body releasing. And by the time he did it a third time, he opened his eyes to see her staring at him.

"I don't know what you just did, but I feel much better. Loads better."

He smiled. "Good. I'm glad it worked."

"Then why didn't you do it out there?"

"Because I needed peace and quiet to open up my senses and also to know that you were in a secure place. I couldn't release my protective energy in order to access yours because it needs to be in a safe environment."

She shot him a horrified look, walked over to the couch, and collapsed on top of it. "I don't know what has happened to my world," she muttered, "but it can stop anytime."

He laughed at the note of disgruntlement in her voice. "I'm glad to hear that because I need to have as much of your fighter temperament back as I can get. Nothing worse than trying to deal with somebody who's in a victim mode, closed off and reeling from trauma."

"I would never have said that I was somebody who would become a victim easily," she noted, "but, when you don't know what is attacking you or even what has happened, it's hard to protect yourself from the unknown."

He nodded. "So, had you never seen that man before?"

"I don't know if I have or not. Whatever is going on, it appears to have been pretty complete."

"That's the problem. It wasn't complete enough, so we don't know if somebody is coming back, hoping to finish the job."

She stared at him and shuddered. "You're a very scary man."

He looked at her and nodded. "This is very scary stuff."

"That's why you do it, isn't it?"

"Yeah. Imagine if, right now, you didn't have anybody who understood this."

"I'm not sure I do have somebody who completely understands it," she admitted, staring at him intently. "You understand something about it, but I don't think you know all of what's going on, do you?"

"No, not yet. But I will get there."

"Because it's what you do," she repeated, with a clipped nod.

"Partly that, and also because whatever is going on is dangerous to you, and I don't want to see you get hurt."

"You mean, get hurt any more that I already have been," she clarified, with a note of bitterness.

He nodded. "Now what I just did, we call it cleansing. It's a way to ward off the negative energy, and what we just did could make you very tired. Feel free to crash there on the couch, while I put away the groceries."

"I'm not tired," she argued.

Yet, when he turned back to look at her, she was flaked out on the couch, already out cold.

He walked over and gently covered her with a blanket. "You may not be tired, sweetheart, but whatever is happening is exhausting you."

CHAPTER 11

J EWEL WOKE ON her living room couch to the sounds of voices. She slowly sat up, looked around, and frowned, when she saw Hurricane at the door, accepting a package. She flung back the blanket, got up, and walked over. "Is that for me?"

"It is," he confirmed, handing it to her. "Were you expecting it?"

She shrugged. "Again with a question I don't know the answer to." But she had answered it humorously, feeling much better. "I don't know what the hell was going on in that grocery store, but I am feeling better now."

"Good," he said, looking at her intently.

She smiled up at him, patted his cheek, and said, "Honest." With that, she walked away, already sensing that some of his worry had eased. "Sorry for being such a trial. Whatever the heck is going on obviously has a pretty good grip on me. Let's see what came in the mail," she muttered.

"Hardly the mail, a courier."

She nodded and opened it up. Inside was another box, a small jeweler's box. She pulled it out and set it on the coffee table, while she searched the rest of the box and the packaging, looking for some clue as to who had sent it. When she found nothing, she looked up, bewildered.

"Do you get orders like this?"

She shrugged. "Not very often, but I guess it's happened a time or two, where somebody I've worked with a lot has sent something, but then forgot to include another element inside. But typically they would contact me by email or phone in order to make sure that I got it. No insurance on this, was there?"

"Yes." He pointed it out on the back of the package.

She pondered that. "No return address, so that's definitely suspicious."

"I can track down where it came from," he offered, "after you've opened it."

She gave him a look. "Am I looking for a bomb?" she asked, her tone gaining in volume.

"I wouldn't think so. Unless you tell me that is something you're likely to receive."

"No, I wouldn't think so, but then none of this is making much sense either."

"Agreed. So let's open it and see what comes up."

Shrugging, she opened up the jeweler's box and froze. She looked up at him. Her eyes rolled back in her head, and she collapsed on the couch.

Her mind was filled with images, images of women screaming for help, images of women just floating in some strange space. The terrible images of women ranged over young and old, but all beautiful, every one of them striking. When she suddenly jerked free of the images, she lay on the couch gasping, staring up at Hurricane, who looked down at her grimly, the box removed from her hand and his hand on her forehead.

She whispered, "Oh my God."

He nodded. "I don't know who sent that to you, but that package packs a punch."

She shuddered. "That's what happened with the pearls, as soon as I started working on them. It wasn't immediate, only after I did my usual thing, and then it, ... it started to get weird. I could see all these women. So beautiful and in terrible pain."

"The same women you just saw now?" She nodded. He hesitated. "Did you get any names?"

"Names? What names?"

"Names of the women, so I could try to track them down."

Tears welled up in her eyes. "These women aren't on this earthly plane anymore."

He nodded. "I got that," he agreed, his tone grim. "However I would still like to know who they were and what happened to them. It would be good to maybe get closure for their families."

Jewel took a deep breath. "First names. I can do first names."

"How about last names?"

"I don't know," she whispered. She stared down at the box, like it was a viper about to strike her again. "I don't know what this is, what kind of power is in that, or how to dilute it."

"I hate to say it, but diluting it means not getting answers."

"You want to know what happened to those women?" she asked him.

He nodded slowly. "If you think you can."

She shuddered. "Maybe the second time it won't be so bad?" she asked hopefully.

"I'll be here," he stated.

"What does that mean?" She widened her eyes and

looked at him. "What can you do?"

He smiled. "Hold my hand."

When she reached up and grabbed his hand, immediately the waves of panic and terror eased back. She stared down at his hand and back up at him. "I don't know what you just did, but I think I want that all the time."

He chuckled. "Use me as a ground," he urged.

"Is that what you're doing? Like helping to ground my energy?"

"Let's worry about explanations later. I'm afraid that whatever this energy is will dissipate."

Obediently she took a deep breath, closed her eyes, and, with his hand in hers, she opened up the parcel and grabbed the jeweler's box, now holding the bracelet. Immediately the same storm swept through her, tossing her into a torrential hurricane of emotions. Almost instantly she understood how that connected to him, but, just as the understanding swept through her, so did more women, more faces.

She started calling out names, "Elizabeth, Rhea, Haley, Anna."

"Last names," he urged.

"Targus, Malone, Robinson, Billings."

The words, the names, they just rolled off her lips, almost like an incantation. When her voice finally fell silent, the storm eased, as if it had finally passed.

She opened her eyes and stared at Hurricane. "Is it over?" she whispered.

He looked down at her hands, now tightly gripped in his, and he whispered, "For the moment."

She closed her eyes, shuddering. "And those women in the necklace? I'm not sure I had names for them."

Hurricane nodded. "If they come later, tell me then."

Jewel shook her head. "It's never over for those women, is it?"

He hesitated and then replied, "I'm afraid not."

She opened her eyes, glaring at him. "What is happening?"

"Somebody has somehow captured these women's souls and enslaved them into this bracelet, the same with the necklace," he whispered. "My best guess is that, when you poured love into it, you came up against the evil that was behind it, and all these women, with your energy at their backs, are now screaming to get out."

Jewel stared at him in horror. "Are their voices knocking me out?"

He nodded slowly. "As far as I can tell, their energies inside are causing all this."

Jewel swallowed. "How do we let them out? We need to set them free," she stated, her voice gaining in urgency. "How do we help them?"

"I'm not sure yet," he admitted, as he stared down at the bracelet in fascination. "Didn't you say something to Stefan about a bracelet?"

"Yes. I thought a bracelet was connected to the necklace, as if he would put more souls inside it. I can vaguely recall it."

"Right, so you already knew that the souls were there."

"I knew, yes, and then I forgot." Frustrated, she shook her head. "How does somebody forget something like that?"

"Self-preservation, if nothing else," he murmured. "You have to remember this was all relatively new, and you were and still are unprepared for this in many ways."

She shuddered. "I work with the light," she stated. "This is not something I've ever come across."

"No, and sometimes the absolute goodness of who you are and what you're doing can attract the exact opposite of what you want."

She stared at him, struggling to comprehend. "You mean, I … I brought this necklace to me?"

He nodded slowly. "It's possible, yes."

"Possible, but you're not sure."

At that, his lips twitched. "In this business, I can't be sure of anything, until we get to the raw end of whatever is going on."

"But what … what other end is there?" she asked in astonishment, staring at him. "What other end could there be?"

He hesitated and looked at the bracelet, back at her, before replying, "I guess the question really is, who sent it to you, why did they send it to you, and is one of these pearls empty?"

"If it's empty, that's good, isn't it?" she asked in bewilderment.

He looked at her and slowly shook his head. "No, it's not good at all."

"Why not?" she asked. "I mean, it would mean one less soul to save."

"Jewel, think about it. It's also one more soul he can capture." He looked at her directly, squeezed her fingers, and added, "And I think you're it."

HURRICANE KNEW THAT he'd shocked Jewel, and that was good. He wanted to shock her. He wanted her to wake up to be as aware as she could be as to whatever was going on. That she'd been targeted, he had no doubt. Why she was targeted was a whole different story. Stefan's voice in the back of Hurricane's head gave him a clue to the answer.

Because she can, Stefan said.

He looked at the woman sitting here, hugging a cup of coffee and staring at the bracelet, like it would bite her.

What do you mean?

She can access the energy. She is one of them. Therefore, she's very important to whoever owns these artifacts.

How would he capture her like this? he asked, bewildered. *I mean, she's sitting on the couch.*

She is at the moment, yes, Stefan confirmed in his head. *But that doesn't mean that something else isn't there.*

As he watched Jewel, she touched her hand to her throat. He remembered her saying in the hospital that the necklace belonged on her neck.

He sat down beside her, and, with Stefan still half in his head, he asked Jewel, "Did you ever wear the necklace?"

She looked up at him. "I put it on once. Something was off about the hasp, so, after adjusting it, I put the necklace on to make sure it would lay properly. Why?"

In the background, he heard Stefan's shocked gasp.

Hurricane ignored Stefan and concentrated on Jewel. "Because I think doing that is what triggered this thing."

She stared at the bracelet, instinctively leaning farther back away from it.

He nodded. "I've written down those names you called out, and we'll see if we can track down any of these women."

She stared up at him, then at the bracelet. "You and I both know that they're not alive. I just don't know if they're in that bracelet, which is way too hard to believe, or if something else has happened to them."

He nodded. "So let me just see what we can find out

about them. I need to get answers on who these women are and what happened to them." He pulled out his phone and called Stefan, instead of trying to get all the names through his head. "Can you contact the detective or maybe Drew?"

"I'll contact Drew," Stefan replied. "You look after her. The artifact is hungry now. I don't know if it's looking for completion or just feels that fresh energy, but it's hungry, so you have to watch her."

"What do I do with the bracelet?"

"Have you got a strongbox?"

"Not here, not with me," he replied, as he turned and looked around. Seeing the battered-up wall, he added, "She does have a safe. I might put it in there with the necklace."

"No," Stefan snapped, his voice sharp. "Do not put them together."

At that, he hesitated. "Are you thinking their energy will just build on each other?"

Stefan replied, "They will undoubtedly feed off each other. Do not put them together, no matter what."

"Good God," Hurricane said. "Fine, I'll find a solution."

"If not, we can send you something."

"You'll have to do that anyway, but, in the meantime, I need a solution for right this moment. Because even now, sitting far from her, it still feels like it's reaching for her."

"It is," Stefan confirmed. "Bind it, bind it as hard and as fast as you can. I know that won't work long-term, but it's an answer for the moment. I'm sending you a strongbox."

"You'll have to send a couple," Hurricane noted, "because if I can't have the two of them in the same place, we'll need to bind both of them separately."

And, with that, Stefan hung up.

Jewel was looking at him, as if he had lost his mind, ...

or she had. "Bind, strongbox, attracted to each other, growing, feeding, reaching." She stared at him. "You do know that anybody else will think I'm strange if not a complete lunatic, right?"

"I know," he murmured. "And if it … if we didn't have some very private corporations behind us as benefactors, you would never have come across anything like this. And honestly I'm not sure it's a good thing that you have, but the fact of the matter is, it's responding to you, and you are responding to it."

"It, as in the bracelet?" she asked, staring at it.

He nodded. "That's very true. For now, I have to find a way to secure it."

"By the looks of it, it can't go in the safe beside the necklace," she stated, with a startled cry.

"No, it can't."

"Because they will feed off each other," she repeated, as if it made perfect sense, and then she gave a wild cry. "Dear God, what is happening?"

He reached out, pulled her into his arms, and just held her. "Listen. I know it's bizarre. I know it's all very beyond the norm. I get that. But right now, I need to find a way to close this thing up, so it can't continuously call to you."

"Is that what it's doing?" she asked, staring at it in horror. She bolted off the couch and ran to the far side of the room, her hands and back against the wall, as she stared at it. "How on earth did any of this even come to be possible?" she murmured.

She watched, as Hurricane picked up the box and packaged it back up in the second box. "Now what? When just in the packaging, it seems so innocuous."

"Until it fed on your energy and realized that you'd already touched the necklace, I suspect," he murmured. "They are bonded, the two pieces. And that brings its own set of dangers."

"And it almost, almost sounds normal," she noted in a low tone. "Then I think about the whole thing in context and understand just how absolutely insane all of this is."

He smiled at her. "It is, no question. Now, why don't you go do something completely normal, completely mundane, and I will wrap this up in energy, and that way we can try and contain it."

"You don't want me to watch?"

"It's easier on me if I do this alone," he replied. "You could get burned."

At that, her eyes widened. "Oh, *great*, now you'll do something that'll burn somebody? What the holy hell is this?" She shuddered and walked away, her movements stiff, but they were as normal as she could make them, and he knew that.

"Tell me when you're done," she said. "I'll just sit over in the corner here and stare at the fridge."

"Why don't you put on a pot of water for pasta?" he suggested.

She shot him a look and then nodded. "Fine, right. You did say mundane." And, with that, she turned her back on him.

"And, Jewel, don't turn around, no matter what you hear."

She froze and then slowly nodded. "Then you'd better do it fast. I'm not the shrinking violet type, and I don't normally listen when somebody tells me to do things like that."

"No, but, at this point in time, I'm trying to keep you

safe. And, in order to keep you safe, I must stop this thing from coming after you."

He stood, waiting until her back was turned, and then, with the bracelet contained within the two nested boxes, he headed toward the safe, knowing that, as soon as he got closer, it would, … he would feel the vibration. He waited until he was just far enough away to try and keep their energy happy, yet not close enough that they could do anything about it, and he started wrapping it up in energy.

However, as soon as he wrapped it, it would unwrap itself. He would wrap it again, and it would unwrap itself.

Frustrated, he heard Maddy in the background, saying, *Remember. It's only energy. It has wants, wishes, and desires too.*

And, with that, he knew how true her words were, and he infused it with love, with energy that could complement love, instead of trying to constrain it. As soon as he changed that tactic, it accepted the energy, and slowly he found he could wrap it.

With that done, he walked into the kitchen, stashed it in a cupboard, and announced, "Okay, it's contained for the moment."

She looked up at him and nodded jerkily. "The pasta water is on. What did you want for a sauce?"

"I'll do it," he offered, stepping in front of her. "You want to make a salad, while I take care of this?" And, with that, he proceeded to make a rosé sauce to go with dinner. He kept an eye on her, and, as a little more time passed, she calmed. As more time passed, she had calmed even more.

Finally she slowly relaxed, her shoulders easing, noting, "The entire atmosphere is different."

He nodded. "It happens that way sometimes."

She let out her breath. "So, what do you do in real life?"

"This," he stated. "Honestly, this is what I do."

"Do people pay you to do this?"

"We do have corporate donors, and we get sponsors to help," he admitted, "but I have money of my own."

She stared at him, and he gave her a knowing look.

"Anybody who has this energy ability has access to money. Why would we not? If money is only energy, we can get what we need at any point in time. It's just one of those universal laws."

Her eyes widened, and she stared at him.

He shrugged. "Once you understand the universal laws, they're really quite forgiving."

"If you say so," she replied in a strangled voice. "Man, I really need to learn how to use that one."

He burst out laughing. "That one I should be able to teach you," he murmured. "If you can hear, see, and feel the energy in that box, all you need to learn are the laws, and you'll be fine."

"Says you," she quipped. She shook her head, turned back to the food, and asked, "Is it time to eat?"

He looked over at the sauce in the pan bubbling gently in front of him and nodded. "Absolutely."

"Good," she replied. "I'm starving."

CHAPTER 12

T HE NEXT MORNING dawned bright and clear. Jewel lay in bed, feeling a set of tumblers going through her head, almost like *clickety-click-click*. She slowly sat upright, knowing that it was important, but she didn't know why. She dressed quickly, walked down to the safe, and opened up the tumblers.

She reached inside, only to have Hurricane grab her hand and whisper against her ear, "Stop."

She froze and looked up at him. "I wanted to check that they're still there."

He gently pulled her hand back, locked up the safe, and put the plasterboard back into position. Then he nudged her down the stairs. "It's the pearls, the energy, calling to you."

Downstairs, she stared up at the safe and looked back at him. "Something *was* calling me, but, like really important, tumblers went off in my head," she murmured.

He stared at her and then nodded. "I'll still put that down to energy."

"Maybe," she murmured. "I woke up feeling so good, so normal, and then all of this played through my head, and it felt so right."

He smiled at her, leaned down, then pulled her into his arms and gave her a hug. She cuddled in close, only to realize that his chest was bare, and he was a furnace of warm, comforting heat. She wrapped her arms around him and just held him. They stood like that for a long moment, him gently massaging her back, his chin resting on her head.

"Will it ever be normal again?"

"It will," he stated, his chin moving back and forth on the top of her head. "It will all go back to normal, whatever that means."

She gave a strangled laugh. "That's the thing isn't it? Whatever *normal* means."

He smiled. "Let me go grab some clothes. I had to bolt to stop you." Turning away from her, he walked to his duffel bag in the corner, his huge muscled body rippling in the early morning light. He quickly pulled on his jeans and then turned back to her, T-shirt in hand. "Coffee?"

Almost dumbstruck by this male specimen of perfection in front of her, she felt an urgent need to create itching at her fingertips. She nodded, but, instead of going to the kitchen, she headed to her workbench and her sketchbook, her mind busy with a design. She quickly picked up a piece of charcoal, and her fingers moved furiously across the page, as she opened up that well in her mind and let her fingers dance across the designs pouring from her soul.

When she took a shaky breath, she took a step back and looked down. Her shirt was covered with charcoal. Her hands were covered with charcoal, and the canvas in front of her was covered with charcoal. She stared at it and then gasped.

He came up behind her, looked at it, and nodded. "*Okay.*" Yet his voice was soft, gentle.

She looked at him. "I came to put a design down on paper."

He nodded and pointed to at least a half-dozen pieces

off to the side, not just the single page in front of her.

Her eyes widened, and he held out a cup of coffee.

"This one's hot," he said, looking at the cup on the table that he'd brought her earlier, which had obviously gone stone-cold.

"How long have I been doing this?" she whispered in shock, as she took the cup from his hands, hugging the warmth close to her.

"About forty-five minutes," he replied. "I've never seen anybody sketch so fast." He picked up the latest image. "Yet you've caught an incredibly powerful look in her eye."

"That's Lana," she stated instinctively. "Molmon."

He pulled a pen from his pocket and a notepad from the other and wrote down the name on it. They went through them one by one—all six of her sketches of the women trapped in the pearls. Trembling, she walked over to the couch and very slowly, cautiously, sat down, feeling as if her bones were so brittle that they might break if she sat too heavily. Then, with her feet tucked up under her, she curled into the corner and hugged the coffee cup against her.

"That's a very good thing you did," he noted, coming over to sit down beside her. He picked up her free hand and just held it. "I can take pictures of these and see if we can get a match."

She looked up at him, her eyes wells of pain. "They were murdered, weren't they?"

He hesitated, then shrugged. "That is what I would presume, yes, but I don't have any proof of that."

She nodded. "He murdered them."

At that, he looked at her, his intensely soft blue eyes, turning deep and sharp with electricity. "Who is he?"

"The man who sent me the necklace."

"Does it feel like the same man?"

She frowned and then shook her head. "I don't have anything to go by, but my gut feeling is no."

He nodded. "Always question what you're feeling to see it if matches with everything else that you know. Instinct is usually our best bet when it comes to this stuff."

"What is this stuff?"

He smiled. "This is energy work, but this guy, the bracelet, the necklace, and all? It's just the darker side of it."

"No kidding," she murmured. "Murdered women, their souls trapped inside pearls, who would ever have thought it? I don't even fucking know if I'm making this all up," she wailed.

"No, you're not. I watched you. No time for you to make anything up. You were simply a conduit for the energy. What I don't know is whether it's the women calling you or their killer."

"Either way, it's a very disconcerting thought," she murmured.

"It is, but one is definitely better than the other."

She nodded in agreement. "Still, it would be nice to think that this was something I knew how to do or had some ability or had seen this before so it wasn't so new and scary."

"Most of us don't get any chance to have practice runs at this stuff," he noted gently. "It hits us when it hits us and not a whole lot you can do about it."

She stared at him, wide-eyed. "That doesn't seem fair." His lips twitched. She shut her eyes and shook her head for a moment. "I get it. Nothing is fair." She pivoted toward her sketches again. "They're really good, aren't they?"

"They're incredible," he stated. "I'm also grateful for the fact that you appear to have caught them in the good times of their life."

Startled, she looked at him. "What do you mean?"

"I do know one energy worker who draws images of the dead, but she draws them as they're dying."

"So, she sees what's been done to them at the time?" She stared at him in horror.

He nodded. "When you want to talk about nightmares, she has a few things to say."

She shook her head, wordless for a few seconds. "That would be horrific."

"It can be, yes, but she does it to be of service because she can bring closure to people."

"How does that bring closure to anyone?" she asked, feeling bewildered.

He hesitated and then explained further, "She hunts the killers with the police, so she basically paints what's happened, including their surroundings and anything else she can give them. Clues and pieces in order to find the killers."

"Has she ever found anybody alive?"

A smile broke free. "She has. A couple people, which made it feel more worthwhile for her, … but it's not easy. None of this is easy. Most of the time, people only turn to somebody like her when they're absolutely desperate, when every other avenue has been closed off, and when it's already too late for the victims. Therefore, all she can do is hope to bring some measure of closure to the families."

"That sounds absolutely terrible." Jewel shuddered. "Definitely … not something I want … ever to happen to me either."

"In that case, you just say no. If and when something like that comes to you, you state you're not interested, and your energy will obey," he replied. "Don't ever feel that you have to be a victim to this."

She stared at him. "How was it I never even considered that I had a choice in this?"

"You always have a choice," he declared. "You might regret it later, when you realize you could have done some good. Yet if it is not of your temperament and you don't think you can handle the information coming in, you are under no obligation to help."

But that felt wrong too. She stared and went back to sipping her coffee. "I can't imagine. … I can see saving somebody and the absolute euphoria that must bring, but the rest? To know that you're too late? That they're already dead? I don't think I could do that."

"Not everybody can," he confirmed, "and I'm not bringing it up to say that you should. All I'm saying is that, should something like that ever happen, just know you have a choice, that you can say no."

"Good," she murmured. "I'll keep that in mind, just in case."

He smiled at her. "You do that." He took the empty coffee cup from her, which she hadn't even realized was empty. "I'll refill it." He got up, poured her another cup, and brought it back. But, when he returned, he snagged up the images. "These are incredibly good. Why are you not just an artist? Why a jewelry maker?"

"I don't know. I guess it's always been the jewelry that called me. The gems, pearls, diamonds, and all kinds of stones. Things that were valuable."

"Ah, an interesting distinction."

"Why?" she asked in a dry tone. "That feels very much like a judgment."

"Absolutely not," he disagreed. "I try to keep judgment

out of my world."

"Yeah, does that work well for you?" she asked, with a note of humor.

"Sometimes. But you are an incredible artist, so I do find it interesting. You might want to consider that energy work and that the gift of being of service is also valuable."

She looked over at him, gave him a wry look, and frowned. "I'm not convinced."

He chuckled. "That's fine. At some point in time, you might change your mind."

"Maybe."

He stood, while she sipped her coffee, and took photos of each one of her sketches. When he was done, he texted somebody, and sent them off.

"Who did you send them to?" she asked.

"Stefan. I also don't know if you realize it, but Stefan is quite an artist too."

She frowned at that and then nodded. "Yes, … I did hear that. I did some research before I contacted him. I'll bet he's got quite a few things in his life that he would like to forget."

"I imagine so," Hurricane agreed. "If you think this is weird, Stefan has seen and done so many things."

She nodded. "Did we already talk about somebody named Dr. Maddy contacting me?"

His eyebrows shot up. "Yeah, and you told me that she did a scan."

"Yeah, she did. If we already talked about it, never mind."

"Did it feel bad?"

"No, it felt freaking awesome. Just a little hard to under-stand what she was doing. She did a visual thing, but, of course, she wasn't even here."

He chuckled. "I know that this is all a huge learning curve for you."

"It is, and yet, in some ways, it feels like it isn't, and I don't understand. I presume that my memories are affecting this—and that, at some point in time, I will figure out why and how. Still, at this moment, it's a bit overwhelming."

He nodded. "Having patience is huge where this is concerned."

"*Right.*" She gave him a headshake. "Like anybody's got patience for this crap."

At that, he burst out laughing. "You're doing great." He pointed at her artwork. "Like, even waking up and prompted to do these drawings would freak out so many people."

She stared at the sketches. "I certainly won't freak out," she murmured. "I used to do a lot of drawing, and I guess that's probably why I stopped."

He stared at her for a moment, not understanding.

She shrugged. "Think about somebody who doesn't know anything about this energy stuff, then have them get up in the middle of the night and start painting images that, … that evoke feelings of such desperation and fear, with no idea where any of that was coming from. Then you might understand why I stopped."

"Because you freaked yourself out?"

"Yeah, somehow it sounds so much worse when you say it."

"Not at all, but, if you've not had anybody who does energy work in your life to help you through that, it can be a bit traumatic."

"Traumatic, yes, and I didn't have anybody in my life to explain any of it. I didn't even have anybody to question, so that made life a little more complicated."

"Of course," he agreed in a soothing tone.

She sighed. "Somehow you don't make it sound any better."

He burst out laughing. "You keep acting as if you're looking for judgment or something. I've seen way too many people who didn't get nearly as far as you in this world all by themselves, and you have done amazingly well."

"What do you mean?" she asked.

"A lot of people in mental institutions are simply energy workers who didn't have any way to express all this energy clogging up their systems. Without getting the proper help they needed, they just slowly go insane. Imagine how traumatic that is for them."

She winced. "That sounds absolutely terrifying."

He nodded. "And, for a lot of people, it is. I mean, I'm sure you can understand that in many instances it drives people crazy."

"You mean it literally, don't you?"

"Yes, literally," he agreed, with a nod. "So the fact that you're doing as well as you are is amazing. Don't ever judge yourself or knock yourself down over it because you are phenomenal."

He watched as she relaxed slightly and smiled. "You're such a good cheerleader."

He rolled his eyes. "Somehow that doesn't sound like anything I want to be known as."

She burst out laughing. "Too bad. So, it's taken me a bit, but I have slowly concluded that you are one of the good guys."

"Yes. And that's half the battle because sometimes, when I do what I do, it may not look like I'm one of the good guys. In fact, it may not look like I'm on your side at all. I certainly don't want to freak you out, but sometimes these things can get really hairy."

"Are you kidding? All of this is pretty hairy, and I would never have understood this much of it, if you didn't explain it."

"Still, somehow you are coping amazingly well, especially for someone who's lost their memory."

At the odd note in his voice, she looked at him. "And yet somehow, that tone of voice …"

"Are your memories changing?"

"No, not at all. … At least I didn't think so." Yet she frowned at that. "It's all just a big jumbled mess."

"That's why I'm not pushing you," he shared gently. "It's far better to just relax, and, when something appears to deal with or to make a decision on, then you'll handle it," he stated. "In the meantime, just relax."

She sagged in place. "Sure," she muttered. "Yet, still all these dead women …" She stared at the face on the drawing closest to her. "I know they're dead, but I don't know how they died. I don't think I want to know how they died, and I definitely don't want to channel or draw how they died."

"Agreed," he replied immediately. "The question is, do you know who killed them? Do you remember ever feeling that energy before? If you're supposed to be next on the list, do you have any idea how to stop it?"

She stared at him. "Next on the list? … As in, inhabiting the next pearl, right? That is absolutely beyond anything I've ever heard," she said faintly. "And, no, I haven't a clue how to stop him because I don't know how he caught these other women in the first place."

"I was hoping that, by seeing them, by seeing their faces,

it would help you understand."

"You mean, how he captured them?" she asked, bewildered.

"If it's that, yes."

"What do you mean, *if it's that?*"

"If it's capturing them, that's the issue. See? I don't know if…" He hesitated and then continued. "Look. Not everybody has to be right beside you in order to kill you."

"Oh Lord," she muttered, sinking deeper into the couch, as she stared at him. "Are you saying that somebody could kill me from wherever they are? Like sitting in their living room, sipping a beverage, somewhere across the world?"

He winced. "In theory, yes, though I've never encountered anybody who could do it." Then he hesitated and added, "Well, actually I probably do know somebody, but they're on the side of right and goodness."

"Thank God for that," she uttered, staring at him in shock. "Because there really should be a law against that."

"All kinds of laws exist, but unfortunately they are intended to keep the guys in check who have little respect for authority anyway."

"Still, what a freaky concept."

"Of course it is," he agreed. "So, let's focus on this killer, assuming of course that it is just one killer?"

"Do you think more than one person is involved in this?" she cried out.

"I don't know. I'm just casting about, looking for answers, so we can take even one step forward."

"I don't have any answers," she declared faintly, then looked at him closer. "Are you really expecting me to help you?"

"For whatever reason, the pearls have ended up on your

doorstep. You've unlocked them, and they're trying to get closer to each other and closer to you," he noted. "So I guess the answer to your question is yes. I'm hoping you can be of help with this."

She just nodded and yet had no clue what she was agreeing to. "Good God, this is all just completely beyond me."

"That just isn't so because they are here, calling out for you, which I can only guess is a cry for help."

She winced.

"Do you think I don't hear them?" he asked. "I've muted their calls as much as I can, but they're strong. They are very strong."

"That's the din in the background, isn't it?"

He looked at her slowly and then nodded. "Yes, it is. You have to make sure that you don't contact them."

"It's too late. I heard them before. I don't remember very much about it, but I know that I could hear them."

He grimaced at that.

"It's already too late for me, isn't it?"

"No. If you're thinking that it's too late and that you'll die from this, you're wrong. I won't let that happen. You need to learn to detach yourself. Try listening without getting attached to them. Just listen and do nothing."

"Can't you stop it?" she asked, staring at him hopefully. "I mean, I sure don't want to end up dead over this whole thing, but I'm already starting to feel very much like a freak."

"Hey, way worse things than being a freak," he stated.

"I know. I know," she murmured. "I didn't mean it that way. It's just …" Then she fell silent, fearing that she might offend him.

"Look, Jewel. I know. I get it."

"It's just … It's just too much, way too much." She gave

a stuttered chuckle and shook her head.

"It is, all of that and more," he agreed.

"Obviously I want answers, and I want to have this over with, but I would like to know a whole lot more about what you do and how you do it," she stated. "You have intrigued me into learning more about something that I'm obviously connected to and didn't know very much about."

"Yet I still wonder about that. And why? Because you contacted Stefan."

"And you keep bringing that up, as if it says I'm some gifted person or something," she argued, "when, in actuality, that has nothing to do with it."

"If you say so," he replied, chuckling, "but I'm not so sure about that."

"I am," she murmured. "Just because I made a phone call, based on some research I did, doesn't mean I was following some energy pathway or whatever it is you want to call it. And, even if I was, so what?"

"I don't know, but I can't help but feel that this amnesia may have been …" Then he went silent.

"Don't stop now," she said in an ominous tone, shifting so she could stare directly into his face. "You feel like what? Like I'm acting? Like this is all fake or something?" she asked, with rising outrage in her voice.

"No," he declared, his tone firm and steady. "That's not what I'm saying at all."

"What is it then? What are you saying? Because it sure sounds as if you think I'm making this up."

"I don't think you're making it up," he stated, his tone still firm.

"What is it then?" she prodded, glaring at him. "What is it you think I'm doing here?"

He hesitated, then, with a nod, spoke freely. "I think you're protecting yourself. I just don't know how much you know about what you're doing. Like how much you're doing consciously and how much you're doing subconsciously."

"Or how much is being done to me? Isn't that what you really mean?"

He searched her gaze, as if looking for something inside her, and then nodded. "Yes, that last thought occurred to me as well."

"But Dr. Maddy already told me that she found no sign of possession," she muttered. "So that still leads back to your thinking I'm just making it up, no matter how you disguise it with your unconscious and subconscious mumbo jumbo."

"No, I don't think that at all," he disagreed, his tone firm and hard. "But, as I said, I'm not exactly sure what's going on. I just know that something is."

"Are you ever wrong?" she asked, as she sank back onto the couch cushions, now looking at him with a fatigue and a weariness that reached deep into her soul.

"Sure I am. … Sometimes. Just not very often."

"Of course not," she murmured. "That would be way too easy."

"Nothing is easy about it. Being wrong in my work can be really hard, with terrible consequences. Being wrong can mean lives are lost."

She stared at him. "We're back to that danger again, aren't we?"

"Yes, we are. We can't minimize the potential of this situation, and I don't want you to take anything for granted. I don't want you to take any messages, any voices, or anything else for granted because it could very well be the last thing you do."

"*Or else?*"

"Yes, or else," he snapped. "Or else you could end up being the next soul in a pearl and the next pearl on that string of tears."

CHAPTER 13

J EWEL WOKE SLOWLY, feeling an odd, weird dryness in her mouth and a sticky scratchiness to her eyes. She blinked several times and then let out a half shriek.

Immediately Hurricane reached out a hand. "It's okay. Take it easy."

She stared at him. "What's the matter?" she asked, and then she slowly sat up and winced. "Why am I so sore?" she muttered, and, then staring around, she cried out, "Why am I in the living room?" She turned and stared at him. "I went to bed last night, didn't I?"

"You did," he stated, his gaze intense. "I watched you go up the stairs and waited for you to fall asleep, before I crashed. You don't remember anything?"

She shook her head and looked around. "No. … What time is it?"

"It's five a.m."

She winced at that. "Good God, that's still nighttime, as far as I'm concerned, and not even close to a normal time to get up, so what am I doing up?" And then she glared at him. "Why did you wake me up?"

He gave a tiny shake of his head. "I didn't wake you up," he murmured. He was crouched in front of her, wearing only his boxers again.

"Do you always walk around without clothes on?"

He snorted. "When people sleepwalk in the night and it's necessary to interrupt them, yes."

She stared at him, her heart sinking. "Sleepwalk?" she repeated, her tone very low, soft.

He nodded, his gaze never wavering. "Has that been a problem before?"

She slowly shook her head. "Not that I know of."

"When you say, *not that you know of,* does that mean not that anybody's ever told you about?"

She realized he meant somebody who may have slept over with her. "No, nobody has mentioned it," she muttered. "I'm not sure I even believe you right now."

At that, he straightened up and walked into the kitchen. "That's great, and you don't have to believe me, but I sure wouldn't mind an explanation."

"Explanation for what?"

He stared at her and asked, "You really don't remember, do you?"

"Remember the part about my supposed sleepwalking? No. What's going on? You seem to think that I did something or that you saw something you're not sure about."

"Oh, I definitely saw something," he confirmed, leaning against the kitchen countertop, crossing his arms over his chest. "The question is, what did I see?"

She just stared at him, not sure where he was going with this.

He added, "Sometimes what I think I see is not always what I see." She blinked. He nodded. "Yeah, that's about how I feel right now too."

With coffee dripping now, he turned back to her and added, "I get that it's early and that you're probably not ready to talk, but I am more than ready to get an explanation."

"If I had one, I would give it to you," she declared in exasperation, standing up. She gave herself a light stretch, realizing that she really was sore. "God," she murmured. "I feel like I've walked to hell and back."

He spun around so quickly that she took a step back, staring at him. "Whoa, whoa. What did I say?"

"You tell me," he replied, his gaze intense.

"Just a phrase about feeling crappy. Feels like I walked to hell and back."

At that, he didn't seem to react quite the same way, yet he still stared at her, as if unsure whether she were serious or not. "So you didn't mean anything by it?"

Her jaw dropped, and then slowly she closed her mouth, taking a moment to realize he was serious. "You really think I might have been serious about that?" She stared at him, frowning for a moment, dumbfounded. "Is that even possible?"

"You'd be surprised," he noted, his tone hard. "The shit I deal with, even a simple phrase like that has all kinds of meaning."

"Not with me," she snapped, glaring at him. "I don't know what the hell is even going on. I went upstairs to sleep in my bed last night, and I wake up, and I'm down here." She tried to keep the note of accusation out of her voice, but she didn't succeed, and his eyebrows shot up.

"So you think I did it?"

"I don't know. I don't have a clue what I'm supposed to think. What I do know is that I'm sitting down here in barely any clothes and freezing, yet you're wearing less than me and are having absolutely no trouble with the chill."

"What chill?" he asked. He walked over, took a closer

look at her, put a hand on her head, and immediately frowned. Grabbing a blanket, he bundled her up. "That's a reaction," he muttered, "but to what?"

"Reaction to what though?"

"Just give it a minute."

She shook her head. "I don't know what's going on here."

"No, I realize that. I'm sorry."

"Sorry for what?" she cried out.

"For making it sound as if you had something to do with this. I mean, I know you did, but I'm just now realizing that you really didn't understand."

"More riddles," she snapped, glaring at him.

"Yes, to you, but really, to me, it's just more questions."

"I have never sleepwalked in my life—that I know of—if that's even what you're talking about."

"That's part of what I'm talking about but not all of it."

By the time the coffee was done dripping, she felt better but still chilled.

"That chill worries me though."

"Yeah, I'm not exactly feeling all that great about it myself," she replied, wincing, as if she were getting worse. Her teeth started to chatter, and she looked up at him in pain.

He made a startled exclamation, set down the coffee, and, sitting down beside her, picked her up, and pulled her into his arms.

Immediately she felt a furnace of heat wrap around her. She shivered harder for a moment, and then the chills seemed to reduce to something almost manageable. Wrapped up as she was, she couldn't talk, though she didn't care about talking. The cold had hit her sideways to the point that she was almost numb.

He worked his hands over her legs and her arms. "You should warm up soon," he muttered.

"I am. I just don't know why or how any of this can be happening."

He held her close but continued to rub her limbs. "We'll give it a minute. You should start to improve soon now."

And, while she was warming up, it wasn't to the point that she wanted to be separated and sitting on her own. So, when he made a move to do just that, she clung to him.

"Easy now, you're fine."

"Says you," she muttered, slowly separating, but, as soon as too much air was between them, she started to shiver again. Immediately he wrapped her back up and held her close.

When the shivering finally slowed down to the point that she thought it safe to move, she muttered, "I think I'm okay now."

"I don't think you're okay at all, but I agree that we can probably try to separate again and see how it goes."

And, with great care, he placed her on the couch beside him, then tucked the blanket around her shoulders and her feet and asked, "Can you handle a bit of coffee?"

She nodded. "I was hoping it was still hot."

"If not, we'll get some fresh." When he held it out to her, he suggested, "This is probably about the right temperature now, so you can drink it right away."

And, with that, she stuck out a hand from under the covers and reached for the cup, immediately taking a sip. As soon as the hot brew hit her throat, she felt the warmth sliding through her. "Oh, Lord, that feels so good."

He just nodded and kept a worried gaze on her.

"I'm fine," she muttered, hating that look in his eye.

"Sure you are," he stated, with a confidence that he obviously didn't feel.

She gave him a wry look. "Guess this doesn't normally happen on your other cases, *huh?*"

He shrugged. "Well, there are cases, and then there are cases."

"Another time it'd be fascinating to hear all about that," she noted, with an eye roll, "but right now doesn't feel like a good time."

"Of course not. Some of it is pretty freaky, and, right at this moment, you're talking to people who aren't here, and you're getting chills, and you have no clue what is happening in that head of yours." She glared at him, and he smiled. "Sorry, but it's true."

"I haven't done anything."

"I know," he added, with a chuckle. "That's partly why this is so interesting."

"Yeah, not for me," she declared, "and it shouldn't be for you either."

He raised an eyebrow at that. "It is what it is. What we have to do is figure out what the heck is going on here and see if we can't get some answers to free you from whatever this energy is doing to you."

"Free me?" she asked, her gaze narrowed.

"It would appear that, in some way, you are quite seriously affected by this energy—or else it's a reaction to your movements in the night."

"Yeah, you keep bringing that up, but I don't know just what it is you think I have done."

He nodded. "When you're a little warmer, I'll show you."

She stared at him. "What do you mean, *show me?* What

did I do?"

"Nothing too crazy," he replied carefully. "But considering we went to great lengths to not encourage this energy, it is a little disconcerting that you felt that you could go change things in the middle of the night."

She just shook her head at him. "You're not making any sense."

"I know that, to you, I'm not making any sense at all. I do get that. Drink your coffee, and let's get you back, so you're feeling a little more normal, and then I'll show you."

Hearing his words, she quickly gulped down the coffee, her mind trying to figure out what had gone on. The memories were blank, just a smoky vision of nothing, as if she had walked forever though. Her legs were sore. Her arms were tired. She looked over at him. "I seriously feel like I did one of the hardest workouts or hikes in my life during the night, and everything hurts."

He nodded. "That is often the case with energy work, particularly if you're fighting against something."

Her gaze widened at that. "I wish all of this wasn't gobbledygook to me."

"Now we're back to the fact that I'm not sure it truly is gobbledygook for you."

She shook her head. "That implies that I'm deliberately trying to fake something."

"No, it doesn't, not at all," he argued, "but you had the foresight to contact Stefan."

"You keep bringing that up too," she stated, looking at him. "And I keep telling you that I didn't know anything about Stefan. I just … He was an expert, a number to call, somebody to talk to."

"But the right number to call, the right somebody to talk

to."

"Surely he has a word for that, like maybe I was fated to contact him or something."

"He definitely has words for that, and he does send out a transmitter message to help anybody in need, to have them come to him so that he can help, since so little exists in this way of assistance."

"Yeah, you're not kidding," she agreed, with feeling. "You'd have to be absolutely nuts to have anything to do with this stuff. Did you ever ask him if he had any dealings with me before that?" she asked curiously.

He shook his head. "No, I don't suppose I did. Not clearly anyway."

"Maybe you should. Maybe I have a history with him that I don't remember right now because of whatever happened to me."

"Yeah, being found out on the highway, alone, naked, and dead? That part's freaky too."

She stared at him. "That alone should exonerate me from any culpability in this. Yet it does feel like it's got to be related somehow."

"Somebody helped you do that or somebody did that to you." She slowly straightened, glaring at him, and he winced. "Okay, my bad, that wasn't a great turn of phrase."

"Helped me to do this?" she asked in an ominous tone.

"I really didn't mean it the way it came out."

"How else could you possibly mean it?" she asked, staring at him in shock. "Do you truly think I had something to do with this? With these pearls, with the women, with me found dead on the side of the road?"

"No," he stated, his voice clipped and clear. "I don't."

She pulled away and stared at him. "I don't even know

what to think about what you just said, but believe me. I don't trust anything you have to say right now because of it." She sank back into the corner of the couch, closed her eyes, and sipped her coffee. When she was done, she stood, and, still slightly cold, she stated, "Okay. What did I do? Show me."

He looked at her and then nodded. "Fine, let's go look at the safe."

"The safe?" She stared at him. He nodded again. She turned to look at the drywall, leaning on the floor. "Why did you open it?" she asked in confusion.

At that, he shook his head. "I didn't. You did."

"I did not," she snapped at him. "We decided it was safer to have the necklace and bracelet apart and intentionally locked that necklace in the safe."

"Oh, I know," he agreed. "So where's the bracelet then?"

"You hid it. You wrapped it up in something energy-related, and you hid it. First you thought it should be put into the safe, and then you and Stefan decided it would be safer if the two pieces were apart."

"Where did I put it?" he asked, staring at her steadily.

She looked around and replied, "In the kitchen, didn't you?"

"So go get it," he urged her.

Glaring at him and not at all sure why he was doing this, she walked into the kitchen, went to the cupboard where he'd put it, and checked, stunned. "It's not there."

"No, it isn't."

She turned and looked back at the safe, shook her head, and said, "Oh, no, no, no, no, no."

"Oh yes. You woke me up when you opened the safe, and you put the bracelet in with the necklace."

She stared at the safe, walked over, found it locked securely, quickly opened it, and, sure enough, there in front of her was both the bracelet and the necklace. She turned to look at him in shock. "Not that I'm saying I believe you, but why? If I did do this, why would I?" He hesitated. She narrowed her gaze at him. "The truth, please."

"I imagine it's because the energy was too strong for you to ignore it. Whatever is going on, … you are connected, and these souls, these pieces of jewelry, they have a hold over you—in one way or another."

"Why on earth would they want that?"

He shrugged. "If you think about it, they already got one thing that they wanted."

"What's that?" she asked, looking at the safe.

"They're together again. More than that, they got you to do that for them."

HURRICANE HAD QUICKLY separated the jewels once again, and this time he didn't show her where he was putting them. She deliberately didn't watch. Jewel had been quiet for the last hour, ever since she had closed the safe and returned to the couch.

When he refilled their coffee cups and sat down in her tiny living room again, he asked, "Are you okay?" He watched as a wave of furious color washed over her cheeks and realized it probably wasn't the best question. "I'm not really sure how to phrase it," he said. "I can't say I've been in this position before."

At that, she hesitated and then frowned. "I keep getting angry at you, and I guess I shouldn't. Who in the world could understand all this energy stuff?"

"You have every right to be angry. Something is manipulating your world, but the question is, what? And I guess the bigger question is, why?"

She nodded at that. "I don't understand any of this. I got an email, asking me if I could repair the clasp and a couple of the threads on the pearls. That's it."

"Did you ever find those emails?"

"Yes, and I printed them out, plus forwarded them to you, right?" And then she stopped, stared at him, and asked, "I did, didn't I?"

He pulled up his email and nodded. "They're right here. And the printer whirred behind your canvases, but I never retrieved those either. Sorry, I didn't have a chance to look at either."

She shrugged. "It's fine. I was just worried I hadn't even sent them."

He ran through those two emails and added, "Okay, so really nothing indicative of a problem in here. So how did you receive the pearls?"

"I told you that too. I got them in the mail, by courier."

"We need to track down who and how that came to be as well," he noted. "Did they come together?"

"No," she snapped, her frustration building. "They came in separate deliveries, which you know very well. The necklace came before any of this started, and the bracelet? … You were right here and helped me open it."

"No problem or no weird feeling when you held the necklace?"

"No, I didn't even realize at the beginning that there was a matching bracelet. He–at least I think it was a male–told me that he had another piece to go with the necklace that needed work as well. It wasn't suspicious. It wasn't different.

It wasn't weird, no strangeness to it, until, as I already told you, … I was finishing the work on the necklace and began adding the positive energy that I always do to help people. I would never add energy other than that, and I didn't even know that it was something you could do."

"No, but, if you think about it, if you can do something one way, there will always be people out there trying to do it the other way."

"You mean, if I'm trying to put good energy into something, somebody out there will be trying to pull it away or to instill bad energy?"

"Yes. Although *bad* isn't the word I would choose."

"Right, you don't mean bad. You mean evil."

"That is a more descriptive word, yes," he agreed, as he nodded. Just then his phone rang. "Stefan, how are you doing?"

"A little tired. I'm sending you some photos of images that I sketched last night. Go over them with Jewel and see if she recognizes any of them."

"Will do," he replied, and then he explained to Stefan about her night.

"Damn," he muttered. "Whatever this is, somehow it's gotten into her space and her energy. We have to keep her safe, while we figure out a way to detach her."

"Yeah, and I'm not sure how well detaching will work either."

"Let's not worry about that just yet," Stefan suggested, and then he yawned through the phone.

"Sounds like a rough night for you."

"Yeah, definitely, but …" He hesitated, then added, "I'll need to talk to you in a little bit about something else."

"Yeah, ditto." Hurricane hung up and waited for the

photo files to open up on his phone, and, when they did, he winced.

"What's the matter?" she asked.

"Stefan was called to sketch last night, and, when he does, they're usually not the prettiest of images."

"No, I don't imagine so." Jewel frowned. "Did he send images?" She scooted closer to Hurricane on the couch. When he held up the first one, she sucked back her breath and stared at it, her face twisting. "Good God, that's just like a photograph."

"And that's the way these images are coming out," he noted. "He doesn't always draw in this clear graphic form, but obviously a message is involved."

"A message?" she asked, turning and looking at him.

"For some reason, the clarity is needed."

"*Great.* Anybody who can do this …" And, when she didn't have words, she groaned, as she stared at the image. "Do you think it's one of the women?"

"That's what Stefan was hoping you could tell us. Do you recognize her?"

"No, I don't." She shook her head. "And that's saying something because, with an image that clear, it would be hard to *not* recognize her, if I knew her."

At that, he flicked to the second image. She seemed to study Stefan's technique and shook her head. "He's incredibly talented," she murmured.

"He is, indeed."

When he got to the third one, she pulled back and stared. "That's Anna," she cried out. She jumped up, raced over to her workbench, and pulled out one of her sketches. "It's her."

But whereas she had done an almost contemporary, almost modernistic image, Stefan had done one in brutal clarity.

Hurricane quickly sent Stefan a text. **Number three is Anna, one of the victims in the pearl bracelet.**

"Are there more?" she asked, looking at his phone and then back at him.

He nodded, hesitated, and then flicked again. She nodded, tears coming to her eyes. "Yes, that's another one. Nellie, from the necklace."

"And he has one more here."

As he flicked it open, she cried out, "That's Rhea. She's in the bracelet." She stared at him. "How could Stefan get the same images as I did?"

At that, Hurricane turned to her and then replied, "Because, for Stefan, this is the energy work that he does."

"Yes, but I don't," she snapped, glaring at him.

"Yeah, I hear you," he said, "but, right now, it seems that you do."

She sank back down beside him on the couch. "Why me? Why these images? Why now?"

"Why you? Because you opened the necklace for energy transmission, incoming and outgoing, it seems. *Why these images* is because you were given the necklace and now the bracelet to repair. Why now? Maybe for no other reason than the fact that somebody who owns the necklace wanted to get it fixed, so that somebody else could wear it again."

She stared at him. "Nobody can wear this," she stated, her voice harsh. "Whoever wears it will die."

"And yet," he began gently, studying her carefully, "When you were at the hospital, you kept asking for a necklace, and you kept reaching to your neck for it. As if you had worn it. And you'd had it on your neck at one time, right?"

She stared at him. "The way my memory is, I can't be sure of anything."

"You told Stefan that you had tried it on, something about the repair. Think of how you work."

"Maybe. It was a beautiful piece. Sometimes they don't lay flat. What difference does it make?"

"I don't know," he admitted. "I mean, I'm grasping at straws here. That you were trying to put loving energy into it was one trigger. However, that you put it on maybe was a bigger trigger. Maybe somebody who would wear it wouldn't necessarily end up as a victim, but maybe, because of what you did, it made you become a victim."

She stared. "Are we thinking that this killer is still out there and that the killer may have sent the necklace directly to me, for me?"

"I can't say that for sure," he told her, shaking his head. "For all we know, the killer is long dead, and this necklace was inherited. Until we can track down these women in your visions and Stefan's, we don't know whether they died decades ago, if not centuries ago. Or maybe the necklace and bracelet were sold in some estate sale, and somebody pulled it out of a dusty dark corner, and that coming back to you has brought it back to life again."

She swallowed hard. "You almost make it sound like this thing is alive."

He smiled gently. "Don't ever kid yourself. It is energy, and energy never dies."

"Right," she murmured. "That's just not very reassuring." She got up abruptly and stated, "I'll go have a shower. It's six in the morning and way too early, but I'm not sure I have much more to give at the moment."

"If you want to go for a nap instead, do that," he suggested. "Otherwise, we've got a long day ahead of us, and we still can't do very much, until the business world opens."

Obviously she wanted to ask questions but, at the same time, probably didn't want to know exactly what he had planned when the businesses did open. She nodded. "I'll go lie down and see if I can sleep again."

He nodded. "Good." As soon as she went upstairs, his phone rang again. He looked down, and, not recognizing the number, he answered it cautiously.

"My name is Drew."

"Yes, right. Hi, Drew. Hurricane here."

"You know me?" Drew asked.

"No, but I certainly know Dr. Maddy."

He sighed. "Such a strange world that everybody knows my wife and my connection to her and that's how I get identified."

Hurricane chuckled. "Not necessarily, but she pushed some of the energy ahead to make it an easier trip for you."

"If you say so," Drew muttered. "Look. This case has really gotten ahold of her."

"It certainly got ahold of Jewel as well."

"Right, and anything that goes bump in the night always has me on edge."

At that, Hurricane had to chuckle. "Not a big fan, *huh?*"

"The stuff that they see is pretty darn crazy, but then I gather you're in the same business."

"Pulled in by the same forces," he said honestly. "It's not as if I can ignore this."

"But you don't have much of a choice either, do you?"

"I don't. Some of my skills are ..." He stopped and then added, "Let's just say, unique."

At that, Drew snorted. "Every one of you guys appears to be unique. This is a world where nobody knows what you can do, and yet you all exist in some weird time-space dimension that makes no sense to the rest of us."

At that, Hurricane burst out laughing at the disgruntled tone in Drew's voice. "I hear you, man. So, is this meant to be a helpful call?"

"What? You mean it isn't?" he quipped on a note of laughter. "Anything that sets Maddy off the way this has will be something that I'm all over, just trying to keep her safe."

"Is she not safe?" he asked hesitantly.

"I'm not sure, but I haven't seen her like this in a very long time. So I'd like to solve it as quickly as possible."

"I'm all for that," Hurricane agreed. "You got any idea what we're supposed to do about it?"

"I've pulled some of the names that you gave to Stefan," he stated. "And I understand from Maddy that I have some images to look at regarding this case. But Stefan's artwork that I've seen before is pretty crazy sometimes—some of it is dead clear, and some of it isn't."

"These are like photographs," Hurricane stated, "and you should be able to get some IDs off them via facial recognition, I would think."

"Particularly if anybody has names to go with the images," he added, a question in his voice.

"In that I can help you."

"Really?" he said. "So whatever psychic is giving us that is somebody I would love to work with."

"Be careful what you wish for. In this case it's Jewel, and it's not terribly easy on her. Something's going on in her space, and, while we're not yet sure, we suspect a possession of some kind."

At that, Hurricane heard Drew suck in his breath. "Okay, how about you give me the names to match whichever drawings. I'll add it to the list that I've got and see what I can come up with."

"Also, can you check into Jewel's incident report? Like where she was found and anything about it that we don't already know, just because you may have access to more information."

"I got the gist of it from Stefan, but that's definitely not the normal abduction."

"We're not sure that it was an abduction."

At that, Drew's voice turned brisk. "That you'll need to explain."

"Not sure I can," he admitted. "A lot of woo-woo stuff goes bump in the night for this one."

"Unfortunately there always is, when it comes to Maddy's cases. I can look into Jewel's case and see if we can come up with anything."

"I was hoping there might be surveillance video and witnesses or something, anything at this point."

"In your dream world that would be very nice," Drew said, "but it's rare to get something quite so clear-cut as that in my line of work."

"Yeah, well, I keep hoping," Hurricane replied. "Now she's started to walk in her sleep, and these objects that are infused with a certain dark energy are calling to her in a dangerous way."

"Right, and that's something that you specialize in, I understand."

"Yes, I don't know if Maddy's mentioned some of the specialized museums we protect."

"I've heard about them, yes. Not that I particularly want

to see firsthand."

"No, I'm sure you don't," Hurricane agreed, with a chuckle. "However, because I do what I do, you don't have to deal with these … artifacts."

"I'm not sure I could do anything that would help with that either," he noted. "This is … There's only so much those of us who don't have any energy-working abilities can deal with."

"Yet, if you're with Dr. Maddy, I suspect you probably have abilities you are using that you aren't even aware of."

"So they say," Drew murmured, with a note of laughter. "Let me just add that I'm not too worried about that pathway."

"It will happen anyway," Hurricane warned.

"Yeah, it already has," Drew admitted, "but still, this is out of my wheelhouse. I'll get back to you." With that, he hung up abruptly.

Jewel sat on the stairs, her chin propped on her hand, looking at him. "Who is Drew?" she asked.

Hurricane was startled, as he wondered how she knew his name, then realized he'd said the man's name at the beginning of their telephone call. "That was Dr. Maddy's husband," he replied, looking at her.

"You said something about possession," she noted, her tone equally soft and controlled.

He hesitated again and then nodded. "Yes, but we're not exactly sure—not sure how, not in the expected ways of possession."

"Is there anything you guys are sure of?"

At that, he smiled, because her voice had a teasing note to it, not full of blame or anger. "I think we know what's going on, yet we're just not sure how it came about and who is involved."

"You really think that I'm being possessed by some-body?"

"It's not like that in the generic possession sense," he began, as he got up and walked over to the bottom of the stairs to look at her. "In a case like this, I think the dark energy has somehow gotten into your system, probably when you opened yourself up to the necklace, and somebody—either connected to these women or the actual killer him-self—somehow managed to get into your energy. If we can track down these names you've given us, even find proof that these women were murdered, we can work on that angle."

"But if they're in my energy, I should be able to get rid of them, right?"

"Absolutely," he confirmed, looking at her with a nod of approval. "That is very important to remember."

"So this isn't a case where I've got them and I have to keep them forever?"

"No, but we need to make sure that we do it in such a way that we don't cause you any more hurt."

"Do you mean *hurt* or do you mean ending up in one of those pearls?"

"That's the ultimate injury, is it not?" he asked softly.

She looked at him, something dancing in her eyes. "I'm hungry." Her voice was garbled. Almost as if the prosaic turn of voice had caught her by surprise, a burble of laughter popped out.

He chuckled. "Now that's a sound I really like to hear," he stated, with a smile.

"I'm not sure I've been laughing very much lately. I feel there's been nothing but one wave of problems after anoth-er."

"Got it. Did you manage to sleep at all?"

"No, when I heard that phone call, that was the end of it."

"Sorry about that. I did give him all the names you came up with. He'll also look into where you were found and see if we can come up with any more information."

"I suppose that would be one of the biggest things. I mean, it's one thing to have whatever you're saying here happening, but it's an entirely different thing to have ended up naked and left for dead out on some highway."

"Exactly," he agreed. "I don't know who or what is involved in this, or why, but I think a couple issues are involved, and solving at least one would help us to narrow down the other one, if only because we've ruled out the other, you know?"

"Well, that's the thing. Is all this related, or are they different things entirely?"

"You never found anything missing when you looked around your house, either the first one or this artist loft, right?"

"No, says the woman with amnesia." She looked at him puzzled. "Nothing outside of my laptop and cell phone."

"I'm just back to wondering if somebody did find something."

She shook her head. "I mean, it's possible. However, if they were looking for the stuff for my show, it was already sent out. That much we gathered from my emails. My jewelry designs were already sent to the show, and the necklace was in my safe. I don't know what to say about the safe, but it's awkward having it open and exposed," she noted, looking at it. "I feel that we need to close it off again."

"We can do that." Hurricane hopped up the few stairs to

where the wall safe was and replaced the drywall, making it look as close to having always been there as he could. "Obviously, if this were a long-term solution, we would be closing this off with proper drywall or maybe cement."

"Or just make it look like a proper safe and not try to hide it at all," she muttered.

"That too," he agreed, looking over at her. "I suspect that's what it was when you first moved in here."

She shrugged. "I'm not sure I have that memory."

"So tell me something. Who would have broken into your house, or, if they saw you passed out, looking like you were dying, who would have dumped your body?"

"That's what I keep coming back to," she shared, puzzled. "Because, to me, they're very separate issues. Unless the break-in was to abduct me? I don't know. I mean, whether my death involved someone I knew or a stranger, why dump me by a highway and why nude like that? So, if I had a lover, a boyfriend, and I'd somehow passed out or died here in front of them. Maybe he was terrified. Maybe he would have taken me out of here, but why not drive me directly to the hospital or bury me somewhere I'd never be found or, hey, how about just calling 9-1-1? Could it be just literally a case of panic?"

He nodded. "I'm not sure that's how I would react, but—"

"Yeah, we can't really say how we would react in that situation. The fact of the matter is, I don't know how even I would react if somebody I was with died suddenly." Then she stopped, shook her head, and added, "Actually I do know. I would call for an ambulance and then would be at the hospital, waiting for news, while doing everything I could to try and help figure out what happened," she stated.

"So, it takes an uncaring person to have taken you out onto the highway and dumped you. The other thing to keep in mind is that whoever did that will be shocked to see you. Alive. Not dead. Although if we could get some reaction from someone in that manner, that would be a game changer and a dead giveaway."

"That would be something, wouldn't it?" she muttered.

"Obviously it wasn't Lucas or Charles. They didn't appear to be surprised to see you at all."

"No. Back to basics though, I definitely need food."

"Good. Do you want me to cook something?"

"No, I want to get out of here for a bit," she muttered. "I want to go for a walk. I want to just go someplace, anywhere. The walls are closing in on me." He hesitated. She glared at him, shook her head, and stated, "No, we're going."

"Okay," he said. "As long as food is part of this equation, I'm okay with it."

She snickered. "As long as you get food, anything is okay with you."

"If you say so." He laughed. "Come on. Get dressed. We'll go for a walk first and then find some food."

CHAPTER 14

A LMOST TWO HOURS later Hurricane and Jewel made their way into a small restaurant. He looked around, smiled, and nodded. "This looks like quite the place."

"It's an artist haunt," she murmured. "A decent place to come, and, while they don't really know me, they do."

"Good choice. Not so close to your loft as to be an obvious choice for you, yet not so new and different as to stand out."

"I don't think anybody ever stands out in these places, but I could be wrong."

They took a seat, and a waitress came over, handed them menus, gave them a perfunctory smile, and then quickly left.

"She didn't seem to know you."

"Maybe that's a good thing."

Sitting in the back, he looked around, as she watched him. "Do you see anything?" she asked him.

Startled, he turned to her and shrugged. "No, not really. Was it that obvious?"

"You're doing the same thing I'm doing. We're looking to see who might have recognized me and who might be surprised that I'm, you know, alive and well."

"The thing is, if they know you're alive and well, would they come and approach you or would they disappear and maybe even pull up stakes and leave town because of what they did?"

She shrugged. "I don't know."

"Would you have taken a stranger home?" he asked after a moment.

She stared at him. "You mean, like, literally pick up a stranger and take him home to my bed? Ah, no, that's not my style."

"I didn't think so, but …"

"No, absolutely no way." He hesitated. She looked at him and asked, "Now what?"

"Just your … relationship status."

"As in, do I have one? The answer is no."

"Okay, and why not?"

"Because the last one was bad, and I didn't want to get into another similar scenario, particularly when I was working so hard on my show."

"You talk about the show as if it was pretty well a done deal."

She hesitated and shrugged. "I don't think it was a done deal at the time, but I think it was definitely … not in the bag, but something I was expecting." Knowing he wanted her to say more, she continued. "And, no, I don't think my ex would have had anything to do with this. He was one of those irrationally jealous types, and, when I started expressing interest in putting together pieces for a show, first he just laughed and scoffed at me. But, when I wasn't deterred, he got really upset and immediately decided I must be sleeping with all the gallery owners in town, trying to get into a show. He went so far as to suggest that I was offering sexual favors to convince them to give me a shot, since my jewelry sucks so much and all."

At that, Hurricane's eyebrows went up. "So, insecure,

jealous, and not nearly as talented."

She laughed. "Something like that. Art brought us together. I don't know what kept us together though," she murmured.

"Circumstance is what often happens. So often people get into something like that, and it just seems like too much trouble to rock the boat and to get themselves out."

She nodded. "I would never have thought that I'd wind up in a situation like that, but I guess we don't really know what we're dealing with, not until enough years go by. Then, at some point, you wake up and look back, shaking your head, wondering what the hell that was all about."

"Yep, that's pretty much it in a nutshell," he agreed, with a smile.

"What about you?" she asked. "Do you have a relationship with someone who doesn't have a problem with you bouncing around the country, helping other women?" Her tone was nothing if not shrewd.

"I don't have one right now, and, in my world, it's probably a whole lot better that way."

"Or at least have one who would understand," she corrected.

"Yeah, is that possible?" he asked, with a smile. "Anyway, some of the work I do takes me all over the globe."

"So she just has to be self-confident enough in who she is to not hate that you're gone a lot of the time. Surely that's not too hard to find."

"I haven't found it yet," he shared, with a bright smile. Just then the waitress came back and poured them coffee.

Jewel immediately pulled hers close and wrapped her hands around it.

Noticing her movements, he asked, "Are you feeling cold

again?"

"No, I'm fine," she replied. "That walk was good though. It's just, now it feels like we have to get back to the other stuff that we really don't want to deal with. We've talked about everything but that."

"Anytime you want to talk about that other stuff, go for it."

"That's the problem. I don't really have anything to say," she stated. "It feels like I should have something to say, and I should know what that is, but I don't."

"I guess the question for me is, do you have any idea who might have done this to you?"

"Done this? You mean dumping me out on the highway? No, I don't. Now I'm wondering if I was drugged or attacked somehow, and yet I didn't know. It's possible, but I don't know by whom or what."

"That's always the question, isn't it?" he noted. "Would you have opened the door to a delivery guy?"

"Well, yeah, I would have. I get deliveries as part of my business. And particularly when you don't know of any looming danger out there, you do it without a thought. I mean, you only become wary after something has already happened. Most of my clients send in deliveries, and I return them in a similar fashion."

"Very true," he muttered. "Okay, and we already know you have no cameras at the loft."

"No, after an incident, when I first moved in, where somebody got drunk one night and smashed them up, they were never replaced after that."

"Of course not," he murmured, with a nod. "That would be way too simple."

"I'm sure you already checked that."

"I did. Right after we got to your place, I checked and had the manager questioned about it. He's supposed to be getting them fixed."

"I've also heard that same story from him a couple times."

"What about your house? You don't stay there at all?"

"No, I don't." She hesitated, now staring at him. "It just feels wrong to stay there." At that, his gaze narrowed, and she added, confused, "I don't really know what that means."

"That's an intriguing statement to say that and then not know why."

"It goes along with the rest of my life at the moment," she noted, with a smile.

"Do you think you lived there with him, this ex-boyfriend of yours?"

"I wondered, but I don't know. If you're wondering if the relationship was violent, I don't think so. I don't have any memories of that, but again I don't really know."

"Maybe you should ask those friends of yours."

Her face lit up. "They would know." She immediately pulled out the phone Hurricane had loaned her and called them. When Charles answered, she asked him about her ex.

"From what we saw, he was pretty abusive to you, but it was more verbal, and you never really understood or saw it. We kept encouraging you to ditch him, but you didn't."

"Great. Thanks for that."

"No problem," he said cheerfully. "Where are you?"

"We're having breakfast," she replied, then named the restaurant.

"Oh, that's a good place. You sound better."

"I'm not sure I'm necessarily feeling all that much better," she admitted. "We haven't really solved any of the issues yet."

"That's all right. Give it time," he replied comfortably. "None of this stuff will happen quickly, at least I've never found it to."

"We're trying to figure out who might have dumped me on the road in the middle of the night. Do you remember if I had a courier or anything come by earlier that day?"

"I don't know. You certainly didn't mention it, but then we didn't talk that much, as you were really focused on your work and the show."

"Right," she murmured. "That's the problem. I apparently isolated myself those last few days, trying to work hard to get caught up, but I ended up left for dead on the road and eventually in the hospital, all with no idea what happened. But, speaking of my work, we did figure out one thing."

"What's that?"

"The show, I'm in it. I was invited!"

"What? Oh my God. That's wonderful news. I can't wait to tell Lucas. But wait, your pieces? Were they damaged when your workshop was ransacked?"

"No, as it turns out, I'd already sent them in."

"So your show's okay?" he asked anxiously.

"It is, though I need to get down there to see how the setup is going."

"When does it open?"

"Not for a couple days yet, though I need to double-check that too. My schedule is a mess, along with everything else."

"Hey, give it time. All of this has been quite a shock. I'm over the moon for you about the show, though wondering why you didn't tell us. Never mind. I already know. You wanted to surprise us, didn't you?"

"That's the current theory. Thank you. I'll be in touch about the show." And, with that, she hung up. "So apparently my ex was abusive, but more verbal than anything else," she shared. "I do remember that we didn't end on good terms. I wonder if that was when I quit staying at the other place. I don't know." At that, she watched Hurricane's face twist.

"We'll check into him." He opened a notepad and said, "I'll need his contact information."

She frowned, thought about it for a moment, and then gave him the name and a phone number from memory. "I hate not having my phone," she murmured. "I wish they had left me that much."

He chuckled. "But then that's practically leaving you everything. If you think about it, our whole worlds are on our phones. Anybody who wanted to cut you off from others in your world would do exactly that."

She gave him a small nod. "Still, it's a pain in the ass."

"Oh, no doubt." He chuckled. "It absolutely is. But you're holding up and managing just fine."

When the waitress brought over their order, she looked at it. "Did you order while I was on the phone?" she asked curiously.

He nodded. "No point in waiting."

"No. Thank you. *Huh.* I just blanked out and didn't even notice." He nodded but didn't say anything. "Okay, you need to tell me something."

"What's that?" he asked.

"Have I been blanking out?"

He hesitated and then nodded slowly. "I'm not sure that I would call it blanking out, but, just like I saw you do the little sleepwalking scenario, you've been like, … I guess blanking out in the midst of conversations."

She took a deep breath. "Any idea why?"

"No, but I can hazard a guess."

"I won't like it, will I?"

"I don't know if you will or not, but I'm not really good at burying my head in the sand or letting things get to me."

She snorted. "I've noticed. You also prefer to employ the sledgehammer approach to getting the job done."

At that, he burst out laughing. "That's hardly fair. Anyway, would I say that the blanking out is all part of it? Yes. Is it somebody else's energy? I'm not seeing any sign of it."

At that, she let out her breath slowly, her gaze intense as she searched his face. "But you're holding something back from me."

He nodded. "I am, but so are you, so we're even."

"What am I holding back from you?" she snapped.

"Exactly who took you out on that highway and dumped you."

Just then his phone rang, and she felt her insides go still, like a calm before a storm that broke everything.

HURRICANE LEFT THAT statement hanging, while he answered his phone. "Hi, Grant. What's up?" he asked.

"The names you gave me, two of them were murdered." He gave a few details.

Hurricane frowned and stared into the phone. "You're sure?"

"Yes," he stated in exasperation. "Of course I'm sure."

Hurricane winced. "Sorry, I didn't mean to insult you."

"Oh, that's fine," he muttered. "When it comes to you

guys, I've almost come to expect it."

He burst out laughing. "Sorry. Sort of. Anything on the others?"

"Still looking, but nothing definitive yet. In the meantime, I wanted to let you know what we're looking at." And, with that, he hung up.

Jewel leaned forward. "What was that all about?"

"Two of the names, Rhea and Anna."

She winced. "Yes, what about them?"

"They were both murdered but on opposite sides of the country. One here in Maine and the other in California."

She stared at him. "Is that even doable?"

"Yeah, sure it's doable, though not necessarily convenient. For somebody who was a frequent traveler, like for work, or was deliberately traveling in order to avoid getting caught, that would be possible. But one problem."

"What's that?" she asked, staring at him.

"The time frame in between is harder to reconcile."

"Meaning?"

"Anna died seventeen years ago and Rhea closer to twenty-seven."

CHAPTER 15

HURRICANE DROVE THEM home, parked, and headed for the loft. She stood by the front door, uncertain, then looked at him and said, "Maybe we should go back to my house."

"Why is that?"

"I don't know, but this feels off now."

"Let's go inside and take a look to see if anything is out of place, and we'll go from there. If you want to go back to the house, we can go back to the house."

"I also need to find time to get down to the gallery to check the display."

He nodded. "Were you planning on putting the necklace in it?"

"No, of course not. It's not one of my designs."

"So it's all pieces that you have designed and created?"

She nodded. "Yes, exactly."

They walked into her loft, and she immediately stopped and sniffed the air. Fascinated, he watched. "That's an interesting reaction."

She looked at him, then nodded. "Soldering."

"What do you mean?"

"It smells like somebody has been soldering in here."

"You weren't, were you?"

"No, of course not." She hesitated and then added, "I

mean, other jewelers are in the building, so I suppose I could be getting the smell through the vents."

He nodded cautiously. "What do you mean, other jewelers here?"

She looked at him. "This whole complex is full of artists, and I'm not the only jeweler."

"Anybody jealous over the whole show thing?"

"Maybe, but I haven't exactly told anybody. I'm not friendly with anybody else here either."

"Right, that's another point to keep in mind too," he muttered.

She nodded. "It is absolutely another point to keep in mind, though I'm not exactly sure what you're going on about."

He smiled at her. "I'm not sure I do either, so let's just keep focused on what we need to stay focused on at the moment."

"Yeah, nothing here, nothing to stay focused on," she cried out, raising her hands in frustration and glaring at him. "Now back to what you were saying in the restaurant. You're wrong. I don't know who dropped me on some highway."

He nodded. "You not believing me isn't helping. You should at least entertain the possibility."

"Ah, well, sorry about that, but it's a little hard to believe you right now. You are driving me a little crazy," she muttered.

He chuckled. "You and me both."

She wasn't sure what to say to that. "Look. I'll go up and have a nap."

"You do that." He walked over to the safe, opened it, double-checked that everything was there, and nodded.

"Is it fine?" she asked.

"It is."

"I still have to give it back."

"Yeah, I know that. I'm just wondering if he'll be the one who comes to collect it."

She stopped, slowly looked at him, and moaned. "Somebody *was* here that day. I remember him now."

"Good." Hurricane walked over, urging her to sit down on the single couch. "What is it you remember?"

"I'm not …" She frowned, stopped. "If I say, *I don't know*, you'll get mad at me."

"I won't get mad at you," he stated immediately, "but anything that you can start to remember is huge."

"It is. I'm just not sure what it is I'm remembering."

"Okay, so why don't you start by telling me what you've got. Don't try to understand it or have it make sense, just tell me."

"I remember somebody at the door that day."

"That's a good start."

"I think he mentioned something about his necklace." She frowned at that. "But I'm not … I'm not getting anything after that. Why am I not getting anything afterward? I mean, if I saw him at my door, I should remember him."

"Maybe. Did he ask for the necklace back? Did he want to see it? Did he want to see the work you were doing? Maybe he wanted confirmation that you were legit and that he hadn't sent the necklace off into cyberspace."

"I don't know." She frowned.

"Why don't you go lie down and get some rest. Maybe, when you wake up from a nap, you'll remember."

Obviously she didn't like that answer, but it was also a decent idea, given that she couldn't seem to draw anything else from her memory banks. Slowly she nodded. "Okay, but I don't like this."

"No, I know you don't," he agreed. "And it's okay. We will get to the bottom of it."

"Yeah, and then you say shit like you did at the restaurant," she noted bitterly, "and I realize you're not here on my side at all. You're here to sort out whatever's going on for whatever reason, and I don't know what that is. You say it's the necklace, but I don't know that you have any right to it. You can't just take something like that, when it's been entrusted to me."

"Wasn't planning on it," he stated cautiously, looking at her carefully. "Maybe you should go have that nap now."

At that, her gaze turned almost mutinous, and then, like a curtain came over her, she nodded. "Good idea." She turned and walked back upstairs to her room, almost in a trance.

Suspicions immediately aroused, Hurricane watched as she headed upstairs and heard as she collapsed onto her bed. He sat in the living room and immediately contacted Stefan by text.

Do you want me to call? Stefan texted back.

I don't want her to hear.

Almost immediately Stefan knocked on the inside door to Hurricane's mind. He smiled and let Stefan in.

Hey, Stefan greeted him, as he stepped in. *Sounds like this one's a little bit weird.*

Getting weirder. Hurricane explained what he'd seen, as she walked up the stairs.

Interesting, Stefan noted. *Do you have any idea what's going on?*

Not for sure yet, no, but I do think somebody else is heavily involved, and I'm not sure that she's even aware of it.

It would make sense that she wasn't aware, Stefan stated. *It's not exactly something she would easily believe or disbelieve.*

Maybe, Hurricane replied. *Yet all of this is starting to rattle her pretty good. Just a few minutes ago, she got a memory and thinks she remembers somebody coming to her door, earlier the day of her abduction. She was just starting to describe it to me, but then shut down, as if—*

She shut them down? Stefan supplied.

Maybe, but if that's the case, why? What is it that she is hiding so well?

I'm not sure that she's hiding it as much as she's in a survival mode. She's keeping the memory blocked to protect herself. Something has terrified her, and it's quite possible that's what this is.

What? You think she's just shutting down in order to not have to deal with it?

Possibly. Could be the energy-worker version of sticking her head in the sand. I mean, we don't know that for sure, but, if you think about it, all kinds of issues going on in her world could be dredging up this response.

Hurricane contemplated that and then nodded. *I guess that's possible too, isn't it? Just because we have experience at this doesn't mean she does, but I keep coming back to the fact that she reached out to you.*

She not only contacted me, she was confident, quite assured, and a very different person than what I'm seeing right now.

So, is she playing games? Was the person who contacted you playing games?

At that, Stefan sighed. *Have patience with her, have tolerance, and we'll get to the bottom of it,* he stated. *But you really need to watch your back.* And, with that, Stefan was gone.

CHAPTER 16

J EWEL WOKE FROM her nap, rolled over to realize that she was in her bed, tucked up under the blankets, but still fully dressed. That was one of the most comforting signs she'd had all day. She sat up and looked around. Everything appeared to be normal, calm, and contained. Normal was a good thing. She got up and slowly walked downstairs to find Hurricane stretched out on the couch. Trying not to wake him, she walked into the kitchen and put on the teakettle.

She was tempted to go visit Charles and Lucas, to just have some normality in her life, but she also knew she should visit the gallery, to check in on the show and to see what was going on, just to ensure everything was ready for her display. Particularly after not having her phone available, especially for those days that she was unaccounted for. Just the fact that she had lost those days was something she was really struggling with, but more so was the fact that she now remembered somebody had come to her door, and she had let them in. She didn't know why; it wasn't like her to do that, but she had. And now there were consequences, whether that person had been involved in all this or not.

It went against the grain to think that his visit here wasn't connected, but again something was different. She couldn't put her finger on it. If those memories were to come back, it would all make sense, but, until then, she was in this dark maze that she couldn't find her way out of. With the teakettle happily buzzing away, she made herself a cup of tea and then walked over to her workbench.

Her little studio was pretty small and not more than ten feet separated the living room and her studio, but, hey, it was her home. At that, she stopped, looked up and around, and realized that was how she felt about this place. Her house was just a house; yet this loft was her home. For better or for worse, this is where her creations came to life. As she looked down at the drawings she'd done of the women, she picked up a pen, filled in a few of the details, and then turned one of them into a cameo on a pendant and kept on working.

By the time she was done; she had a couple new designs that put a smile on her face. She looked back over to see if Hurricane was awake, but she still saw no sign of him stirring at all. Matter of fact, something was weird, otherworldly about it. As she got up and walked closer, she also realized that his skin was pale, the color off, too much different than before.

She reached a hand down and then drew back, wondering if she should even touch him. She'd heard all kinds of weird things about psychics, when they were off doing things. Obviously he wasn't just sleeping anymore, but also just as obvious was that whatever he was doing wasn't normal. And was that on his own, or was it something else entirely?

She hesitated and then determinedly gave him a hard shake. His shoulders and chest rolled with the movements, but she got absolutely no reaction from him. She nudged him again, harder. "Hey, wake up," she cried out. "Wake up, wake up."

No answer. Nothing. Just that same vacant look on his

face, everything lax.

She immediately pulled out her phone and called Stefan. When he answered, she said, "Something is wrong with Hurricane."

He hesitated. "When you say, *something wrong*, what do you mean specifically?"

"I just got up from a nap. I thought he was napping on the couch, but he's really pale and doesn't look right. I tried to wake him, but he won't. I can shake him and move his body around, but it's as if he's not even there. His face is … His skin's pale. It's … It's very strange. It's damn freaky."

"Hang on a minute," he snapped, "and don't hang up. Just wait right there."

And, with that, he was gone. Even as she held her phone, she stared down at Hurricane, watching. Something seemed to reach out to slap him hard. When no reaction came, she felt fear choking her. She glanced around, wondering what she was supposed to do, but there just didn't seem to be any answers.

Stefan hadn't returned to the phone either. Not knowing what else to do, she hung up then called out, "Dr. Maddy. Dr. Maddy, I need you. Something's wrong with Hurricane, and I don't know what to do." Almost immediately this calm, serenity-infused energy swept through her.

Take it easy, said a voice in Jewel's head. *We're working on him. Sit down, and let us take care of him.*

Not sure what that meant, she dropped obediently into the chair beside him, wondering why she should listen to a voice in her head and not have a problem with it.

You don't have a problem with it, Maddy stated, *because you've done this before. You just have to remember.*

Jewel frowned. Absolutely nothing inside her confirmed

that she'd done this before. Nothing inside her said any of this made sense. But, as she watched, Hurricane gave a sudden jolt and slowly opened his eyes to stare at her. She bent down to kneel in front of him. "Hey, are you okay?"

He blinked several times. "I will be. Give me a minute." She waited cautiously for him, and then finally he opened his eyes, smiled, and said, "Yeah, I'm okay. Thanks for calling the troops." When he seemed able to focus and more coherent, he stared at her and asked, "How did you know?"

She shrugged. "How did I know what?"

"To call Stefan."

She snorted. "Is there really anybody else?"

"I don't know," he admitted, with a smile. "Yet, once again, you called the right person for the job."

"I don't know about that," she muttered. "This is all very freaky, and I'm not sure anybody should be called. I really don't think you should stay here. It's obviously too dangerous."

"Really, and in what way is it dangerous?" he asked, his gaze boring through her.

She stopped and stared at him. "I don't know. What happened to you? Maybe that would help me, … if I could understand."

"Let's just say I went for a trip and got caught in a maze."

"A trip? A maze?"

"Yeah," he replied. "A space that wasn't really a space, yet it looked like a space."

She blinked. "Space?"

He nodded. "That's about how I felt. I've been doing this for a long time, and, if anybody had told me that a space like that was out there, one where I could get lost in, I would have laughed. But I was there, and now I'm not sure what it was or if it was a trap set for me."

"For you? You specifically?"

He nodded. "And now that I have some idea of what that was," he declared, with a feral smile taking over his features, "I can tell you that I quite possibly have found an avenue to go forward."

At that, his phone rang. He answered it and then said, "Thanks, Stefan. Yeah, I'm back in the land of the living. I can explain some of what happened." And he gave him the cryptic version of what he had just told her. "I know. Things like that aren't supposed to be there, so I presume I walked into a void of somebody's making, but it was strange because a lot of energy surrounded it, as in energy being constantly fed and sustained," he clarified. "I'm not sure how or by whom though."

Hurricane and Stefan talked some more, while she sat here, chewing on her fingernails, and finally she looked at him and burst out, "It's all related, isn't it?"

"It is, indeed," he confirmed, sagging onto the couch. "It is, indeed."

HURRICANE STAYED ON the couch for a long moment, until he was ready to stand, hoping the energies had calmed down enough that it wouldn't make him so dizzy or wipe him out. He used the wall to support himself and made his way slowly and carefully to the bathroom, as he was not at his full strength. Jewel watched him with quiet concern. He gave her a reassuring smile, before closing the door to the bathroom. He used the facilities and then stared at himself in the mirror. "Dear God," he murmured.

He'd seen things in his life as an energy worker, but that torrential cyclone of faces was something he'd never expected to see and surely didn't want to see again. He had been met with this darkness and a blackness that he figured was just energy, and he'd walked toward it and got sucked into this vortex of its swirling energies. Just as he was about to open the bathroom door, Stefan stepped into his mind.

Are you all right?

"I am," he murmured, out loud, too drained to speak telepathically.

You don't look like it.

"Thanks for that," he replied, with a hard laugh. "I'll be fine."

What the hell was that?

"I'm not sure, but I think it was a trap, set by the souls."

Silence came first. *Souls?* Stefan asked in a calm voice.

"Yes, as in the souls of the necklace and the bracelet."

And yet why you?

"That's the question. I don't know why me. I'm also not sure what I did that took me to that spot."

I'm thinking that's because of her.

"That makes sense. Of course it is about Jewel, but what does that mean?"

Did you sense danger?

"Absolutely, more than that, a panic, a franticness, an urgency, maybe coming from these souls."

Urgency, Stefan repeated, his voice flat.

"Yeah, I don't know how else to describe it."

Well, that's describing it pretty well, he muttered.

"And yet, in a way, it isn't. It doesn't describe what I'm trying to get at or what that vortex was trying to convey. I do know that Jewel is connected in a big way, and that something is trying to get to her."

Of course, but what is it? We've been assuming that, whatever it is, it is trying to get her to be part of the necklace.

"Yes. Did Drew get ahold of you about any of those names?"

I was about to contact him because I know he's got some information. But, when I found out you got sucked into this new issue, I had to table that conversation.

"Yeah, well, thanks for coming to the rescue." Hurricane laughed. "I am fine."

Are you though?

"Yes, I think so. It's certainly not what I expected, and I'll certainly be better prepared the next time."

She won't want to see a next time.

"She doesn't know what she wants at this point, except she wants answers. I'm trying to get the answers, but, more than that, I'm also trying to stop anyone else from getting caught up in this. The question at this point really comes down to who is doing this and how do we stop them?"

I got no arguments there, Stefan murmured. *Let me contact Drew, and I'll get back to you.*

Hurricane opened the bathroom door to find Jewel standing right in front of him. She raised an eyebrow. "You look like hell."

That brought a laugh and a shrug. "Sorry about that. I didn't mean to scare you."

She crossed her arms over her chest and refused to move out of his way.

He reached down, his hands wrapping around her tiny waist, then he picked her up and set her off to the side, even as she let out a shriek. "Sorry, but it looked like you were trying to stop me."

"And if I was?"

"You're at least one hundred pounds too light to do that," he noted, with a smile. "But, as it is, I do need food and soon. I burned through a lot of energy."

"Doing what exactly?"

"It felt like I was getting sucked into a vortex, by all these other souls."

"You think they were the ones sucking you in?"

"No, not necessarily," he replied cautiously. "Motivation in something like this is highly suspect. I … I would imagine whoever put these souls into the pearls in the first place was intent on trapping me."

She shook her head. "That's beyond creepy," she announced.

"It's terrifying, and it's something that we have to stop."

She looked back at the safe on the wall. "What if we destroyed the necklace?"

He stared at her. "It may or may not work."

"But why not? If they're captured within a pearl, surely we can shatter the pearls and release them."

"They've been held captive via energy, so I don't think it's as simple as physically smashing the pearl."

She frowned at that, her fingers thrumming against her forearm. "So, do you know anybody who can talk to the dead, so that we can get them over to the light?" She wandered into the kitchen, opened the fridge, and started pulling out sandwich fixings. "Hopefully a ham and cheese will work, while you answer me."

"Sandwiches are good, and the answer to your question is … maybe."

He joined her and saw she had pulled out two slices of bread. He grabbed six more, lined them up, and pointed.

"These three sandwiches are for me."

She stared at the bread, looked at him, shook her head, and went back to working on the two slices in front of her. "As long as you can eat them, it's okay with me."

After a moment, as they fussed away on the sandwiches together, he said, "They've been tethered to the pearls, and, if we undo the tether, I don't know what happens to the souls."

She shuddered in front of him.

He nodded. "Exactly. "At least tethered as they are, we have a way of knowing who they are and where they are. I feel like, if we break that tether, we'll lose that."

"Drew?"

"Stefan is calling him now."

"*Great*," she muttered, half under her breath. "I heard you talking in the bathroom."

"Yes, Stefan was talking in my mind, but I was still too burned out to reply the same way."

She shot him a look, and he just gave her a droll smile. "Come on. Don't tell me that you didn't contact Maddy the same way."

"Of course not," she declared, looking at him, startled. "I called Maddy. On the phone." And then she stopped, pulled her phone from her pocket, stared at it, and hit Recent phone calls. "At least I thought I called her—or yelled out for her."

"You did call for her," he agreed comfortably, as he reached for the ham, placing two slices on each of his sandwiches. "But you called her through your mind."

She slowly put down her phone and stared at him, disconcerted. "How would I know to do that?"

"That's the million-dollar question," he stated, as he

slapped cheese on top and then lettuce and tomatoes.

By the time he had the three sandwiches on a plate, all cut so they fit, he looked around for where to eat. Either the two stools at the counter or the bench seats at the dining table or the coffee table in the living room. He snagged a bottle of water and sat down in the living room. She came over and sat beside him, with her single sandwich.

She sat sideways on the couch, picking up half a sandwich and took a bite, chewing slowly, but her gaze was intent on his face. He deliberately didn't look at her but continued to focus on his plate of food. He had burned through way too much energy, and that fact had terrified him more than anything because he didn't think that was normal.

"Why did you burn through all that energy?" she asked him. He shot her a surprised look. She shrugged. "You say how you do this a lot, and, if you do this so well, then how is it that this time you ran into a problem?"

He snorted. "There can always be a problem," he muttered. "No way to know from one scenario to the next what I'll come up against. In this case, I encountered something that wasn't expected."

"And that was what?"

"The souls," he stated succinctly.

"What difference does that make?"

"You asked how I ran out of energy or how I burned through so much energy. I think they were taking it from me," he replied. "Those souls, they're looking for energy, a source, from anybody who has it to offer. They really aren't asking," he added, his tone hard. "They're demanding it and taking it, whether you want to give it or not."

CHAPTER 17

I T HAD BEEN several hours since Hurricane came out of the vortex session, or whatever he wanted to call it. Just as Jewel sat down, studying her designs and trying to get her mind to focus on anything other than what had just gone on, his phone rang.

Turning to look over at her, he put it on Speakerphone and said, "It's Drew. He wants to talk to both of us."

She shrugged, joined him on the couch, and replied, "Hi, Drew. It's Jewel. Nice to meet you."

"Hi, Jewel. How are you feeling?" he asked, his voice unexpectedly gentle.

Because of the gentleness, it was much easier to answer him. Yet she hated that softness and how she wanted to give in to his tone. "I'm doing okay. Can't say this is something I'm particularly used to."

"That's good," he muttered. "Seems like everybody around me is used to this stuff way more than I am."

"Yet they always seem to think that I know something about it."

"Do you?" he asked.

"I don't think so, but I don't know," she muttered. "I'm still missing just so much in my memory banks."

"That's part of what I wanted to talk to you about," he began. "There were no marks on you when initially found.

There were no personal effects. We have nothing except an image of the person who brought you to the hospital. … I'm not sure if you'll recognize him at all."

"Either way, I'd like to thank him," she noted. "He saved my life."

"I have an image and a name. I'll send it to you, when I'm done with this phone call. Now let's focus on those women in your and Stefan's drawings."

"Yes, did you find any of them?"

"I found two, two more rather, since we already had a couple. The question is, and maybe this one should be more directed at Hurricane, considering he got sucked into whatever it was. Is there any way to know if those souls have been dead for a very long time? Do they look any different?"

"Ah, yes," Hurricane replied in a slow tone. "Generally they do, but I can't guarantee that all of them do."

"Do you guys ever give straightforward answers?" Drew asked in disgust.

"Rarely, as you well know."

"I do know," he muttered. "However, in this case, I was hoping for a little more."

"Why?"

"It seems like one of these cases was an unsolved murder victim, from fifty-two years ago."

"Oh my God," she cried out. "Don't tell me that she's been locked up in that pearl for fifty-two years."

A moment of silence came from the other end. "That part is well beyond my expertise," Drew muttered. "And, yeah, I'm just as horrified at the thought as you are. I want you to have a look and to see if it's the same woman you may have seen before, Jewel. I have several images that I'll email to you. A couple that I think we're pretty close on, but all I have is a picture, no DNA collected back then, and we just have anecdotal evidence about what happened to her. I guess part of the reason I'm calling is to see whether this is even something that's possible or if it's just too far out there to be connected with Jewel's case."

"It's all too far out there," she snapped, "but then nobody's listening to me."

At that, Drew gave a lusty laugh. "I feel your pain," he replied, his tone commiserating, but comfortable.

"But you seem to be okay with all this," Jewel told Drew.

"Experience has given me a *very* different viewpoint. And my experience is completely tied up in the things that I have seen with my wife."

"Yeah, that's pretty freaky. I mean, not everybody has that kind of exposure like you do, so maybe it's a blessing for you."

"Maybe, but sometimes it doesn't feel like it."

"Yeah, I hear you there," Jewel agreed. "So, what is it that we're supposed to do now then?"

"I'll keep tracking down these other names. I've got the files on the first four who have been ID'd the conventional way. I'll send those over to Stefan and to Hurricane. Go over the details, see if anything gets your attention. See if anything makes any sense. Ultimately we're trying to figure out if it's possible to figure out who did this and if the same guy killed all these women."

"Of course, and that's where the problem lies," she immediately interjected. "If somebody killed a woman some fifty-two years ago, we're assuming they must have been at least sixteen years old, and that would make them sixty-eight now at the least."

"Yes, and, if they are still alive, I'd be surprised, but it's possible."

"Do we really think that this same person killed all these women and somehow found a way to tie them up into the pearls on the necklace?" Jewel asked him.

"That's what Maddy and Stefan are suggesting," Drew confirmed. "For me, I'll keep an open mind. It's better than thinking only along that one line."

"No, I agree with you there," she muttered. She looked over at Hurricane, who was even now still munching away on a sandwich. "Hurricane doesn't appear to be terribly bothered by any of this."

"Hey," Hurricane piped up, "it's not that I'm not bothered, but I've seen a little bit more than you guys, and, if this is what it is, this is just what it is."

"But it can't be," she argued. "He'd be too old."

"No, I don't think so, not at all. And given the time frame we have, it is feasible that he was sixteen, yet not likely, but even if he was twenty, twenty-two, twenty-four, I mean, even that is not out of the realm of possibility. We have a lot of serial killers who have escaped detection for that long and more. Right, Grant?"

"Yes, unfortunately, and we're still looking for quite a few who have yet to be caught. Anytime we would get a lead on some of these, something happens, and they manage to slip away."

"Do you think they could be using energy to get away?" she asked.

"I'm not saying yes, and I'm not saying no. All I can say is they have escaped detection, and it seems like there was absolutely no reason for it, yet they found a way to do so."

"Right, so if there was a way to do it, this guy may have

found it."

"Exactly. But you also have to consider that, depending on what he did for a living back then, he may not need to do very much to escape detection. If he traveled a lot, or frequently relocated, he could remain under the radar. Plus we didn't have DNA, nor internet, some fifty-odd years ago, nor any communication between the different authorities within counties. I mean, disappearing under the radar could have been a pretty simple case for him."

"That's a scary thought too," she muttered. "Okay, I'll take a look at the file when it comes in."

"Good enough. And consider the fact that one of the things we need to determine is the timing of the death of his most recent victim. Is this something that he has continued to do, or is this something that he did in a crazy spree and then stopped doing some years ago? Like maybe he lost the ability or something like that," he muttered.

She laughed. "You're stretching. I think you're looking for an answer just as much as I am, and one that has nothing to do with the boogeyman."

"I'm always looking for an answer that shows me a flesh-and-blood criminal," he stated. "I leave the spooky wispy ones to my wife." And, with that, he hung up.

She looked over at him. "Does Dr. Maddy really deal with these awful criminals?"

Hurricane smiled at her. "Very few people can even comprehend that a criminal element happens to be on the other side of flesh and blood," he shared. "So, if such a thing exists, you must have people who can look after, or at least find some way to protect, people on this side."

She gave herself a hard shake, and he nodded.

"I know. Nobody wants to think about it, and that's fine

and dandy, until you come up against something, like you just have. Things that go bump in the night make no sense, so we still have to come up with answers to try and keep people sane and to not have them freaking out every time they turn around."

"I'm in the freak-out category right now," she stated, staring at him. "The fact that people even exist, doing what you do, is just terrifying."

He smiled at her. "And yet if I didn't …"

She nodded. "If you didn't, there wouldn't be anybody to fight the evil energy workers. I get it."

"And I know you don't want to hear this, but I'm still not at all sure that you're as innocent in all of this as you say."

At that, she glared at him.

"I know, and I'm not saying that you killed anybody. I'm not saying that you had anything to do with these people being locked up in the pearls, but I am concerned that something is going on here at a much bigger level, involving you, that even *you* don't understand."

"It would have to be something I don't understand because no way I would be involved in something like this if I did understand."

"That's all good to know," he said.

"Did you ever doubt it?" she asked, staring at him. And then she frowned. "If you don't believe me, why is it that you would even have anything to do with me?"

"I didn't say I didn't believe you," he stated, "and what you do consciously versus what your body and your mind are doing subconsciously is a completely different story."

She winced at that. "We're back to that whole *taken under somebody's power* thing, aren't we?"

"Not even that so much as understanding what you have a will to do, what you might have done willingly, and what you don't have any will to do, and what you might not know to be doing willingly."

She frowned at him. "My eyes are crossing on that one."

He burst out laughing. "Yeah, I'm not sure that was terribly clear for you or for anybody, honestly," he admitted. "But, the fact of the matter is, sometimes people are under the control of somebody else, and they don't know it."

"Like this killer guy?"

"If he has imprisoned these women into the pearl necklace and bracelet, obviously he did it without their permission. Agreed?"

She nodded slowly at that. "Agreed, and that's something at least."

"Exactly. And, if something like that has happened, then he had abilities to make them do something. Now I don't know whether he murdered them and somehow captured their souls or somehow got their cooperation to do some ritual ahead of time, so that, when he did murder them or they died, maybe even by their own hand, he ended up getting control of their souls regardless."

She winced. "That's almost like a devil's pact, where you get my firstborn son if you give me unnamed riches."

"People have signed up for things like that generation after generation," he noted smoothly. "I'm not saying that would do it. I'm just saying that maybe, in a case like this, something more is here that we need to examine."

"You go ahead and examine it all you want." She stared at him and then looked back at the safe with loathing. "I'd just as soon have nothing to do with any of it."

"You may not want to, but you will have to deal with it.

It has a hold on you," he stated.

"Says you. I only have your word that I walked in my sleep."

He smiled. "I have separated them, so we'll see later today how that works."

"I'm not exactly sure what that means," she noted, "but, if you've separated the necklace from the bracelet, and so far it's been fine, then nothing should happen tonight."

He shrugged. "We'll see."

She nodded. "I'm almost ready for bed anyway."

And, with that, she took her plate into the kitchen, washed up the dishes, walked back toward the stairs. "I'll have to check out my show setup later. I'll just have a shower and crash."

"You do that. After that vortex session today, I'll be up for a while." He followed her to the stairs.

She hesitated, then asked, "Are you sure that you're really okay?"

He looked up, reached out a gentle hand to capture one of hers, and said, "Yes, and thanks for caring."

She stared down at their hands. "I'm not sure exactly what brought you into my life, but thank you for staying. I don't want anything to happen to you because of me though."

"I appreciate that." Pulling her into his arms, he gave her a gentle hug, dropped a kiss on top of her forehead, and said, "Now go to sleep."

She laughed. "Now I feel like a child, being sent off to bed."

"Hardly a child," he noted, with a twinkling gaze, "but certainly, for the moment, it's much safer if I think of you that way."

Snorting, she looked at him. "Yeah, I highly doubt you're looking at me any other way, particularly if you think I'm involved."

"I don't think you're involved," he clarified. "Still, something is definitely going on."

She shrugged. "I don't know what that could be."

And, with that, she turned and headed upstairs.

HURRICANE WATCHED JEWEL as she went to bed. She might not know what it could be, but an element inside her energy was fighting for something. He just didn't know what it was fighting for, making him beyond wary. She was a fascinating woman because she was this constant contradiction that fascinated him, yet worried him at the same time.

He pulled out his laptop, wondering why she had ignored the facts that she wanted to visit her show exhibit and see the files that were coming in from Drew for her review— or maybe that much was willfully sticking her head in the sand on her part. He'd seen people much stronger have their stomachs turned by some of what they would be looking at now because, if these were murders, chances are they were hardly the *take some pills and die in your sleep* type.

People had a tendency to get violent, and, once that violence erupted, things got ugly quickly. He sat down and pulled the laptop toward him, then downloaded the zipped files from Drew. As soon as Hurricane opened it up, he found twelve separate folders. He went to her case first and scanned through it, finding everything was as he already had pretty well known. Nothing terribly surprising in there.

Another file identified a C. Hardy as the man who brought her supposedly dead body to the hospital.

She could contact him later and thank him, if she still wanted to when this was over. She had mentioned thanking him at one point, and maybe that would be something she'd follow up on. Hurricane didn't know. Then he started in on the murder cases.

He had the files for Rhea and Anna in front of him. He opened them up and saw that Rhea was murdered twenty-seven years ago in Maine, and the other one murdered seventeen years ago out in California. When he read the even older murder files, strangulation appeared to be the favorite killing method. Strangulation was also up-front, personal, and took a great deal more skill and strength than most people realized, and that was something to consider.

Hurricane instinctively wanted to say that the person behind all this was male, but that was a little too blasé of him to count on. Profilers utilized all kinds of science in order to make their best guess as to who could be killers, and, sure, more often than not they were males, but Hurricane didn't want to discount any possibility just yet.

Then he stopped, thought about the energy that he had felt inside that vortex, and realized he really couldn't discount it anyway because all that energy had been female—powerful, angry, furious female energy, raging inside that torrent. He shook his head at that and deliberately disconnected from that memory, so he could continue to research the paperwork in front of him.

When Drew phoned him an hour later, he asked, "Did any of it make sense?"

"I'm still going through the files," he replied, "and, yes, it does make sense. Jewel's gone up to her room. I don't think she really wants to get too involved in this part."

"I can understand that," Drew stated, "but I was hoping

that you had gotten to the pictures."

"I have sketches that she drew of some of the women, and two of them definitely match up."

"That's depressing," Drew replied.

"And here I thought that's what you wanted."

"I did, yet I didn't. Yes, we want confirmation that these IDs match up with the photos of the murdered women, yet that woo-woo confirmation isn't the kind of confirmation I really want."

At that, Hurricane laughed. "No way you have lived with Maddy all these years and not come to terms with this."

"Sure, but I prefer a criminal I can lock up and throw away the keys, not a criminal I can't even see."

"Regardless, so far as the records we've got, Anna's seventeen-year-old murder case would be the most recent we can confirm."

"That's not very recent at all," Drew muttered.

"If we don't find out who had possession of this necklace over this time span, then we can't really begin to link the murders to the pearls, much less track down this one lead to find out who on earth was doing the killing."

Drew replied, "One of the things I have is an email from Jewel of the person who contacted her, but he sent the necklace by courier. I contacted the courier, and they don't have anything other than a P.O. box number and the name John Smith on the end of it."

"Which, of course," Hurricane muttered, "is not likely to be his name at all, and the P.O. box was probably closed right afterward, I suppose."

"Indeed," Drew agreed cheerfully. "But this is exactly the kind of criminal I deal with," he noted, "so I'm happily off on a hunt for him, while you can go off into the ethers and hunt all you want. But let me know if anything else gets your attention or if you can confirm any of these other victims."

"Will do," Hurricane agreed. And, with that, they ended the call.

Just as he was about to start on another folder, he heard an odd sound. He looked up to see Jewel coming down the stairs, but, from the look on her face, she wasn't exactly conscious. He set aside the laptop, got up, and raced up the stairs, his cell phone camera videotaping her, as she headed to the safe. She immediately opened the safe. Then, leaving it open, headed to the kitchen, bypassing him on the stairs, not even acknowledging his presence, and heading to where he'd hidden the bracelet above the fridge.

He hadn't even realized that she had known where he'd put it. And even now wasn't sure if she knew or was following some energy trail, without even being cognizant of what she was doing. As he watched, she took the bracelet out and immediately carried it back to the safe, putting it inside the safe, before locking it up and heading back upstairs.

As soon as she was back in her room, he quickly separated the two pieces again and hid the bracelet, knowing she wasn't even available to see this transfer. Plus, this time, he wouldn't inform her beforehand. As a test it wasn't great but something. Then he sat back down and waited.

Sure enough, not an hour later, she came back down the stairs again, her eyes wide open but completely disconnected from the world around her. Again she removed the bracelet from where he'd hidden it and took it back to the safe.

This time he stepped in front of her, as she went to go back upstairs, and called to her gently. "Jewel, wake up."

She stared up at him, but her eyes were blind. He reached out a gentle hand and slid just a feather-light brush of energy toward her. She just stared, motionless, her body not moving forward or back, frozen in time, almost buried in her own mind. He frowned at that and reached out again, gently increasing the energy surge. She flinched and stepped back.

"Jewel, wake up," he ordered, his voice commanding. But again nothing.

He reached out a hand and gripped her shoulder, and this time she didn't flinch, she didn't do anything, she just stared up at him. "Oh, crap." He peered into her face. Then he gave her a hard shake and called to her. "Jewel, Jewel, wake up. Snap out of it!"

When she blinked and stared up at him, comprehension finally coming into her gaze, he shuddered with relief and pulled her into his arms.

"What happened?" She spoke in a whisper against his chest.

"Yeah, I'll have to show you that on video."

He led her to the couch, sat her down beside him, then opened up the video that he had taken of her that showed her as she first came down the stairs, went to the kitchen, then removed the bracelet, only to go and put it back together with the necklace.

"Oh my God," she whispered, staring at it in shock. "How?"

"As I said, you're connected to it somehow. I assume because of all that's happened to you. Now you have this connection to it, and it won't let you go. It's using you to bring the rest of the pieces together."

"What happens when they're all together?" she asked, looking up at him.

"I have no idea, but the energy that's in there is dangerous, and it's highly explosive."

She winced as she stared at him. "How come the term *explosive* was never mentioned before?"

He smiled. "Because most people don't want to think about that type of explosion," he murmured. "However, when you get something as volatile as this, it is dangerous."

She stared down at it. "What happened after that? What did I do when I was done?"

"You went back upstairs, so I hid it again," he told her, "and look what you did again." He showed her the second video, and she stared at it in shock. "That's when I woke you up, and honestly it took a lot to do that."

She reached up and scrubbed her face. "My God, I don't even remember having a shower."

"Your hair is dry. Did you have a shower?"

She frowned. "I don't know. I went and laid down, but it's like this singing came in my head."

He straightened and looked at her in concern. "What were they singing?"

She shook her head. "I don't know, just music. Some music, nice, soft, and gentle."

"Like a lullaby?"

"Yeah, that's what it was," she agreed, looking up at him with a smile. When Jewel noted the look on his face, her smile fell away. "You're telling me that's not good."

"I don't know," he admitted cautiously. "Do you normally have lullabies in your head?"

She shook her head. "My gut says never. At least never before. Wait. … I heard it earlier. I heard it when I was working on the necklace."

"That should tell you something right there," he stated. "That is just one more sign that this is all connected."

She nodded and stared toward the safe. "I need it out of here," she cried out.

"Oh, I hear you, but one of the things I would suggest is that you contact whoever gave it to you, tell them that the job is done, and have them come collect it."

She looked at him eagerly. "Yes, we can do that." Then she frowned. "Yet the job isn't done."

"How much damage was there on it?"

"Not a lot. Just some of the threads were getting bare and needed to be reinforced, so I was rethreading it," she explained. "I … I'm pretty well done. That's why I was doing the energy work. I was trying to make it better."

"Of course you were, and don't worry about that. At this point, we need to have a talk with whoever it is who sent you the necklace."

"You don't suspect him?"

"I don't have any reason to—unless that memory of that man at your door, asking about the necklace, is the owner?"

"I don't know," she wailed.

"I'll be here with you the whole time. Just remember that. Otherwise, setting aside a partial and unsubstantiated memory, the necklace was damaged. It came to you to get repaired. Outside of the fact that Drew can't locate him through a trace of the original necklace delivery—"

"That may not mean anything though, if the pearls were stolen as some point," she suggested.

"Has that happened to you before?"

"Yes." She nodded. "I was asked to repair an item that was stolen, though I didn't realize it at the time. When the police came to my door, we found out that it had been stolen quite a few years earlier, and, when the supposed owner came to collect it, the police caught him."

He stared at her for a long moment. "You didn't mention that before."

"Why would I?" she asked, looking at him. "It's just one of the hazards of doing this work."

"How did the police find out?"

"I happened to post a photo of it on my website, as a piece that I was working on," she noted. "It never occurred to me not to. Nobody said anything about keeping it quiet. Like, *Hey, this is stolen. Can you keep it under wraps?* Anyway, I guess somebody recognized the piece and reported it. So the police came, checked it out, and took it away." Jewel shook her head. "A hard lesson. And I no longer put things on my website like that. Not trying to be shady, just not wanting any trouble. I also didn't get paid for the repair of the item. Since a fair bit of work had been involved, that sucked. Yet, at the same time, it was stolen property, and it went back to its rightful owner. So that, at least, felt good."

"Except for the fact that you never got paid for the work you did."

"One of the hazards of being self-employed," she stated. "I mean, just because I expect to get paid doesn't mean I will."

"Yet you should have."

"I should have, yes, but I didn't. So what am I to do?" She shrugged. "That's life, and it isn't always the way we want it to be."

He smiled at her. "Do you know who that customer was?"

"Sure. I don't remember his name right off hand, but I've got the files."

"That's good. We could at least double-check that it has nothing to do with this matter."

"Why would it?" she asked. "It's not as if that client had anything to do with what I was doing with this client."

"I'm glad to hear that. How long ago was this?"

She pondered his question. "Maybe a year and a half ago."

"I can always get the detective to look into that." He pulled out his phone, quickly sent off a text, and asked, "Do you remember anything about the stolen piece?"

"A pendant," she murmured. "I think the police had told me something about it being part of the Royal Crescent heist." He typed that into the text and sent it off. She got up, wandered around the living room, then stopped and looked at the safe. She turned and wandered around some more, then stopped and looked back at the safe again.

"Is it calling to you?"

"It is. I feel like I want to take them both out of their cases and put them together." She held out her hand and shook her head. "However, that seems like a bad idea."

"I would think so, but I can't be sure. When you go back to sleep, I plan to separate them again."

She nodded. "Well, you can, but it doesn't seem that it'll make much difference. Based on your two videos, it's likely that I'll just keep putting them together again. And, if I don't, if I try to do something to keep them separated, it feels like the power is building and heading for some sort of collision."

"Agreed," he murmured. "I'm just not sure what that collision is trying to do."

"Explode all of the souls free, I'm hoping," she replied, "but I guess it could be an implosion too." She turned and frowned at him. "Right?"

"Yes." He nodded, with a grimace. "Can you go back to

sleep?"

"Sure. Will you leave them in there so I can sleep?"

"I could do that," he suggested, "as long as they're in there and separated as much as they are, maybe it's okay."

She pondered that, then shrugged. "I need sleep either way." She reached up, gave him a gentle kiss on the cheek, and said, "Thank you." Then she ran lightly up the stairs, heading straight for bed.

CHAPTER 18

J EWEL WOKE THE next morning, with a stronger sense of well-being than she'd had in days. Feeling remarkably better, she headed downstairs to the kitchen to find Hurricane already there, drinking coffee, his laptop open in front of him.

He looked up, smiled, and asked, "Hey, how was your night?"

"Peaceful, relaxing, and calm," she stated, returning his smile. "Yours?"

He shrugged. "Maybe not quite so good as that, but fine." She frowned at him. He smiled again and added, "I'm fine. It's okay, Jewel. You're the one who needed it."

"And you didn't?" she asked. "After what happened in the vortex maze thing?"

"Nope, I didn't," he stated, "at least not yet."

Not at all sure what that meant, and not willing to ruin her morning by asking questions with answers that wouldn't help, she walked over, poured coffee, returned to the kitchen table, and sat on the bench beside him. "What are you working on?" she asked.

"A timeline of the victims."

She winced. "*Great,* that sounds like a lovely thing to wake up to."

"You don't have to look," he said immediately. "Enjoy

your coffee."

"Yeah, I'm not sure that's even possible, now that you've brought it up."

"Didn't mean to," he replied in a cheerful tone, "but it's not something I can really put off. Time is going by pretty fast on us."

"Am I the only one who thinks that the time will be an issue?"

"No, I'm pretty sure we all are considering that. Whatever is going on has a time frame, either for the energy to be the strongest or for something to happen that will change this completely."

"All because I unlocked the energy?"

"Yes, but not because you opened the pearls."

"Right, and definitely a difference there, correct?"

"Exactly. You can't torture yourself for having done what you did. It's not as if you did so knowingly."

"Good thing. Imagine the chaos I could have created if I had known." He just smiled. She hesitated and then added, "One of the thoughts I woke up with this morning was how, in all the sleepwalking or whatever, it felt like it had an element of trying to help them."

He canted his head, then shook it. "I wouldn't be shocked at that. Believe me. I don't think you were trying to hurt anybody, when you inadvertently started this."

Relieved, she nodded. "I did wonder, since you keep mentioning that you think I'm involved."

"That's not really fair to you. You may be unconsciously involved. I just know that something is calling to you, and I just want to ensure that you stay safe."

"Yeah, me too," she agreed, with feeling. "Yet, at the same time, a part of me is horrified about what these women have experienced, and, if I thought I could do something to make their lives—eternity or whatever you want to call it—better somehow, I would do it in a heartbeat."

He looked at her for a long moment. "Do you think that's what you were doing when you were putting the two pieces together?"

"They were lost," she tried to explain. "They were lonely. They were calling for each other." When his expression stilled, she gave a headshake. "No, forget it. I don't know where that came from," she muttered. "Probably makes me sound even crazier than before."

"No, it just confirms what I already mentioned about you being connected."

"You keep saying that, but what does it even mean?"

"We don't really have an answer yet, but we're working on it," he stated. "You keep trying to do your best and believe that we will find out."

"Sure," she muttered, as she stared at him, "but that's really not all that helpful."

He smiled and gently stroked her cheek. "You just look after you, and I'm helping you to look after them."

"Are you though?" she asked, looking at him intently. "Sometimes I feel like you're much less concerned about those poor women than you are about this whole scenario."

"You mean, about the fact that it's weird and wonderful and all that good stuff?"

She nodded slowly. "I really need to know that you're here to help the women."

"I am," he declared emphatically, "but, at the same time, we have to balance that against the potential for you getting hurt."

"That's not likely to happen though, is it?" she asked

curiously. Then she frowned. "That's a stupid question. Sorry. Of course it could happen. Spending eternity imprisoned inside a pearl isn't how I want to spend my life."

"Thank you," he muttered, "because it really could happen. Will it? I don't have any answers. And in order to get those, we need to find out who sent the necklace and bracelet to you and get ahold of them."

"How fast? I'm supposed to let him know when they're ready." She stared back over at the safe, frowning.

"That would be good," Hurricane said. "At least if we can do that, we could see if he's connected with this."

She stared at him. "You're not really suggesting we have a modern-day soul stealer or something, are you?"

"That's not a thought I want to entertain," he replied, "but don't you want to make sure that your client, whoever he is, is not the person who did this?"

She frowned and then abruptly nodded. "Yes, that I do want to know. I'm not at all sure how to protect myself from the usual con artists after my money, my designs. However, in this case, I want to know how to protect myself and other women from this dark energy. And, if my client thinks I'll be one of his next victims, he's got another think coming." Then she laughed, almost hysterically. "Listen to me. I'm talking as if I actually know what I'm saying."

"You *are* speaking as if you know what you're saying, which is kind of an interesting point," he noted.

"Back to that whole *I might be involved* thing?" She frowned at him, starting to get angry. "That is getting irritating."

He smiled. "I imagine it is," he agreed. "Drink your coffee."

She snorted but picked up the cup and had a sip. She

sighed happily, as the hot brew slipped down her throat. "Wow, I don't know what you did to my coffeepot, but this tastes extraspecial."

At that, he stilled, then turned and stared at her. "Yeah, how? In what way?"

"I don't know. It's just hitting the spot today, I guess," she replied lightly. She looked over at him and said, "I didn't mean to imply anything odd, different, or abnormal about it."

"Okay," he replied agreeably, turning his head back to his laptop.

It suddenly felt like she was walking through a minefield, her words registering for him very differently than the way she intended. "Would it mean something if the coffee were very different?" she asked, not being able to stop herself.

He smirked. "You mean, besides the fact that I've obviously mastered the art of your coffeemaker?" But his gaze was watchful.

She sighed. "*Ugh*, I hate this. I feel like everything I say is misconstrued. Each word is being judged and weighed in ways that I don't intend."

"Only in the sense of my experience and anything that I've come across up until now," he confirmed. "Have I sensed anything more about you? No. Do I have a clue if you're involved? No. So let's just keep working and see where we end up."

On a sudden impulse, she hopped up and asked, "Are you up for bacon and eggs?"

"Are you kidding? I'm always up for bacon and eggs," he muttered, as he clicked away on the keyboard.

"Good enough. I'm hungry, like, really hungry." She headed around the island counter to the kitchen, where she opened up the fridge. She knew instinctively that he was watching her, with that ever-intensive gaze of his. She sighed. "Am I not allowed to be hungry either?"

"Hunger is a good sign," he stated, his tone suspiciously neutral.

She glared at him. "Somehow that's not making me feel better."

He flashed her a cheeky grin. "I said it's a good sign."

She relaxed and smiled. "Thanks for that. I'm starting to get a complex about everything I say to you."

"I don't want that to happen because it could impede sharing some crucial information," he murmured. "It really is good that you're feeling better. No memories back though?"

She shook her head. "None that I can really think about, outside of what I told you earlier about contacting the client when the repairs on the necklace are done. I'm supposed to send an email and arrange a time for payment and a courier for delivery. But that's just standard business practices. No big revelations there."

"Any idea how he would pay? And does he always want a courier?"

"No, we didn't get that far," she replied. "He was in a bit of a rush about it all, so I'm surprised he hasn't contacted me yet."

"Maybe he has," he suggested.

She frowned. "Maybe. I didn't see an email from him yesterday, but today's a new day. I did go to bed early last night."

"It wasn't that early," he noted lightly.

She smiled as she reached for the bacon. "If you say so."

He chuckled. "I do say so. How's that bacon coming along?"

"It's not, as you can see and smell," she quipped, with a bright grin. "Just give me time, and I'll get there." She sensed his gaze again, as she headed over to the stove and got started. By the time the bacon had mostly cooked, and she was cracking eggs to scramble, then she whistled gently. She was feeling really good, if she were honest, suspiciously so. At that she stopped, frozen. She slowly turned to look at him, frowning. He was staring at her. "Okay, what the hell's going on?"

His eyebrows shot up. "What?"

She shook her head in a slow, heavy motion. She almost felt like a rhino about to charge, but she had nothing to charge at. He continued to stare at her quizzically, when she took a deep breath, then slowly released it. "I'm feeling really good," she stated emphatically.

"Good." Now he was frowning. "Why is that cause for concern?"

She hesitated and then spoke. "As in, I'm feeling better than expected, like suspiciously good."

He slowly let out his breath. "Ah, so you're afraid that something is wrong? As in, did I do something to you?"

"Yeah," she admitted. "Did you?"

He looked at her and stated, "Tell me exactly how you feel."

"Like I had a great sleep, a great night and everything, in a way like I'm on the top of the world."

"You're not used to feeling that way?"

"No, never," she admitted. "That's not true. I mean, not *never*, but it just seems like it's been a very long time since I felt comfortable, happy, and not stressed. I should be stressed. Look at what's going on in my world," she noted, "and yet … I'm not."

"I would take that part as a good thing," he replied. "I get that we have a tendency to overcomplicate things in our lives, but there really isn't any need, especially if we don't have to."

She nodded slowly. "If you say so." She turned back to the bacon and flipped it again. "So, are you saying you didn't do anything to make me feel really good?"

"No," he confirmed, "but you did sleep. Maybe something in your brain just reset because you got some restorative and uninterrupted sleep."

"I'm not sure I want to know what that means," she muttered.

He chuckled. "No, I can see that, but, at the same time, let's not bury your head in the sand just because you don't want to face the truth."

"That's not really my style, I think," she muttered, "at least not before, before all this crap was let loose."

"I didn't think so. However, when dealing with too much—and we still have a lot of unanswered questions—we need to just take it easy, take things one by one, as much as we can. So maybe take the fact that you feel really good right now as a gift and go from there."

"I can do that." She quickly removed the bacon from the frying pan, put it on a paper towel, and tossed the scrambled eggs into the bacon grease. When she turned to see him looking at her with amusement, she glared at him. "Now you're laughing at me."

"I just never thought you'd be somebody who loved bacon grease."

"I do love bacon grease." She checked the pan, frowned, and asked, "Is it too much?"

"Not by me. I'm totally okay with it. It depends on how

many eggs you put in there."

"There wasn't a whole lot of grease, and I'm really hungry," she muttered. "So I threw in seven eggs."

"Four for me and three for you?"

She stared at him with stunned surprise and then shrugged. "I guess, if you're that hungry."

"I'm definitely that hungry," he replied immediately.

She laughed. "Okay then, I guess that's the way it works. … Unless you want me to throw in some more?"

"Only if you'll take some of mine," he replied, with a smile.

"No, I'll be good with three. However"—she faced him again—"is an appetite like this a sign of anything having to do with energy?"

"It certainly is for me. I need to eat when I wear down, but I was going on the assumption that you had a good night's sleep and weren't doing things in the night."

"Did you stay up and watch?" she demanded.

"Not the whole night. On the other hand, I did set up the camera."

Turning off the eggs, she finished tossing them around until they were done, then quickly served up breakfast and put a plate in front of him. "We'll look after we eat."

"Good, I can't wait."

She stared at him. "Have you seen it yet?"

"No, I haven't."

"So you don't know if anything's on there or not? You're just being suspiciously you?"

His eyebrows shot up. "I'm always being me. I can't help it."

"Yeah, I know," she agreed. "Sometimes it's good, and sometimes it's damn irritating."

He burst out laughing. "You're not the first person to tell me that."

"No, I wouldn't think so," she agreed, with a half smile. "Still, it's a little disconcerting."

He nodded. "It's all good. Remember. None of this is bad news, just gathering facts."

"Yeah, says you," she muttered. Then she handed him a fork and said, "Let's eat."

AS SOON AS Hurricane and Jewel were done eating, he got up and came around to her side, crouched down beside her and opened up the recording on his phone. He logged in, and, as soon as it started to play, nothing happened for the longest time.

She sat back, relaxed, and smiled. "It's all good then."

All of a sudden, in a mad scramble on the video, she raced down the stairs, looking a little wilder than he was expecting. She sucked in her breath. "Good God," she whispered. "I look like I'm crazy."

He patted her hand and pointed. "Let's just watch."

She came downstairs as far as the safe, quickly opened it, and then raced around the kitchen, heading first directly to the two different hiding places she'd retrieved the bracelet from earlier, then finally came back with it and slowly, carefully, put it back into the safe. As she did so, she murmured something to it and then quickly locked up, tossed one final glance in his direction and raced back upstairs again.

"Good God," she whispered. And they continued to watch on Fast Forward, until the video was over. "What did I say to it at the end?"

"I'm not sure, but I think something about staying safe."

She nodded slowly. "That sounds about right." She stared off in the direction of the safe, and he wondered just what was in her thoughts. "I have no idea what this thing is doing, but it really does feel like I'm trying to keep it safe," she murmured.

"I get it," he agreed, "but from what?"

"I'm presuming from the dark energy worker who had put them in those pieces." She looked at him. "What else?"

"I'm not sure. That's why I'm asking you." Obviously she didn't like the way he had phrased that question.

"And you lied to me. You told me that you would keep the necklace and the bracelet together, so I could get a good night's rest."

"I said, I *could* leave them together, hoping you got a good night's rest. I made no promise, so I didn't lie to you. I just didn't tell you my plans beforehand. And, even though I separated the pieces, even though you put them together again, you did sleep well, didn't you?"

She continued to glare at him, but she didn't say anything else, which was good because he was still trying to figure out just what he'd seen. The fact that she had looked as harried and as half wild as she had really concerned him because it certainly wasn't her that he was seeing but something else entirely.

"Is that what you expected to see?" she asked him.

He nodded.

"So how do I disconnect from this thing?"

"I think we have to disconnect everything from it," he guessed. "I don't think it's simply a case of disconnecting just you. We have to disconnect all of the dark energy from it."

"I don't have a problem disconnecting. I just don't know

how."

"When you were asleep, did you recognize that you were being called?"

"No, I don't think so," she recalled softly, "but then I wouldn't have expected this to happen either."

"Even though you knew that it had happened before."

"Sure, but I slept well. I slept great." And then she frowned and looked at the safe. "Do you think they had anything to do with it?"

"They?" he questioned.

She flushed. "I mean the pearls, or the souls within the pearls." She winced as she said it. "God, it sounds terrible to speak it out loud. The fact of the matter is, I did sleep well. I do feel good, and yet I shouldn't. I mean, I should have been more than a little irritated, upset, and stressed at the separation of the two pieces, but instead—maybe because of that reuniting, maybe after that—I slept like a log and woke up feeling quite refreshed."

"Let's not worry about the how and the why for the present but just be grateful to be feeling so much better," he stated, hoping to keep his tone noncommittal. He could only wish that she wouldn't sense it, but unfortunately she did.

"Now you are definitely not telling me something."

He hesitated, then shared, "I just worry that, if your deep restorative sleep was brought on by these souls, what is it that they want?"

"Obviously they wanted to be together," she stated, staring at him.

"Sure, I get that part, and it makes sense. I mean, if they've been separated for an eternity, then maybe they would want to be together. Maybe they want to be together just because they're the same, because they have been through the same tragedy, and their victimhood is their connection. But, if it were you, would you want to be in there?"

"No, of course not." She frowned at him. "So I'm not sure what you're asking."

He smiled. "What's happening is the same as what was happening yesterday," he pointed out. "It's nothing different. It's nothing new. We just have something, a connection to this scenario, that doesn't make either of us very happy."

"I would feel much better if I weren't being affected by it, and they didn't catch me while my guard was down." Then she froze.

He stared at her. "What's the matter?"

"Something in my mind, something's there."

"What?"

She stood up slowly and looked over at him again. "I have to be crazy now. No, I mean, it is crazy. It can't be."

"Let me decide that, please, and I can't make any truly informed decision if you don't tell me what's going on."

She frowned, then asked, "Do you have any idea, any details on these murders as to how they were found?"

"Why? Does it matter?"

"Yes, it matters," she stated, her voice getting faint.

He pulled up the files on his phone and said, "I've got some of them here, but I don't have all that much data, since I just received a truncated version of the police records."

"Call Grant," she stated, her voice urgent. Hurricane stopped to study her, and she shook her head. "Now you have to trust me. This is important. Get him on the phone."

He immediately dialed Drew's number. When he answered, Hurricane began, "I'm not quite sure what's going on here, but Jewel has some urgent questions."

"Okay. Hey, Jewel. What's up?"

"I'm not sure what's up, but we're back to the woo-woo stuff."

"*Great*," he said, with a note of humor. "I thought you had some questions that I could answer."

"The women," she said, "the ones you do have the case files for."

"Yes, what about them?"

"Do you have any information on how they were found?"

"I have a little bit here. Why?"

She hesitated and then replied, "Particularly Anna and Rhea. Those are the ones I have the strongest connection to."

"Yeah, what about them? I'm bringing up the files on my computer now. Give me a second." She heard the clicking of a keyboard, then he came back and said, "Okay, I've got those two files ready. What is it you want to know?"

"How were they found?" she asked urgently.

"Looks like they were both found on a highway."

"Right," she replied. "Don't tell me. Let me guess. They were naked and tossed on the side of a highway."

Drew sucked in his breath, even as Hurricane stared at her. "Yes, that's exactly what Anna's case file states." He hesitated and then asked, "Isn't that how you were found?"

"Yeah, that's exactly how I was found."

She looked over at Hurricane. "It sounds like a bigger connection here than I'm, … than we were aware of."

Drew asked, "What does this mean, Hurricane?"

"I'm not sure," he admitted slowly. "Yet the fact that she was found in the same situation as these two women is very concerning."

"Yeah, you think?" Drew quipped. "That's a distinctive

MO, linking these cases. You won't let her alone anytime in the next while, will you, Hurricane?"

"No, that's a given," he confirmed. "How about Rhea? What was her situation?"

"Let me check." After several clicks on the keyboard, then he sighed. "Same thing. She was found nude, comatose in this case, almost dead but not quite, on the side of a highway."

"What color was her hair?" Jewel asked.

"Jet-black hair, alabaster-white skin." And then Drew swore. "Didn't I see something in your file that your hair was dark and that your skin was pure white?"

"Yeah," she whispered. "That's exactly what you read. Only it wasn't before all this happened. I used to be a strawberry blonde with peaches-and-cream skin, definitely not jet-black hair and alabaster-white skin."

"So, what the hell's going on?"

"What's going on is that someone is trying to make me into the image of these other women, likely so he can add me to his collection."

CHAPTER 19

AFTER THE PHONE call with Grant, Jewel asked Hurricane if she could use his laptop for a bit, then buried herself in work. When her email refreshed, she found a message from the client regarding the necklace repair. She looked over at Hurricane. "The guy who couriered over the pearl necklace is asking when he can get it back."

He nodded. "Anytime."

"That's not reassuring," she whispered. "So both the necklace and the bracelet? He can't have them back, right? Or can he?"

"Nope, he can't, but we sure need to talk to him."

"What do I say to him?"

"Just tell him that you need to show him some damage on the necklace to determine if he wants you to try to fix it or not."

"I'm not sure I can."

"I'm not sure I want you to touch it at all," he added, with even more force. "However, that doesn't change the fact that we need to talk to him." She hesitated, and he just stared at her steadily.

"Fine." She quickly sent an email message back, saying that she'd like to show him some of the damage in the necklace and to explain her recommendations for repair. His immediate response was that he didn't care. He just wanted it fixed.

She winced at that, looked over at Hurricane, and asked, "Now what?"

"Tell him to come pick it up," he stated. "We need to see him. I'll let Drew know."

"*Great*," she whispered. She crafted what she hoped was a genial customer service email, telling him it would be ready when he came to pick it up. Instead he sent a response right back, saying he'd send a courier. She winced at that. "I don't know what you want me to do now, but he doesn't want to come in person."

"Of course not." Hurricane frowned, sharing a look with her.

"I don't have any right to keep it, except for the fact that it's dangerous."

"It is dangerous," he confirmed. "Hang on a second while I call Drew again." He got up and headed off a few steps.

She wasn't sure what to say to this client, yet obviously wanted to meet him and to see if he had any idea what was going on and to see if he matched her memory of some guy at her loft, asking about a necklace. Yet she had no right to hold the necklace. So, if he asked for it, she pretty well had to return it, although she was almost positive that Hurricane wouldn't let that happen. And yet how could he not? Was there any way that they could hold it?

When he came back, he smiled and said, "Drew will track it."

"Once the necklace leaves, it won't be easy to do anything with it."

Hurricane nodded. "A part of me would be quite happy if it leaves, especially if it frees you up."

She frowned at that. "But will it? Even the thought of it leaving is making me nervous."

He studied her for a long moment. "Doesn't matter whether it is or not."

"I get that," she replied defensively. "I get that being connected is not a good thing, but I'm not sure that it'll be within our power to get rid of it."

"I know. It'll be one of those things that we get a chance to test, whether we like it or not," he admitted. She frowned at him. He still smiled. "Drew says to pack up the jewelry box but not the necklace itself."

"So then what? I'll just keep it?" she asked, her eyebrows going up. "That won't be very good for my business."

"Do you want to send it off?"

"No," she stated emphatically. "I don't."

"Do you have another suggestion?"

"No, that's what you're supposed to come up with."

He chuckled. "We can't let it go without finding out who your client is and what his connection to that necklace is. If it's stolen, we need to know where it was stolen from. And, just so you know, that was my suggestion." He winked at her.

"My customer's not likely to know. He's probably a private collector," she murmured, "maybe not too interested in an accurate provenance on a piece."

"We still need to find out."

"Got it. So, what do you want me to do?" she asked.

"You'll pack up the empty box and send it off, and we'll track where it's going."

"He gave me a P.O. box address."

"Of course he did. What is it?"

She quickly gave it to him. He nodded and passed the

info to Drew. Just a moment later Hurricane read an incoming text. "Drew says it's registered to an export company."

"Which means nothing," she murmured.

"Exactly, he's doing a rundown on that company right now."

"I don't want to let the necklace go," she murmured, staring at the wall safe again, beginning to get angry.

"Why the anger?" he asked. "It's coming off you in waves."

"Because it doesn't belong to anybody else," she stated, staring off. "It belongs to me."

He whistled suddenly. "Whoa, whoa, whoa, don't even go there."

She focused on Hurricane now. "I don't think I have a choice. If I hand it over, something bad will happen."

He sucked in his breath. "To you?"

She nodded slowly. "I think so."

"Yeah, you think so, *huh*? In that case we're definitely not handing it over, not until we figure out what's going on and until we track down this guy who supposedly owns both these pearl pieces. Drew will track the package and have the courier picked up for questioning. Meanwhile this customer of yours hopefully will be the one to come and collect the package. If it isn't him, it'll have to be somebody he hires."

"You think he'll come?"

"Somebody will. We can count on that."

"Says you," she murmured. She quickly packed up the empty necklace box, adding a few glass beads she had for weight. When the courier came to the door, she handed off the package, already preaddressed. He took it, smiled, and left. She didn't think the courier had anything to do with this, but what did she know.

At that, Hurricane looked over at her. "Stay here."

Giving her that one simple instruction, he was gone out the door, before she could ask him anything else.

HURRICANE RACED FROM the building, hopped into his truck, and followed behind the courier at a safe distance. With the panic rising within him and that weird sense of disconnect from her, it felt wrong to be following the courier. He quickly picked up his phone and called her. "Stay inside and lock the door," he snapped, as soon as she answered.

With that, he disconnected the call and quickly punched in Drew's number.

Drew greeted Hurricane with an update. "We're already at the courier depot."

Hurricane replied, "I didn't even know you were in town."

"I'm not, but I have somebody there," he explained. "So you won't know who they are, although they have some idea of who you are. Regardless, they're waiting for the courier."

"I'm on his tail, so we should be there in a few minutes."

"Good enough," Drew replied. "We'll connect as soon as it's been handed over." And, with that, Drew disconnected the call.

Tossing the phone down on the seat beside him, Hurricane drove carefully through traffic, until he got to the courier depot. He hopped out, watching as the courier drove around to the back. He walked around to the rear of the building to keep an eye on what was happening, but the parcels were being unloaded into the back of the store. He frowned at that because, from here, until the person picked it up, he had no way of knowing who would appear for this particular package. He looked around, but the place was mostly empty.

One person sat in a vehicle off to the side, Hurricane immediately tagged as one of Drew's associates but couldn't be sure. They had no idea who was involved in this, and it would not be smart to knock off anybody at this point.

He texted Drew. **I'm here. Parcel's gone into the building.**

We have somebody inside. Just hold on.

Hurricane waited but, of course, had no way to know if the supposed owner would come and pick this up right now or later. He assumed it would be a fast shipment, but it also didn't mean it wouldn't be sent right back out again for another delivery. He pondered that. **Can you access the online tracking for it?**

We do have a tracking number for it. So far it's not registered beyond being returned to the courier station.

Where is it going from here?

It says it's being held for pickup, Drew sent back.

Good, I'll stay then.

Are you sure you want to do that?

Yes, I don't want to see that disappear anywhere.

"We're on it, you know," Drew stated, calling him now. "Look. I don't have your woo-woo powers, but are you really okay with leaving her alone right now?"

At that, he swore. "No, I'm not. It's like an itch in the back of my mind."

"Then get back there," Drew stated. "We'll track this. For the moment it'll just sit here or be held at the counter for a pickup, so nothing you can do until somebody comes to get it. They've already been alerted that we are interested in who is picking this up, so again leave it to us."

And, with that, Hurricane had to be satisfied. He hopped into his vehicle and picked up his phone yet again and called Jewel. When she didn't answer, he swore and started the engine and quickly drove back to her loft again. He kept trying her all the way there.

He broke the speed limits as he raced to her. He could only hope that she had fallen asleep on the couch and was ignoring her phone. That was the best answer. Grim, he pulled up in front of the loft building, raced up the front steps to her place, and let himself in. As he walked into the living room, his steps swift and hard, his gaze searched frantically but found no sign of her on the couch. No sign of her anywhere. As he stood in the middle of the room and slowly turned around, he called out, "Jewel, where are you?"

He bolted up the stairs to the bedroom, but again no sign of her. He opened the bathroom and again nothing. On the way down he stopped because the drywall to the safe had been disturbed. He quickly plucked it free to find the safe not even closed, which was why the drywall had been at an angle. And he didn't have to look very hard to realize that both the necklace and the bracelet were gone.

"Shit, shit, shit," he cried out. He pulled out his phone and called Drew. "She's gone. So are the necklace and the bracelet."

Silence. "What are you thinking?" Drew asked cautiously. "Because, if it were me, I'd be thinking she stole everything."

Hurricane plunked down onto the bottom step and pinched the bridge of his nose. "That makes no sense," he cried out.

"Maybe not, but, at this point in time, obviously something's going on."

"Yeah, something. Any news there yet?"

"Nothing, but then we haven't had very much time yet," he noted.

"No, I know. I've just gotten to her loft. That word of warning you gave me sent me here as fast as I could, and I still missed it."

"Missed it, missed her, missed what?"

"I don't know," he cried out. "I just don't know. I'll call Stefan." And, with that, he hung up on Drew and called Stefan. His wife answered. "Is Stefan there?" he asked, with a note of urgency.

"He's been painting all morning. Let me see. I gather it's urgent?"

"Yeah, isn't it always?"

"When you call, it tends to be," she noted, with a chuckle, "but then so much of our life here is like that—hurricanes and then the calm."

"This very much feels like the calm before the storm," he stated, "but I'm not sure we'll ever get through it at the rate it's going."

"That bad, *huh*? Here he is."

There were muffled voices, and then Stefan came on, his voice tired. "Hey, I've been working in the studio all morning."

"She's gone," he admitted baldly.

A shocked silence came on the other end. "When?"

"In the last forty minutes."

"How?"

"I have no idea." Hurricane quickly relayed what had happened and that Drew's people were standing by where the parcel had been taken.

"But it was a fake in the parcel, correct?"

"Yes, just the necklace case, not actually the pearls."

"And she knew that?"

His heart sinking, and feeling like a fool, he murmured, "Yes, and I know you'll say that she stole it, but—"

"But what?" he asked curiously. No judgment was in his voice, just an honest need to understand where Hurricane was coming from.

"I don't feel like this is something she would have done."

"How well do you know her?"

"Not well enough," he bit off.

"Does she have a vehicle?"

He froze. "Yeah, we tracked that down. It was here all along. Shit, I should have checked that first. I'm checking that now."

He walked to her garage unit, where she kept her car. "It's not here."

"Do you think the client would have contacted her privately? Would he have taken her at gunpoint?"

"I suppose," Hurricane replied, "but wouldn't he just take the jewels and not her? And how would he know they're still here? I'm worried."

"He's taken her away in order to either imprison her or to just destroy any threat to his anonymity."

"If we're following the theory that she's not involved in this, then that makes the most sense, doesn't it?"

Stefan asked, "Give me a few minutes. I'll call you back." And, with that, he disconnected.

STEFAN DROPPED GRACEFULLY into a cross-legged position, his back against the front hallway wall. He opened up his senses wide, wider than he would have liked to, but he was too tired after the art session not to. He could sense Maddy's surprise jolting him.

Whenever he went into this mode, it sent an alert to her. She poked her head into the energy, but he gave her a gentle wave, signifying he was okay. However, instead of disappearing, she sat in the background and gently funneled energy in his direction. He smiled because there was a genuine love here that went way past humanity. They were bonded in so many ways. Their own skills, needs, and desires to help the world around them had bonded them in a wonderful friendship. He sent images of what had gone on to her. Rather than waste the energy, he immediately headed out of his house into the ethers, looking for Jewel.

He'd already caught her signature from much earlier, and, when she'd phoned him, there had been already an awareness in her voice, as if she was well versed in this art of energy work. So had she been hiding this skill the whole time or had she ended up with some psychic attack that had blinded her?

Maddy's voice whispered behind him, *Careful. This isn't what it seems.*

He took that under consideration but had no choice but to follow through. If for no other reason than the fact that Hurricane was sending him frantic energy, the waves pounding against him in such a way that it was all Stefan could do to buffer them back, so that he could function.

Maddy immediately said, *I'll take care of that.*

She quickly put up what was essentially cotton batting in an energy form, to stop Hurricane's incredibly powerful waves from reaching out and shaking Stefan. She lined the energy with love, sending waves of calm energy back to

Hurricane, to get him to ease the storm inside him.

Stefan immediately headed out into the ethers, tracking Jewel's signature. It didn't take long, but where and how he found her was something he'd never seen before. He slowly brought himself out of his trance, picked up the phone, and called Drew. "I know where she is," he began, his voice exhausted. "But you won't believe it. I'll call Hurricane right now." He disconnected.

Stefan called Hurricane. "Go to this address. She's there. I'm sending an ambulance too." And he hung up without saying anything more.

CHAPTER 20

J EWEL OPENED HER eyes and stared, her gaze blurry, her body exhausted, as if she had run an ultramarathon and had pushed herself to the absolute end of her limits but had succeeded in some fight. She lay here, shivering against the cold.

A blanket was pulled up over her, and she murmured something, turning her head into the pillow. She tried to raise her eyelids, but they kept closing again. A hand reached out and grasped her fingers. She smiled, not knowing how she knew but knowing who it was. "Hurricane," she murmured.

"Yes," he answered, his voice thick. "Sit tight."

"What happened?" she asked.

"That's something you'll have to tell me," he said, "but not right now. We're getting you checked over first."

There were sounds, mechanical sounds, movements, and the fresh air that had surrounded her now included antiseptic smells and an odd sensation. Then a door slammed. She tried to open her eyes again, but it hurt. "My eyes," she whispered.

"Keep them closed," he ordered. "Stay calm and stay quiet. If you've got any energy to heal with, then use it."

Such an odd thing for him to say. She curled up into the blanket and just rested. Her body was being jostled from side to side, and it was all so very weird. She wanted to ask him more questions, but it was hard, beyond hard; she was just so tired. She drifted in and out of consciousness, and then suddenly, amid bright lights, loud noises, she was being rushed somewhere.

She felt her body starting to argue with it all. A voice in her head kept saying, *Fight, fight, please dammit, fight.* Then out of the blue, suddenly her chest hurt, as shockwaves pounded against her ribs, and she cried out. But she couldn't hear her voice; it was just in her head. In the distance, somewhere far away—and yet close enough that she could register the sounds—she heard somebody call out.

"Again!" More voices, more shock treatment, and then suddenly she was back.

She let her eyes drift open. However, the bright light hurt, so she slammed them shut again. But not before she caught sight of Hurricane. She whispered, "Where am I?"

"You're in the hospital," he said. "Don't try to talk, just rest."

She reached out a hand and watched through her lowered lashes in shock, as her hand lifted away from her arm. Separated, distinctly two different pieces, as if she were only a ghost. She went to sit up and realized she was peeling her way out of her body.

Hurricane's voice came back sharp. "Lie back down."

She stared at him, only to realize her eyes weren't open, but she was staring at him anyway in this ghostly form.

"I don't think I want to," she whispered.

"Please," he added, his voice emotional. "Please lie back down."

And then he did something she'd never seen before, but this wave of gentleness, love, and caring washed through her, filling her from her toes to the top of her head, then all the way down to her fingers. "Why?" she whispered. "Why do you care?"

"I don't know, but I do, and that's enough for me," he stated immediately. "Please, lie back down."

Her eyes opened wide, she contemplated it for a long moment, then slowly sank back into her body and drifted back out on the ethers, once again out cold.

HURRICANE SAT DOWN once more on the chair beside Jewel's hospital bed, his gaze locked on hers, her face almost ethereal, as he studied her features.

Stefan stepped into his mind. *She appears to be doing better.*

If you say so. She's been here forever.

It's been less than twelve hours, Stefan corrected, with a note of humor. *It just feels like forever.*

What the hell happened? Hurricane cried out softly.

I'd say it's the pearls. I just don't know what kind of hold somebody has over Jewel or how we can track a killer who, so far, has escaped detection for decades, Stefan murmured.

But why her? Why was she chosen?

I suspect because she could work the magic on the actual pearls themselves, Stefan replied. *It's about the only thing that makes sense. For whatever reason she had that affinity and once he realized that …*

At that, Hurricane shook his head. *To even think that something like this is possible …*

We all know that a lot is going on out in the ethers that we don't know about yet, much of it horrifying and beyond comprehension, but it goes on regardless.

I don't think … I've never seen anything like this. Then Hurricane stopped and shook his head. *Stefan, have you?*

No, this is a new one for me too.

What about Drew? Did he find anything?

No, the parcel is still sitting at the courier shop.

Damn.

Stefan smiled, and Hurricane felt the emotion.

Are you thinking what I'm thinking? Hurricane asked.

If you're thinking that her client knew the delivery was a fake, yes, and that would mean that he is connected to the actual pieces as well.

He couldn't be in the pearls himself, right? Hurricane asked.

At that, Stefan paused. *I won't say no, but how would that make any sense?*

It doesn't. Never mind.

We shouldn't discount it completely, but we need to put this into perspective.

I don't know, Hurricane murmured. *I'd hoped that at least, if we could find out who had sent the parcel, we would have some idea where to look next.*

I know, Stefan agreed. *Drew sent me a text, saying that he had some information, but I haven't managed to connect with him.*

Disconnect now then, Hurricane ordered, *and one of you get back to me when you find out what he's got.*

With a light chuckle, Stefan, in a cool sense of withdrawal, disappeared from Hurricane's mind. Hurricane got up, wandered around the small hospital room once again, and stared at her as she slept. "What the hell happened to you?"

As soon as he had a chance, he would go buy security

cameras to place them all around her loft and all around this hospital room, so he could track if something else happened. Would give him time to sleep a bit. Until the hospital caught on and threw a fit. HIPAA be damned in this case. Somebody hadn't fallen for the delivery ruse and had taken the chance while Hurricane was gone to move in. Nice and simple. And the worst of it was that he himself had let it happen and had, in fact, helped orchestrate the opportunity. As he sat here, chastising himself, a soft whisper reached him.

Stop.

He looked over to see her eyes still closed, her breathing slow and steady. He frowned, closed his eyes, and asked, *Who is this?*

A moment of startled disconnect came, before the voice replied, *It's me. What do you mean, who is this?*

He looked over toward the hospital bed again but nothing gave the appearance that Jewel was awake, alert. *You who?*

What do you mean? she cried out. *It's me, Jewel!*

He got up, slowly walked over to the bed, and asked, *Where are you?*

What do you mean, where am I? she murmured. *I'm with you.*

I know you're with me, he replied cautiously, *but I need to know where you are physically.*

After a moment of confusion, she asked, *Am I not physically there with you?*

He smiled at that. *You are,* he confirmed, with a slight chuckle. *I'm just wondering if you're awake enough to recognize what's going on.*

Probably not, judging by the way you are acting, and it's making me feel very odd.

Can you open your eyes?

At that, another disconnect came, and then she stated, *They are open.*

Open your other eyes.

She seemed stunned for a moment, and then she said, *Oh God.*

Oh God what? he asked, wanting to laugh, but didn't want to freak her out.

Am I dead?

CHAPTER 21

J EWEL SLOWLY OPENED her physical eyes and stared around at the hospital room. Then her gaze caught sight of Hurricane standing at the end of her bed. *Are you okay?* she asked him.

"I'm okay," he said out loud, his mouth moving, reassuring her that something was back to normal. "How are *you?*"

I'm okay, she replied, with a smile.

"Good. In that case, you may want to use your vocal cords." But his gaze was intense, studying her, as if trying to figure out just what she was doing.

She stared at him, and then slowly, as if a huge amount of pressure was required, she opened her mouth and slowly rotated her jaw, as if killing her. "Hurricane?" she asked, and her voice croaked. She stared at him in shock. "Is that my voice?" she asked in a still raspy tone.

He nodded. "Yes, that is definitely your voice."

She closed her eyelids and asked, "What happened?"

"You apparently had a stronger connection in the spirit side of life than in the physical. You appear to have opened up a pathway or somehow allowed part of you to communicate with others on the ethers."

Her heart sank. That statement should be a shock, and yet it wasn't. This was normal; she just didn't know how to explain it. *I think this is the way I'm used to talking.* She sensed his surprise and realized that, once again, she'd whispered in his mind, not out loud physically. She opened her eyes and stared at him. "Things are very confusing right now." She frowned and struggled to regain control of her physical mouth. As soon as she could get the words articulated, she asked, "What happened?"

He sat on the side of her bed, picked up her hand, and just held it. "Maybe you could tell me that."

She blinked at him and slowly shook her head. "I don't have any memory of it."

He nodded. "I was afraid you would say that." But his tone was almost absentminded, as if heavy in thought in other ways. He looked down at her again. "How long have you been able to do this?"

She frowned at him.

"No," he said, "I need to know."

"I don't know. It just feels like it's …" She frowned at that, hoping her voice would ease up because it hurt to talk. "It feels like it …" She tried again, then struggled once more.

"Feels like what? Feels like it's more comfortable, feels like it's natural, feels like it's something you used to do but haven't done in a long time, so it's rusty?"

"No," she whispered. "It feels more comfortable to speak in my head." She swallowed and winced, like her throat hurt. "Like it's what I used to do, like what I'm used to doing." She hesitated, then added, "But physically speaking is what's rusty, like I haven't done it in a long time. … What is going on?"

"I'm not sure. It could be that you've connected with a victim, and she may have been isolated to the point or gagged to the point that she was never allowed to talk, and that's what's happening to you now, and you're just manifesting her symptoms."

She stared at him with her physical eyes, and something about that rang true, but something about it didn't. *Something in here, something I'm ... I've never really understood before.*

"What's that?"

I used to do this. I used to speak in my head all the time.

"Speaking in your head to yourself is very common," he murmured. "However, if you have somebody else you could speak with in your head, that makes it very uncommon."

She blinked several times, then spoke out loud again. "I think I did, but I don't know who it was."

"That would be very helpful to know," he stated, his gaze watchful. "It might help explain why you were picked."

"What do you mean?" she asked, her voice gaining strength. She shuffled in the bed and slowly sat up. Looking over at the glass of water, she pointed.

He got up immediately and moved to hand her the water. "Was there an incident in your childhood or somewhere in your life, where you were held captive?"

She shook her head. "Not to my knowledge."

"Are there any periods of your life that you don't have any knowledge of? Like big blocks of time you are missing or time frames missing from your memory?"

"I don't think so." Jewel stared at him. "That's a freaky thing to think about."

"It is, but it might explain some of this."

"I don't think it explains anything. All it does is raise way more questions."

"That's often what happens," he agreed, with a smile. "Yet, if we could figure out what's happening to you, we might have a chance of figuring out how this other person is involved."

She sighed. "I don't know of anything that ever happened to me," she murmured. "My life is an open book."

He stared at her. "Where were you born?"

"Illinois."

"What year?"

She reeled off a number.

"Who were your parents?"

She gave him the names immediately.

"Siblings?"

"None."

"Where'd you go to school?"

She gave him the elementary, middle, and high school info.

"Who was your first boyfriend?"

At that, she stopped, then looked at him and frowned. "I don't remember."

He nodded. "So, what I'm about to tell you is a bit out there, but you have to consider the possibility. I asked you questions, and the other answers came fast, really fast, as if they were by rote. Many people would have to stop and think about the name of their elementary school, for example, but that information was almost at the tip of your tongue. I'm afraid you may have been fed information known to the public that could be retrieved easily at a later point in time."

He pulled out his phone and said, "I'll talk to Drew for a minute. You sit here, sip that water. And rest."

"Wait," she called out, as he went to the door. "Where did you find me?"

He stopped and turned, his face grim. "Out on a highway, completely nude, without a mark on you."

After dropping that bombshell, he turned and stepped out into the hallway.

HURRICANE QUICKLY CALLED Drew.

"Hey," Drew answered. "I've been waiting for you to call."

"Yeah, sorry, it's been a bit of a shit show here."

"Hey, we found Jewel. That's what counts."

"That's the thing. She has no recollection of what happened," he murmured.

Drew paused at that. "Of course not," he replied, his tone slightly off. "That would be a good excuse for her behavior."

"I know what you're trying to say, and I don't believe she stole the pearls and faked her abduction," Hurricane stated.

"I know. I'm only warning you that, just because it seems like she's sweet and innocent, there's a possibility that she's not."

"I get that too," Hurricane replied, rubbing his temple with his free hand. "It's very frustrating. You haven't seen her the way I have, and right now she's in there, completely bewildered at what's happened."

"At least we found her this time, before anybody else did. Plus we also have a better idea of what to expect, since it's the second time over."

"Do we though?" Hurricane asked.

"We'll watch out for those bruises, in case they come back. She healed from the first abduction rather quickly, as I recall."

"Yes, she did. Once I pointed out to her that they were

odd, she healed pretty quickly. That's not very much to go on at the moment."

"I presume she'll get released into your care soon."

"I don't know. I haven't talked to the doctors yet, but I need to. Did you do a full check into her background?"

"Yeah, I should have done it from the beginning," he admitted. "Honestly, if I had had two seconds, I would have, but you were so sure that she wasn't involved."

"I'm still pretty confident she isn't involved, at least not of her own volition. But when I asked her questions about her early life, the answers come immediately, fast and smooth, without a moment for a thought."

Drew paused. "That's normal."

"No, more likely rehearsed, as if she was fed those lines and schooled on it. But just because she was told what her childhood was like doesn't mean it's the truth."

"No, maybe not," Drew agreed thoughtfully.

"Thus the need for a proper background check."

"Noted. Damn, I hate these woo-woo cases."

At that, Hurricane burst out laughing. "But they do keep us hopping," he noted.

"Yeah, too much so. Anyway, I'll do what I can on that and get back to you." And, with that, he hung up.

CHAPTER 22

W HEN HURRICANE STEPPED back in Jewel's room, she didn't turn to face him but asked, "Did he have anything new to say?"

Her voice was slowly returning to normal, a little bit raspy, but not bad. "No," he replied, "but he'll run a background check."

Her eyes widened, and she turned to face him. "Oh? I am bonded, you know."

"You are?" he asked.

She nodded slowly. "I handle pretty high-end jewelry."

"Yes, of course. That makes perfect sense," he noted. "Not sure how this could even play into it. So tell me. What was your childhood like?"

"I would have said, *Just fine*, but now you've got me wondering."

"I don't mean to set you off. I'm just trying to figure out where we're at here."

"Good for you," she replied listlessly. "When you find out, let me know. God, why the hell was I found nude on the highway again?" she burst out, clearly upset. "Wait? Where are my clothes? My car?"

He gave her a half smile. "Honey, if I could tell you that, I'd be a very happy man." She glared at him, and he chuckled. "I'm not against having you naked under the right circumstances. Believe me. You're absolutely stunningly gorgeous, but these attacks have to be stopped. Can you remember anything after I left?"

She frowned. "I remember telling you to be careful and you warning me to lock the door."

"That's a good start," he noted, "because I absolutely did do that. So then what happened?"

"I slept."

"Anything else?"

She stared at him, her gaze turning inward.

He watched intently but couldn't see any signs of another energy or any deceit on her part.

"I remember lying down on the couch, and ..." She stopped.

He stared, as her face worked, while she tried to get things back into her focus. "And, within hours, I ended up on a highway completely nude again," she stated, somewhat bitterly.

"Yes, but we did find you right away."

"How did you find me anyway?" She turned to him, clearly curious. "Last time I was found by a complete stranger. This time you found me."

"Stefan," Hurricane shared. "He followed your energy." She blinked at him, and he smiled. "You have that way of looking at someone almost owlishly, as if what we're saying doesn't make any sense."

"It doesn't really, if you think about it," she murmured. "But, then again, you guys appear to be very coordinated in skills that most of us have never heard of."

"That's the part that we're still not sure about."

She didn't say anything, just relaxed into her bedding. "So, what does it take to get kicked free of this place again?

And soon, I hope."

"We need the doctor's okay to ensure nothing health-wise is wrong with you—and to get you some clothes."

"Or you could run back to my place and get me some," she suggested hopefully.

He shook his head at that. "No, but I could ask somebody else to go get some for you."

"Why won't you?" she asked, puzzled.

"I'm not leaving you alone again."

"It's not your fault," she said, her voice very soft.

"Are you sure about that?" he asked in disgust. "The other thing that worries me is that the pearls are gone."

She frowned at that. "What? How?" she asked, shifting in the bed eagerly. "Did you see who came to collect the parcel?"

"No, we didn't. He didn't show, or at least not at the point in time that I last spoke to Drew. He has somebody staying and watching the parcel."

She winced at that. "What if it was all just a ruse to get me out of the house?"

"I don't know about getting you out of the house, but it certainly got me out of the house."

"Right," she agreed, after a moment. "And that's not quite the same thing, is it? With you gone, I was basically left vulnerable."

"Which is why I'm not leaving you again," he repeated, hardening his tone.

She looked at him and smiled. "You aren't responsible. You know that, right?"

"Somehow it still feels like I'm responsible," he argued, staring at her. "You might let me off the hook, but that doesn't mean I will."

"I never hired you as a bodyguard. I know that you have stepped up and taken on that role, but it's not as if it was assigned to you."

"I don't take assignments. I just do what I think needs to be done."

"Whether I like it or not?"

"Whether you like it or not," he declared, with a nod.

As she went to stand up in her hospital gown, the door opened. A nurse stepped in, appearing startled to see her on her feet. "Hey." The nurse walked over to Jewel. "This is a lovely sign."

Jewel smiled at her. "Thank you for looking after me," she stated, her tone more formal than Hurricane was expecting.

The nurse looked at her closely. "I do want the doctor to take a look at you, and then, if he clears you, I expect you'll be released to go home."

"Yeah, I'm hoping that somebody can arrange for clothing," she added, looking down at the hospital gown.

"Right, seeing as we've already stripped out the Lost and Found for you once."

She winced at that. "I can return those clothes too. I'm sorry. I should have done that before now."

"Hey, it wasn't very long ago that you were here before," the nurse noted, shooting a look back at Hurricane.

He winced at that. "We're doing our best."

She stared at him. "No offense, but doesn't sound like your best is good enough. She's been attacked twice now and taken to the same place. How hard can it be to figure this out?"

"We do have the cops on it," he added.

At that, Jewel looked at him. "Did you let the detective

know?"

"Of course. He's been consulting with Drew."

"*Great*, the police and the FBI."

"Good," the nurse declared in a severe tone. "We've had enough of this crap," she muttered. As she quickly walked out of the room, she added, "Give me a moment, and I'll get the doctor."

At that, Jewel looked over at him. "Clothing?"

He nodded, and just then his phone buzzed. "Hopefully that will be word on your clothes," he shared. He stepped out of the hospital room and held the door open, while a kind-looking man in a white jacket came in.

He looked her over. "You're in far better shape at this point than compared to last time."

She nodded. "Maybe because I was found earlier, and maybe he didn't get a chance to do something to me that he wanted to. I don't know."

"Again no sign of sexual assault," he noted. "I'm not sure what this guy's plan was, but, so far, you appear to be surviving his attacks—although I can't say I'm terribly impressed that it's happened a second time."

"Nobody is," she agreed gently, "but I can't really blame Hurricane."

"Maybe not," the doc admitted, "but you need to be careful to ensure we don't get a third repeat of this. You've had two skates over thin ice, so—"

"I got it," she said, adding a smile. "No guarantee that I would survive a third."

"Exactly," he murmured. "Now let's have a closer look."

He gave her a good once-over and nodded. "You appear as healthy as a horse now," he stated. "I'm not even sure, at this point, if he knocked you out or gave you something, but there appear to be no ill effects, either way. No new bumps to your head, and all of those bruises that came up post-mortem—I mean, after you came back to life again—have all disappeared, but keep an eye out to see if the same bruising happens again."

"I will, but I'm really hoping the answer to that question is a no."

"You and me both," he said cheerfully. "Strangest thing I ever saw."

With that, he stepped out, and, almost like musical chairs, Hurricane walked back in again, holding up a bag for her. "A change of clothes," he announced.

"Oh, thank heavens." She took the bag from him and, heading into the bathroom, quickly changed. She intentionally avoided the mirror, but, as soon as she changed, she stopped, took one close look, and scowled. It's like the veins clearly showed under her transparent skin. Her skin had gone from being alabaster white to almost translucent. She shook her head, then managed to grab a glass of water, and rinsed out her mouth, washed her face, and ran her fingers through her hair, trying to get some semblance of order. Quickly she put it into a braid and tied the ends loosely together. It would only stay for a little bit, without a hair clip or a ponytail holder, but it made her feel a lot better.

Back out in the room, Hurricane nodded approvingly. "Also a pair of sandals are in the bag, I think," he said, noting her bare feet.

She looked back in the bag, pulled them out, and slipped them on. "Nice, thank you." Then she put the empty bag with the hospital gown on the bed and said, "Let's go."

"In a rush?"

"Absolutely," she murmured. "I want to get out of here,

before something else happens."

He stayed silent as he walked outside, straight to his Jeep.

She sighed. "Were there any changes at the loft?"

"I don't know. Believe me. I didn't hang around long enough to check. You weren't there and both pieces of the pearls were gone. That's all I cared about."

She nodded. "You never found the jewelry, did you?" He shook his head. "Good enough. Let's go home, but we'll need to get some food in the meantime."

"You hungry?"

"No, that's not even the word for it. I'm absolutely ravenous," she muttered. "I don't remember being this hungry before, not in a very long time."

He looked at her sideways and suggested, "I can hit a drive-through."

"Only if it's real food. Otherwise we're going home and cooking."

"If we order Chinese, it would probably be about ready by the time we got there to pick it up."

She nodded and then clapped at her pants and looked at him. "My phone's gone again?"

He winced. "Yeah, it is."

"*Great.*"

He pulled one from his pocket and handed it to her. "Good thing I keep spares." It didn't take her long to locate a Chinese food place, and, when she called them, she placed an order that she knew would shock Hurricane with the sheer volume of food. When she put away his phone, she sat back, and her stomach growled.

The sound was loud enough to raise his eyebrows.

"I said I was hungry," she noted, half mortified.

"Yeah, I got that," he murmured, looking at her. "Loud and clear. Apparently very hungry."

He followed her instructions to the restaurant. When he pulled in and parked, she raced inside, with him on her heels. He quickly paid for the order, and they brought several bags back to the truck.

He didn't say anything, but, as she looked at it, she admitted, "Maybe I overdid it."

"That's all right," he said. "We can warm it up later. Nothing better than leftover Chinese food."

"That would work." As she got back in the passenger seat, she asked, "Do you mind turning the heater on?"

Surprised, he looked over at her, and, realizing she was serious, put the heater on immediately. She settled back but was getting even more chilled. When her teeth started to chatter, he swore and cranked the heat up even higher. "We're almost home, just hold on a minute."

He quickly pulled around a couple more blocks, then parked in front of the building. He hopped out, came around to her side, and pulled open the door, only to find her shaking so much her teeth were literally knocking against each other.

He shook his head and said, "Grab the bags, if you can."

When she scooped up the bags in her arms, he picked her up, bags and all, then slammed the door shut with his hip, and carried her up the front steps.

"Is it locked?" she asked him, as they were now in the public hallway leading to the private lofts.

"I didn't have a key to lock it, so no."

She reached down awkwardly and opened the door, then he carried her across the threshold into the loft. There, he placed her on the couch, took the bags from her, and put them up on the kitchen counter.

"Do you need a hot bath first?" he asked.

"I need food," she whispered.

He didn't say anything but immediately opened up all the bags, bringing out the half-dozen dishes that she'd ordered. She had followed him into the kitchen, snagging two plates, but was still shaking so badly that they clattered against each other with every movement she made.

"Go sit down," he ordered, taking them from her.

She did and watched him like a hawk, as he opened up the containers and quickly scooped out food from all six of the packages, then handed the plate to her. She hardly waited before she shoveled in the food. He stopped and stared, as she shrugged and went back at it. "I'm hungry," she muttered.

He didn't say anything but served himself a modest plate and sat down beside her. She didn't worry about it until the contents of her plate were gone and her shaking had calmed down enough that she'd managed to eat, but she found herself looking at her empty plate and then over at his.

"You want more?" he asked, looking at her. "Go get some. Or should I do that?"

She got up slowly, unsure as to whether her legs would hold her, but, realizing the worst of it had passed, she walked over to the counter and scooped up a second serving, quite a bit smaller but still a substantial amount. "I'm not sure what's wrong," she whispered. "I don't eat like this normally."

He didn't say anything, just continued to watch her, as he ate his own meal. By the time she was done with the second plate, her stomach was almost distended, and she groaned. "Now I feel like an idiot."

"Are you uncomfortable?"

"No, not at all. It's just that I'm not used to consuming that amount of food. I'm sure my digestive system will go into overdrive trying to handle it."

"Maybe, but, if you were that hungry, I'm sure it's prepared for it."

She shrugged. "I gather they didn't feed me while I was at the hospital."

"They didn't feed you, but you weren't gone long enough to need to be fed either."

She nodded and curled up sideways on the couch to look at him. "You're eating awfully slowly."

"I'm not," he disagreed, with a wry look at her. "I'm eating normally."

"In other words, I inhaled mine. Is that what you're saying?"

"Yeah, pretty much," he agreed cheerfully.

She stared down at her hands and said, "They look like they're almost invisible now," she whispered.

"That is of concern to me," he stated.

Startled, she looked up at him. "I figured it was just the cold and the lack of food."

"Maybe," he replied.

"Is there something you're not telling me?"

"Maybe, but I think it goes along with whatever it is that you're not telling me."

She frowned. "I don't understand."

"You've kept something hidden all this time, and it's burning through a lot of your energy, and you don't really have it to spare. So if you would stop trying to hide it, it would be easier on you—and me and the rest of us."

She blinked at him. "We're back to that again, *huh*?"

"Back to what?"

"That you don't trust me."

"I trust what I can see, and right now what I see is your body burning through energy at a rate that is not normal but *is* consistent with what happens after a heavy psychic burn," he explained. "So call it whatever you want to call it, but something is going on that either you are deliberately hiding or you really don't know about."

She shook her head. "You're expecting me to tell you something?"

"Yes, absolutely I am," he said. "The truth would be a hell of a place to start."

HURRICANE WASN'T KIDDING. The only way that she could have worked up that appetite and become that cold, that chilled, like she had so fast, was to have gone through a ton of energy. A blast and burn, so to speak, followed by a massive drop in energy. He'd done it himself a few times, and he always tried to avoid it at this stage of life because it was difficult to come back from, but she'd bounced back like a pro. And that just brought up more suspicions of the sort he'd been thinking about earlier. Something funny was going on here, and she either didn't know or was not prepared to share it, yet he couldn't stop that suspicion in the back of his head.

Stefan whispered in his head, *You need to broach her about it. You'll never feel safe in her presence without trust.*

Hurricane sighed, put down his plate, sat back, and continued. "I really need to push this line of questioning."

She stiffened and glared at him. "I don't know what you're talking about."

"I'd feel better if I could believe that," he replied. "The trouble is, I'm struggling with it." At that, he looked at his empty plate and sighed. "That's enough food for me for tonight." He looked at her and asked, "Coffee?"

"Oh, yes, please," she murmured. She hopped up, then came around and looked at the food left in the kitchen. "I think I'm good for the moment."

He raised an eyebrow but didn't say anything. She'd outeaten him probably three to one. He put on coffee and turned to find her sitting on the stairs, looking at the safe. She'd gotten over there so fast and so quietly that he hadn't even noticed. So either he was rattled or he was too tired to even have recognized what was going on, but it made him extremely nervous. He walked closer and asked, "What do you think?"

She stared at him, but an odd look was on her face. Her features worked, as if she were trying to speak, but couldn't quite come up with what she wanted to say, so she pointed.

He raised his eyebrows, then walked up, opened the safe wider, so he could take look, and swore. "Damn."

"The pearls are back, aren't they?" she asked.

He nodded.

"What the hell's going on?" she cried out.

There it was, in her stare was almost a connection, an avidness that he hadn't seen before. "Do you want to try them on?"

She looked at him and then nodded in joy. "Yes, yes, I really do." She immediately reached into the safe, pulling out the pearls. She picked up the necklace, and, before he had a chance to do anything, she had placed it around her neck.

He swore at that.

"What? You suggested it."

"No, I asked you, and you went at it so fast I didn't really have a chance to stop you."

"It's on now." She preened, turning her head from side to side. "Isn't it beautiful?"

"It is beautiful," he replied, but he wasn't looking at the actual necklace. He was looking at her. "But you could wear anything, and it would look beautiful." A warm flush rose up her cheeks. He was enchanted by it. "I didn't know women still blushed."

"I didn't know I could," she replied immediately, and then smiled at him. "You do say the nicest things."

"Sometimes"—he nodded—"and sometimes I don't. It all depends on the person and the situation."

She chuckled. "I keep confounding you, don't I?"

"That's one word for it."

"Do you want me to take it off?" she asked immediately.

"Yes, I do."

Her hands immediately went up to the back of the necklace to take it off, but then she stopped. "They don't want to do it."

"I know," he stated. "That's all the more reason for it to happen."

She looked up at him and frowned. "I think you'll have to do it."

He braced himself for what he knew would come, but he reached behind her to pull off the pearl necklace and got the shock of his life. He gritted his teeth, as the arcs flashed against his hands, and—better for her, worse for him—he got it off.

She cried out, screaming and kicking, looking at him. "My God, what was that?"

Slowly, feeling the burn going through his hands, he

pulled the necklace away from her and held it up for her to see. Sparks ran through him, grounding into him.

She screamed and scooted a few more steps up the stairs. "Oh my God, what the hell is that thing?"

"It's the energy of the necklace, and my guess would be that it is what has been affecting you, and that is what wants you to put it on."

"I had it on," she said, her hand going right to her neck. "It felt right. It felt like it belonged with me."

He nodded. "I've asked Drew to check into your history. … I'm wondering if you're related to one of the victims somehow and if, in some way, she's using you to reach out."

"But she wants me to join them," Jewel replied. "At least that's what it feels like. Why would she want that?"

"Somebody does. I'm just not sure who though."

With her arms wrapped around her chest, staring at the necklace with loathing, she asked, "Has it really got that power over me?" She shuddered. "Lock it up, please."

"You tell me about its power," he urged. "Before, you told me that you had been wearing it and that it felt right."

"Yes, before, when I was working on it. I had tried it on, and it did feel right."

He canted his head. "Particularly since you were working on the clasp. I think the necklace itself is attracting energy, energy that it can use, that it can feed on. I don't know what the end game of this is—presumably to have another soul on this string—but, for you, it's dangerous, very dangerous. Don't ever put it back on again, no matter how much it calls for you. Do you hear me? You have to resist it."

She looked up at him, bewildered, and then slowly she nodded.

He carefully placed the pearls back into the box and put

it back in the safe, closing and locking it in front of her.

She hesitated and then asked, "Is there any way to secure it better?"

"I've put extra energy on it, and Stefan's putting an energy lock on it as well," he told her. "We won't know if it'll be enough, until somebody attempts to access it, but we're hoping it will be enough to keep its energy calm and quiet, instead of going Thor on anyone who touches it. To me, it felt like it was hungry."

"Hungry," she whispered, staring at him in shock. "Is that why I was so hungry?"

"I don't know," he murmured, his gaze intense. "Maybe."

She swallowed and looked like she was about to upchuck, and he reached for her hand. "Steady. We'll figure it out."

"What kind of influence can all this energy have on me?" she whispered.

"A whole lot more than you might think or might even want to consider," he replied, his voice soft and gentle. "Can it make you hungry? Yes, energy definitely can. Can it make you burn through energy? Partially, hopefully not fully. Maybe you were fighting the energy of the pearls. Or maybe you were trying to become one with the pearls. I don't know because I wasn't there. I couldn't see or read the energy. But right now, an odd energy is around you in your aura, trying desperately hard to make it seem like it was such a good idea to put on that necklace. You didn't hesitate. You jumped at it, and, the next thing I knew, you were wearing it."

"And you shouldn't have let me." She glared at him.

He gave her a half smile. "Believe me. I'm better warned now, aren't I?"

She shuddered, got up from the stairs, and asked, "Is that coffee ready? I think I need a gallon right about now. Just the thought of going to sleep and letting something like that kind of boogeyman take over is scary."

He nodded. "It is scary, but we're slowly getting an idea of what's going on," he stated. "And that helps give us better tools to try and protect you."

She murmured, "Tools, protection, energy."

"I know." He grabbed her hand firmly.

"It sounds like something out of the twilight zone."

"Unfortunately, in this case, it really is something out of the twilight zone, but you'll be fine, and we'll work hard to keep you safe. But no way do we get separated again."

She squeezed his hand, smiled up at him, and nodded. "Now that I can agree with. I do not want to wake up in the hospital for a third time."

"No," he replied, his voice even softer. "But neither do I want to be called out to the highway to find out that this time there's no way you'll ever wake up again."

For Hurricane, he knew getting Jewel relaxed, calmed down, and settled in again would take time. He swapped the coffee for tea, had her relax on the couch, and sat down beside her.

She stared at him. "Why don't you just ask?"

His eyebrows shot up. "Ask what?"

"You want to do something, but I don't know what it is," she murmured.

He hesitated, his gaze going to the safe and then back to her. "I want to go into your mind, into your energy, and try to figure out what it is that I'm seeing."

She stilled, and then her breath escaped so very softly that he hadn't realized she had let it out. "What is it that you think is in there?"

"I'm not sure. What I can tell you is that it feels off. It feels …" He hesitated, not sure how to explain it. "It feels like a blockage."

She slowly sat up, cross-legged on the couch, her gaze never leaving his face. "A blockage?"

He nodded. "Yes, exactly that, a blockage."

"I see." Her gaze went to the safe. "Do you think it's related to the pearls?"

"I don't know whether it's related to the pearls, what's happening to you, or your history and the history of a victim."

At that, one eyebrow went up, and her gaze zinged back toward him. "What would this process be like?"

"You remember how we spoke in the hospital, before you woke up?"

"Yes," she replied cautiously.

"It would be similar to that."

"If similar to that," she murmured, "then you would have done it at the hospital."

He winced. "I could have done it then, yes, but I would never do it without your permission."

CHAPTER 23

S HE SETTLED BACK and took a sip of her tea, while she contemplated his words and the look on his face. Something was direct about that gaze, something clearer.

He said softly, "You're changing."

She snorted at that. "Events like this have a way of making that happen. I've been found twice on a highway completely nude, and thankfully this last time I wasn't already dead."

"No, and that's the good thing, but it was looking very dicey there for a time," he noted. "I want to think that we're getting ahead of this, but, because I've caught sight of something in your energy, I need to go in there and take a look at it, and I can't go alone."

"Oh, wow," she whispered. "Who is it that you need to go with you?"

"You, for one, and Dr. Maddy would be the best."

At that, she straightened. "Dr. Maddy was already in my aura. She already plowed through most of it."

He nodded. "But she was looking at something very different than what I am looking for. Plus she noted a blockage, but she didn't delve into it, not wanting to breach your privacy or put you at risk."

"So you're saying that some people can see things, and some people can't see them?"

"That's one way to look at it," he replied. "Another way is to also realize that there are different layers, different colors, different vibrations. Dr. Maddy was trying to help you through a very traumatic experience and wouldn't have intruded beyond that. She did say to Stefan that the blockage was something odd and that she would need to go back at some point to examine it further. Also only with your permission."

"But there hasn't been a whole lot of time," she added.

"Exactly," he agreed, with half a smile.

"Would it be as painless as when she did her search?" When he didn't answer right away, her gaze narrowed on him.

"I don't want to lie to you," he began. "I don't know. That we will have to see."

"I'm really not into any more pain," she murmured.

"No, and we would do our best to not hurt you."

"Have you talked to Dr. Maddy about this?"

"No," he stated. "I mentioned it to Stefan, and I know that he was talking to Dr. Maddy about your case."

HURRICANE COULD TELL that she didn't like that word. "My case, *ugh*. Don't think much of that," she murmured.

"I know, but, when you think about it, a lot of cases are involved, a lot of women involved, a lot of crimes."

"Do we know that for sure?" she asked, her tone silky, almost deceptive.

"See? Right there. Something's odd."

She frowned. "In my question?"

"No, in the energy with which you asked that question."

"You told me there was no possession."

"I did, and I stand by that, but something else is there, and I don't know what it is."

She let out a deep breath and said, "Fine. When do we have a go at it?"

"I vote for right now."

She bolted to her feet, spilling tea everywhere. She put down her cup, grabbed a tea towel, and quickly mopped up the spill, without saying another word.

"Sorry. I guess I should have warned you."

"Yeah, that would have been nice," she snapped. "Especially considering you've just sprung this on me, and I haven't had a chance to determine what I want to do."

He smiled. "No, you haven't had that chance, but I'm not sure we have a whole lot of options."

At that, she glared at him. "You told me that it was a choice, that I had to give permission."

"It is a choice, but not doing it would also be a choice."

"Meaning?"

"Meaning that, if something's in there, in your energy, that you're not willing to have me go in and look for, that is a choice on your part. A choice that says you don't want to find out the truth."

At that, she sank onto the couch cushions and stared at him in shock. "That's not fair," she cried out softly.

"No, it isn't," he agreed, "and I'm sorry. That isn't how I wanted this to go, but no doubt we need to do something, and we need to do it fast."

"Before I end up on the highway again."

"Exactly. You know yourself how quickly that second event went down, and we still don't even know what happened. I do want to set up cameras here though, but I am afraid it won't be enough. I'll need your permission for that too."

"Cameras?" she repeated, sidelined by the question. She looked around. "In here?"

"Yes."

"Why?" He just waited to let her catch up on the truth, and she frowned, understanding dawning on her. "In case it happens again," she noted reluctantly.

"Exactly, and I know that's not something any of us want to consider—"

"But it's pretty hard not to," she finished for him.

"Yes. I'm sorry. If there was any other way, I would be quite happy to do that."

"Yet you're not sure."

"No, I'm not sure at all, and that's also why I would want to bring in a specialist."

"Dr. Maddy?"

"Yes."

"*Great*," she muttered, hesitating. "Have you tried to contact me the way that we did in the hospital?"

"I have," he confirmed, "and you don't appear to be answering."

She blinked. "*Great*, it's like learning another language, and apparently I've already missed some of the basics."

"I think you jumped into something that you probably knew before, but, for whatever reason, you have pushed away your skill set."

"That doesn't sound terribly good." She frowned. "Is that what this is all about? Are you trying to figure out who and what I was before?"

"That's part of it. I mean, when you think about it, an awful lot is going on here that we don't understand, but I think you do, somewhere underneath it all."

She leaned back into the couch and just stared off into the distance.

He studied her energy as closely and as best he could, but this wasn't his field, not his forte. Now, if she would create a storm of energy, that was a whole different story. He could jump into that and lasso it into something usable, no problem. But this? This was something he didn't have a clue how to deal with. He was just working with his hunches, hoping to punt it all to Dr. Maddy or Stefan. Hurricane watched and waited.

"How long would it take to set it up?" she asked.

"I would need just Dr. Maddy, and that is dependent on her time frame."

"She's one busy lady, isn't she?"

"Yes, she is, and trust me, not just locally but globally."

Jewel blinked several times, as she tried to decipher what he'd just said. "Right. Because, if she can do whatever it is you want her to do from wherever she is, she can probably do it for people all over the world."

"Exactly," he murmured. "So the question is, do I have your permission?"

"Tell me something, Hurricane. If I say no, what will you do?"

He hesitated and then spoke. "I would probably keep trying to convince you and also try to get Stefan in to help persuade you."

"It's that important, *huh*?"

"Yes, but the question you really need to look at is why discovering these answers isn't important to you."

CHAPTER 24

J EWEL STARED AT Hurricane, her thoughts confused, and yet, at the same time, she heard that kernel of truth in his words. Eventually she nodded. "Fine," she whispered. "If that's the case, the sooner, the better."

He got up and pulled out his phone, as she sank back into the couch, drawing the blanket around her. If it was as simple as what Maddy had done before, then it should be over quickly, and she might not have any problem with this. The fact that ending up on the highway naked might repeat again and again in her world was terrifying. If she had some *block*, as he'd called it, something that was beyond comprehension, she wanted to know about it. And, if it had something to do with her own erratic actions, as he clearly suspected, she needed to know about it. Above all else, she needed to understand the root of this evil.

She was still curled up on the couch when he returned.

"Thankfully, it's good timing," he murmured, as he sat down beside her, adjusting the blanket so it covered her better. "Maddy is just getting prepared."

She nodded. "I can't imagine what her life is like."

He flashed her a grin. "All of our lives are different," he noted, his gaze still intent on her, as if looking for a sign that she was something other than what she really thought she was.

"And Drew is really her partner?"

"Her husband. They got married in a quiet ceremony on an island off the coast, a special island at that. They stayed for almost a week, out in the middle of nowhere, just communing with the animals."

"Animals or mammals?"

"In this case, both," he replied, with a chuckle.

"That would have been very special."

"It was. I can always take you in some day and meet them."

"That would be lovely," she said, and then she frowned. "But that would mean that you wanted to stick around and to get to know who I really was, without all this stuff going on."

"I absolutely do," he confirmed, looking at her. "Or have you really not figured that out by now?" He laid his hand beside her, palm up.

Instinctively she put hers into it, looking at their joined hands. "It seems half the time that you're suspicious of me, so that has made me wary of you."

"Of course, and I don't know that *suspicious of you* is quite how I would put it. Suspicious of what's going on, definitely," he explained in the gentlest of voices.

"You always talk to me like I'm some injured twelve-year-old," she said. "I'm really not, and I'm much stronger than you think."

"That's good, and I hope so because it looks like we'll be heading for some kind of a rough finish."

"Tonight?" she asked, bolting upright.

He squeezed her hand and, with his other hand, gently nudged her back down again. "No, this is more of a fact-finding mission."

But something in his voice made her feel that there was more to this than she was sensing. "What if you find something?"

"It depends on what we find."

"Right." She turned her gaze to look at the safe. Even now she felt the artifacts calling to her. "I hate to say it, but I still want to grab that necklace and put it on."

He nodded. "That's one of the things I'm hoping to break you free of."

"Tonight?" she asked, her gaze going back to him once again.

"Not so much tonight, as throughout this process."

Not a whole lot she could argue with in that.

"But I have to have your permission."

"You have it for that," she said. "I don't know what this is." She waited for him to add something more.

When his phone buzzed, he looked over at her.

She swallowed. "I presume that means it's time."

He nodded. "It's time, so I want you to just lie here and relax."

She stared at him. "If our positions were reversed, would you be able to do that?"

He thought about it for a long moment, shrugged, and admitted, "I believe I would buckle down and give it hell."

She gave him a feral grin. "Yeah, I am working on that." She closed her eyes and went through a series of mantras to try to get herself to relax. When he gently unfurled her clenched fists, she realized she was failing terribly.

"It'll be fine."

She didn't open her eyes but squeezed his hand. "If you can keep holding my hand like that, it will make this easier." He did, and she relaxed slightly, feeling some semblance of calm easing over her. She didn't know if it was him, Dr. Maddy, both of them, or neither, but regardless it was working.

Jewel took a deep breath and sank farther into the couch. She took another breath and another, and, before she realized it, she was floating in some weird space. She heard Hurricane in her mind, saying, *That's perfect, just stay like that. Relax, float, and think about happier times.*

She didn't respond, unsure if she was supposed to, and just watched as clouds floated overhead and the sun beckoned in the distance. It was peaceful, warm. There was a light breeze, and the air smelled fresh and felt easy, as it glided over her skin, feeling alive under its touch.

She looked down at her hands, noting that she still held Hurricane's hand, even here. Then she realized an energy flow going from her hand to his. Like a bright light, she was lit up like a Christmas tree, with a million strings running up and down her body. As she looked over at his hand, she realized his arm extended into the distance, as if not an arm so much as … She wasn't sure, but like a thread—or a cord perhaps.

She sure didn't know how it all worked, but the energy from his hand to hers flowed easily, and then went back up his arm and disappeared into the distance.

Despite the bizarre lightning threads, it felt right. It felt like this was meant to be. She closed her eyes and let out a happy sigh. If she could just stay here, like this, she knew that her life would be peaceful and calm forever.

At that thought, her eyelids popped open. Maybe this was forever. Was this heaven? Was this hell? Or was this just the stasis in between? She had no idea; she'd never been dead before. She almost laughed at that because of course she had.

She'd been dead for a couple days, according to what the doctor had said during her first of two recent hospital stays. And now here she was, floating in this weird space, wondering if she'd been here before.

She searched her surroundings to see if anything was familiar, if anything made her heart smile with recognition. Something was comforting about this place, but it wasn't so much that she knew it as much as she recognized it. Maybe from a book or a dream or even a vision.

She wasn't sure how to put this recognition into words. The three energy workers all seemed to think she had more skills than she would acknowledge, but she had no idea what they were talking about. Yet she'd managed to lift her soul, her spirit up and out of her body in the hospital this last time, plus had spoken with Hurricane mentally. That was a telepathic connection, according to the research she had done, when he wasn't watching.

That research had taken her down a rabbit hole of various kinds, but she knew none of those research papers or articles in any way described what she was currently experiencing. The sense of well-being continued, and her body glowed with this golden light. She wasn't sure whether that was her light or Dr. Maddy's or even Hurricane's. When she heard Dr. Maddy's comforting voice in her mind, she smiled. *Thanks for acknowledging your presence.*

Hey, it's the least I can do, the other woman replied softly. *We're really here to help. You know that.*

You are, she murmured. *I'm not sure about Hurricane.*

At that, a jolt in the energy stream came from him to her. *You better believe it,* he replied, his voice strong and caring. *I wouldn't be here if this wasn't what was best for you.*

She smiled. *Every child feels the same way when their par-*

ents force them to take their medicine because it's good for them,* she murmured.

I get it, he noted. *This is very foreign to you.*

At that, Dr. Maddy whispered, *Or maybe not so foreign at all. You're very in tune with this. You're very … comfortable, and you seem to have already adapted. I can flow through your system easily.*

That's a good thing, isn't it? Jewel asked, then noted Maddy's hesitation. *Not such a good thing then?* she asked in a dry tone. She wondered at no one being upset or even questioning her words. *You tell me then,* she murmured. *What does it mean?*

Dr. Maddy hesitated still for a moment, then murmured, *I sense a wall here. I sensed something when I was in last time, but I was more concerned about helping you to heal and to get back to full awareness of what was going on.*

Is this wall blocking my memories?

It could be, yes, she answered, *and it could also be blocking your history. It could be blocking what happened to you when you died, and it could be trying to keep you safe.*

So, it is my own creation, or … is it something somebody else has done?

What you need to remember, Dr. Maddy began, her voice hesitant, yet soothing, *is that, even if it is from somebody else, you have allowed it.*

At that, Jewel sucked in her breath, but immediately Hurricane sent more calming energy to pacify her fight-or-flight response.

It's all right, he told her. *We're working away on checking everything out. I know what Dr. Maddy just said came as a bit of a shock, but, even if it turns out to be somebody else's energy, it really just means that it's probably somebody you knew, somebody you cared about. It's very common within relation-ships to have an exchange, so to speak, of energy.*

And in bad relationships? Jewel asked.

In that case, Maddy explained, *we have what's known as hooks, and hooks can exist in good relationships too. The trouble comes when it starts becoming more about one person versus the other.*

What do you mean? Jewel asked.

When somebody is needier than the other, they'll have a hook that drains a little more energy from the one person, and sometimes you give a little too much to that needy person, so you feed that hook a little more than you should. So, when they leave, you're tired, or, when they go to sleep, you can cut back that flow and rest and reenergize yourself.

But there isn't anybody in my life like that.

No, so that means it's from your history. This wall of yours, Dr. Maddy noted, her voice sounding more distant, *I'm standing in front of it.*

What? You are?

Dr. Maddy replied, *Think about me, think about the wall, and picture yourself standing beside me.*

Jewel blinked at that, but suddenly she was there, look-ing at a beautiful woman standing beside her. *Maddy?* she asked.

Yes, that's me, Maddy replied. *It's hard to see my features though, isn't it?*

It is and it isn't, Jewel noted. *You're tall. You have long dark hair. Your skin is beautiful, but it's the glow around you that I recognize.*

At that, Dr. Maddy laughed gently. *That's my energy. Now, with me beside you, turn and look at the wall in front of you. You will have to think that you are actually looking at it.*

When Jewel turned, this craggy monster of a cliff sat in front of her. *Good God.* She reached out a hand and Maddy grasped it in hers.

Maddy said, *Take a moment to look at it first. Do you see that it's sheer-faced, so you can't climb it? Do you see that it's smooth, so you can't reach for anything to hang on to? Do you see how hard it is, without even touching it?*

Jewel nodded. *It looks like rock, like granite of some kind.*

It's darker than that, but it could be, Maddy noted. *This is in your mind, and it's been here all this time.* Then Maddy stopped, uncertain. *Hurricane?*

I'm right here.

At that, Jewel looked on the other side of Maddy to see Hurricane physically, just as she would have seen him in the loft, if her eyes were open. He stood there, his hands on his hips, staring at the wall.

What's the matter with the wall? he asked curiously.

It gives the appearance of being old, Maddy noted, *but here's the kicker. It's not.*

No, it's not, Hurricane agreed, pointing to the edges, where they were still being formed.

So, who's creating this? Jewel asked, stunned, as she watched the wall get bigger and wider right before her eyes. *Why is it building up more and more, when I want to clear it down?*

Because it knows we're here, Dr. Maddy stated softly. *It's preparing to withstand an attack.*

But wait. Hang on, Jewel cried out. *This is my … It's my head we're talking about.*

It's your soul, Maddy corrected. *It's your energy.*

So, if it's preparing to withstand an attack, and if it knows it's us and that we're all standing here, … then who is it that's building it up? Jewel cried out.

They both turned to look at her.

My best guess, Maddy replied gently, *is you.*

Hurricane looked at Jewel and added, *You are fortifying the wall, even as we stand before it.*

HURRICANE WATCHED THE shock waves hit Jewel.

She immediately held up her hands, trying to disconnect from the whole thing. He reached out and grabbed both of them.

Easy, he said. *Remember. We're not here to attack it. You don't have to fight us off.*

She stilled, then looked up at him, her gaze going from Maddy to him and back to Maddy again. *But it feels like an attack. Everything inside of me is shrinking.*

They both nodded.

Look around you, Maddy said.

The wall was still craggy, dark, and foreboding in front of Jewel, but, as she looked back and up, the rock seemed to be expanding all around her. The meadow was gone. The sun was gone. The fluffy white clouds were no more, and, instead of the light breeze, there was darkness and a ravaging storm.

She tilted her head and could feel raindrops splashing on her face, but they came faster and faster, until it came in a sheet, a hard pouring deluge from the storm.

Hurricane whispered, *You're creating this, Jewel. You're doing this.*

She shook her head in denial. *That's not possible. … I can't be. I don't know how. I'm not like you two.*

At that, Dr. Maddy reached out a hand to them, joining

theirs, which were still entwined. *You are an incredibly powerful energy worker,* she declared, *and at a skill level I find astronomical.*

Jewel opened her eyes, and, with a head jolt, the storm completely stopped. She stared at Maddy and Hurricane, their eyes glowing like orbs. *You're the ones who handle the energy in here. Maybe that was you two.*

Hurricane shook his head. *No, but—because I can recognize that kind of energy, that storm of strong emotions—that's how I know it was you.*

So what's going on? Jewel whispered. *If I can do all this, why have I not torn down that wall? I wanted it gone, so, why is it growing?*

Hurricane spoke. *You haven't torn it down because you're the one who built it. Whatever is behind that wall is something that you don't want us to see. You especially don't want to see it yourself.*

CHAPTER 25

EVERYTHING HURRICANE AND Maddy had said buffeted against Jewel, like a different storm, wave after wave after wave. She squeezed their hands. *I feel like I'm being torn apart.*

You are, Maddy confirmed. *Whatever is going on here is tearing you apart in so many ways. You'll have to let go and tear down that wall. I mean, not some half-assed effort, but really take it down for good.*

No, I can't, Jewel screamed. *You don't understand.*

No, we don't understand at all, Hurricane agreed, *but we want to, and we're here to help.*

At that, Jewel continued to scream.

He gently stroked her temple, and something soothing and calm immediately spread through her.

She opened her eyes. *That's you,* she whispered.

Yes, it's me. You need to calm down, so we can deal with this.

She shuddered. *Can't you feel the danger? Can't you see it? Can't you sense it?*

He stiffened, looked around, and, in a low tone, whispered, *Maddy?*

Yes, she replied, *I see it too.*

At that, Jewel turned, staring around in confusion. Then she saw dark shadows, creeping in toward them, and she cried out, *See? They're there. They're all there.*

They absolutely are, Maddy agreed. She whispered to Hurricane, *I might need to call in Stefan.*

Hurricane nodded. *You do you,* he said. *My hands will be very full, very soon.*

Maddy watched as he stared, his gaze glowing. He studied the shadows, the darkness all around, crouching stronger and stronger.

It's him, Jewel cried out, shuddering.

Hurricane gripped her hands. *Push back against the darkness, Jewel,* Hurricane prodded her urgently. *Fill yourself with love. Fill yourself with joy, sunlight, sunshine, think of happy things. Think of puppy dogs and kittens and all the good things in life,* he whispered, staying calm, yet he was quick with ideas, hoping something would trigger her to be happy. She stared up at him, and he demanded, *Do it now.* She blinked and tried, she really did. Just so hard to get control of her thoughts, especially when all this had triggered such an overwhelming fear, and it was all crowding her.

Now, he murmured, again and again.

Slowly, with the thoughts and his help, she pushed back against the darkness, feeling her soul and everything in front of her open up and push outward, sending the darkness, the shadows, or whatever it was, whoever it was out there, back into the darkness again. She shuddered, collapsing against him.

He held her, filling her soul with energy, and whispered, *See? I knew you could do that.*

I did it, she said triumphantly. She looked up at him and grinned. *But…* Then her smile fell away. *He knows that we're here.*

Yes, he does, but so do you.

She stared at the wall. *Are you saying I have to go behind that wall?*

No, I'm not saying that at all, Hurricane replied. *We are definitely not going behind that wall.*

Why not?

Because, if you do, if we do, none of us will come back out anytime soon. You need to bring it to the ground, once and for all.

How do I do that? She looked around and shook her head. *I don't have any tools, not even a hammer. But you almost need like a bulldozer or something to smash this to bits.*

That would be one way, yes, Hurricane agreed, *but chances are you would rebuild it faster and faster anyway.*

Is that possible? she asked, her voice turning distant. She turned to look at where Maddy was earlier, wondering if she could help. But the golden glow, with the light mint green that was Maddy, was almost stilled, vibrating in place. *What is Dr. Maddy doing?* Jewel asked.

She's trying to get the tone, the melody, of the energy. It's a relatively new thing that she's working on.

This energy, it has music to it?

It has notes to it. It's held together and sends off a vibrational sound, and, if Maddy can disrupt that vibrational sound and weaken it slightly, she might help you to bring it down.

What about Stefan? Jewel cried out. *Maddy said she would get his help.*

Yeah, and it's with Stefan's help that she's doing this right now.

Jewel grabbed Hurricane's hands. *I'm scared.*

He pulled her close, so they both stood in the same golden light, then whispered, *I know, but we can do this. For your sake, you need to do this. No other way for you to ever be free.*

She let out a slow deep breath, feeling that same sense of knowing inside her. *No, you're right. It's hard, like I don't … I don't even know what to say. But you're right, it's time.*

Maddy turned, and, without any sign of a physical body, the words came from her, almost menacing, *Yes, it's time.* She reached out a hand, yet it wasn't a hand so much as a glowing wisp of energy.

Hurricane lifted both of Jewel's hands and moved them toward Maddy. *Reach for her,* he told Jewel. *Reach for Maddy.*

Jewel knew it was time, that some storm waited for her, and yet she must do it. This storm was inevitable, but she grabbed on and clung to Hurricane. *Don't let go.*

I won't, sweetheart. Don't you worry. I won't. This is my specialty.

She reached out with her other hand and connected with Maddy. Instantly she was tossed into a violence that she hadn't expected, her body buffeted from side to side, up and down, a storm raging over her and around her. She cried out, *Hurricane?*

I'm here, sweetheart, he replied, his voice steadfast.

I'm here too, Dr. Maddy whispered.

Farther away, Jewel heard Stefan. *I'm here too. We're all here to help.*

Maddy turned Jewel gently toward the massive wall in front of her. Even now, she could barely see through the wind blasting at her eyes. The wall itself looking even worse, more impenetrable than ever.

How do I release this? Jewel asked.

Close your eyes and step into it, Maddy instructed. *You cannot tear it down. You cannot go around it. It continues to build wider and wider,* she noted. *You must go through it.*

The words made Jewel laugh because, of course, the only way was to go through it—metaphorically, but physically? That was also impossible to do. They were asking her to do an impossible thing. But somehow, with their supportive force behind her, her feet moved her closer and closer toward this horrific wall of darkness. Even as she got closer, it began its creepy, almost slimy movements that made her cry out in fear.

Just touch it, Stefan stated. *Feel the recognition as it hits your soul, understand what this is, and realize you are already one with it. You don't have to do anything. You are already here. Just be with it, be one with it.*

With Hurricane and Maddy speaking over and over again, almost like a mantra, Jewel slowly reached out with her hand, the one still holding Hurricane's, and touched the wall. As soon as she did, she was caught up in the middle of it. Stuck between the walls.

She cried out, *It's got me. It's got me.*

Yes, Hurricane agreed. *It's got you, and it's got me.*

She turned to find he was here, caught in the same storm that she was. *Can you get us out?* Her cries were urgent.

No, he replied, yet his voice calm. *I'm not getting us out, not without your assistance. You'll have to help me get us out.*

No, I can't. I can't, she wailed. *This is what you do, fight storms, right? You're supposed to do this.*

I can't, he stated. *This is your energy. This is all you.*

You need to do this, Jewel, Dr. Maddy whispered.

Need to or have to? Jewel asked.

Both, Hurricane said. *Otherwise we are stuck here together.*

For a moment she wondered if that would be so bad.

But he squeezed her hand and whispered, *Yes, it would be terrible. A whole life awaits us out there, a life together.*

She shook her head. *You don't know anything about me.*

Honey, I know a lot about you, and the rest I'm willing to learn over time.

She wanted to believe him. She wanted to believe that something good would come of all this that was salvageable.

Close your eyes, Hurricane whispered. *Just try. Take another step forward and then another, until you get through to the other side. But don't just go through. Think of it crumbling down, away from you, forever.*

She closed her eyes and willed her legs to move forward, first one and then the other, but they wouldn't budge. She struggled, feeling everything closing in on her.

Don't struggle, he said urgently. *You command this space. You* are *this space. Don't let it walk all over you. You can do this, Jewel. Don't let yourself become a victim of your own consciousness.*

She stilled at that. *You mean, I need to take control.*

You need to take control, yes, he agreed. *You can do this. You've done it many, many times. You're incredibly powerful. You're incredibly capable. This is your creation. Don't let fear choke you right now, not when you're on the cusp of finding out exactly what's going on.*

She slowly nodded. *I can do this,* she said, but it lacked conviction.

You can *do this,* he repeated, bolstering her up. *Close your eyes, take a breath, realize who you are. Claim it. Claim what you can do, what you've already done, and take control of this.*

She opened her eyes, closed them again, and whispered, *I can do this. I can do this.* As she repeated it over and over again, it was like a ball of energy building up, higher and higher inside her, getting stronger.

She flung her arms apart, tossing Hurricane's hand aside,

and cried out, *I can do this.*

A series of explosions came all around her.

Hurricane immediately grabbed her hand, pulled her up tight, and whispered, *Hang on, sweetheart. It'll be a rough ride for a bit.*

She was picked up, still in his arms, and the two of them were tossed into the hurricane, flung from side to side, and spun out of control. She screamed and tried to hang on, but his voice guiding her kept her sanity intact.

He whispered, *We're almost through it, just hold tight.*

She shuddered, closing her eyes against the maelstrom threatening to completely destroy her, as she clung to him with all her might. A sheer force exploded from her, and suddenly the wind stopped, and the pressure was gone. She lifted her head and looked around and looked up at him.

We're in the eye of the storm, he noted gently.

She shuddered. *You say that as if that's a good thing.*

It is a good thing, he confirmed.

No, it means we still have to get to the other side.

He wrapped his arms around her, leaned down, kissed her gently. *Absolutely, and that's even more important now because we can't stay here.*

Why not? she cried out. *We could just stay. It's perfect. We wouldn't have to deal with any of this. We wouldn't have to deal with any of life. We could just be here and exist in this space.*

No way, Hurricane argued. *I want everything out there available for us to exist in the real world, not like this, not as a fragment of ourselves.*

She stared up at him, and he immediately shook his head.

No, we are not cowards. We will not hide in the shadows.

We will take control of this and will let it take us to the safe harbor on the other side.

You promise there will be a safe harbor? she murmured.

Oh, I promise. He smiled and immediately stepped her forward into the other side of the hurricane.

Once again, she was buffeted by this world, the storm, the cold, icy shards hitting her constantly. Then suddenly silence came again. She peeked out, and they were in this weird gray world. She looked up at him. *Where are we?*

He frowned and shook his head. *I'm not sure.*

At that, she stiffened, looked around, and asked, *Are we lost?*

No, I think, more to the point, we're found.

I don't think I like the sound of that.

No, maybe not, he agreed, his voice cautious. He looked around and said, *Call for Maddy.*

Maddy, are you there?

Only silence came.

What does that mean? Jewel cried out. *Where's Dr. Maddy? Where's Stefan?*

Oh, they'll be around here somewhere, but it seems like, for some reason, we've been isolated from them.

She shuddered. *That's not good.*

No, I don't think it's good at all. The better question is, what is so bad about it?

Nothing, a stranger said behind them. *It's a perfect place to stay, and I am so glad you could join us.*

HURRICANE, HOLDING FAST to the woman in his arms, turned slowly to stare at another woman in front of him. *Rhea, I suppose.* He felt more than saw Jewel stiffen in his arms.

Rhea looked at him, then slowly nodded. *Oh, this is lovely. You know who I am.*

No, not really, Hurricane corrected her. *I know of you.*

Right, some of those files were a little bit confusing, weren't they?

More than a little, he replied cautiously. He looked down at Jewel, who stared at the woman. *Do you recognize her?*

I don't know, Jewel said hesitantly.

You can do better than that, Rhea replied, with a laugh. *I mean, it might take you a little bit to clear the cobwebs out of that brain of yours, but that brain has always been pretty impressive.*

Then Hurricane knew, and he stared at her. *You're her mother.*

Rhea looked at him intently, and her eyes glowed with an otherworldly knowledge, as she nodded slowly. *Wow, I really wasn't expecting this. Finding out that she could come here is one thing, but finding out that you could come here with her is something completely different. But finding that you know who I am?* Rhea stopped and contemplated him. *I must think about this.*

No time to think, he stated instantly.

Why not? Rhea demanded. *It's not as if you're going anywhere.*

But behind Rhea, Hurricane saw a slight glow of energy. *Not true. We won't be staying.*

Yes, you are, Rhea declared, then laughed. *Do you really think I would allow you to be here if this wasn't where I wanted you to be?*

Maybe, Hurricane said, *but she's your daughter. Is this really the life you want for her?*

Of course. She's more powerful than I ever was. Rhea shrugged. *She just hasn't come into her full power yet.*

Yet that full power is for Jewel to wield, not you.

Rhea glared at him. *That's not true. Out there in the world, we had no power. We were just victims all the time. Victims of men, like you, taking advantage of us. How fair is that world? But here, we are somebody. In here we have something, have everything.*

He noted other faces were slowly forming around him.

She nodded. *You really don't know anything.*

No, but I'm starting to. They're your victims, aren't they?

She stiffened. *Like hell,* she sneered. *Typical male, who thinks he knows everything.*

He knew he was close, he just didn't quite understand it all. *Why don't you explain it to Jewel, give her a choice?*

No, because she's not mine yet. She's still confused. I need a little more time to convince her of all this. But look at what we've created.

He turned to see at least a dozen women, if not twice that, surrounding them. He kept funneling out strong, loving, healing energy, trying to give Stefan and Dr. Maddy a pathway to find him and Jewel. He still held several of their strands of energy as a guide for them to get through this to him, and he could see bits and pieces, but they were being crowded out by all these other energies.

It's not good enough, Hurricane said. *She deserves to live a full life, not this shadow existence.*

She doesn't know what she wants, but what I know is that she is very strong and that she could do all kinds of things for us. And we're only now understanding how much we can do ourselves. Rhea laughed. *We can't give up that kind of control.*

You mean, you won't, Hurricane argued, his voice harder. *They are following you, but maybe you didn't even give them a choice.*

They have no choice here either, she murmured. *We are all victims.*

Some of you more than others, Hurricane stated, looking at her. *Some of them don't have a clue what happened. Others don't want to look at what happened.*

Rhea burst out laughing. *Oh, well done. Don't you think you're clever?* And she chuckled again. *Look. Even my daughter is numb to all this. It'll take her quite a while, years really, to sort through what's just happened. We'll have to work on her, but I've already prepped the others that she was coming, and, now that she's here, we can help her, just like I helped them.*

Like you helped them to death, to this existence?

Better than what they had, she murmured. *But you wouldn't understand that. You were part of that world that took advantage of us.*

He could only surmise how bad it was from what she said, but obviously it had made quite a difficult life for her. *And your daughter?* he asked. *Is this really what you want for her?*

Absolutely, and I didn't even know it until I felt her energy. We were dormant for so long, and then that fool sent us to her for repairs. The best thing he ever did. Of course I might have had a hand in that, but, hey, he doesn't know anything about it. He doesn't have a clue what's going on, and that's the way we want to keep it. She's my daughter. She's special to me, not to him. He doesn't get to have her.

So, that's all you want? Possession? You don't care about what's important to her? You just want to make sure that you have what you want, so you can use Jewel's power? Hurricane asked.

Rhea shrugged. *It's only fair. I didn't get to raise her. I didn't get to have all those years with her.*

No, she was raised by your sister, wasn't she?

Rhea sniffed at that. *My sister is a mess.*

Still, she raised your daughter, doing the best she could.

Sure, but that wasn't my fault.

Wasn't it? I mean, the fight, when it happened, your death when it happened, did you not try to grab Jewel to try to save yourself?

Of course I did. Rhea stared at him. *Why wouldn't I?*

Oh, I don't know. Maybe you should have been a real mother and tried to save her, instead of just yourself.

But she was young. I was going to take her with me, Rhea explained, her voice more contemplative than upset.

You would take her with you into death?

Why not? It's not as if life offered us anything. She gave a hard laugh. *And, by the way, all your attempts to drag out the time here isn't working. We'll go now, but you on the other hand?* You *we don't need. We don't want you at all.*

Why? Because I'm male?

Partly, and also because you're too strong, and we would never be able to control you. I'm not even sure how you got through all those storms as it is.

Because it's what I do. It's who I am.

She stiffened and glared at him. *Now we definitely don't want you.*

Too bad because I'm here, and I'm not going anywhere without Jewel.

You can't take her. She's my daughter. I have the connection to her, and you don't.

You're wrong there, Hurricane argued. *She has a connection to me, to her life back there, and we need you to separate, so she can come back and live a normal life. So she is free to rejoice at being good at what she does. She's a hell of an artist and a jewelry designer. You know that, right?*

Of course, she's my daughter, Rhea replied carelessly.

But you don't care about her. You only care about gaining her energy and gaining her ability. That's all you want.

Rhea stiffened and glared at him. *That's why you want her too,* she snapped, *but she's my daughter, and she comes with me.*

No, I don't think so. Hurricane already felt energies tugging at the woman in his arms. He whispered to Jewel, *Remember. Love is the answer. You cannot fight these women. Hurting people tend to hurt other people. They're in pain. They've suffered a lot. They're crying out, attracted to the goodness of your energy. She was your mother for a short time, but she's not anymore. No true mother would do any of this to their child.*

He felt Jewel stiffen in his arms, but he stroked her gently, trying to fill her mind with joy and love. *You need to get to the other side of that wall and see what's there. To really see what's there.* She looked up at him, shuddering, her eyes overwhelmed in pain, and he nodded. *Let me help you.*

He could see the storm, the argument, the fear, and then the acquiescence, and she nodded. *Help me,* she whispered. *Help me now.*

Hurricane closed his eyes and thrust the two of them together back into the storm. Almost instantly he heard the screams behind them, as somebody tried to rip Jewel from him. But he bound her as tightly as he could, knowing that Rhea's dark energy was so strong and had survived for decades, fueled by hate and revenge, just waiting for this opportunity, waiting for the chance to steal Jewel, to deny her a true life.

Just the thought of what Rhea could do, what she had already done, was enough to terrify him.

Energy swirled angrily around them.

Hurricane pushed harder and faster, calling out to Maddy and to Stefan to help get them to the other side of the storm. Hurricane felt dark energy clawing at his back, clawing at Jewel.

He wrapped her up, looked down at her, and whispered, *Hold this thought.* He lowered his head and kissed her, pouring love and his soul into her being, entwining the two of them so tightly together that they were one, one energy that only something so equally powerful could pull back on. It was one thing to pull a single energy; it was another to pull another one like him, especially as grounded as he was, grounded in the knowledge of all the things he'd seen over the years. Grounded in the knowledge of what souls tried to do, even when there was no reason, no rhyme, and no possibility of success.

The same dark forces screamed at him, and then Jewel did something that warmed his heart. The absolute soul of her, the specialness that made her who she was, suddenly poured upward, kissing him back, filling his body with her soul, filling his soul with her heart and the specialness that made them each so unique in this world.

The two of them wrapped up together were a force to be reckoned with, and then Jewel reached out a hand and whispered, *Maddy, Stefan.*

Suddenly the four of them were together, and the dark energies screamed with one last powerful push, then drained away.

Jewel stood shuddering in Hurricane's arms.

And he held her, then whispered, *Open your eyes.*

She looked around and asked, *The storm is over?*

We're on the other side, he told her. *We survived that.*

She laughed, stepped back slightly, looked up at him, and her eyes twinkled. *That was a hell of a storm you created, mister.*

I didn't create it, he replied.

At that, her voice dropped deep, as she whispered, *Was that really my mother?*

Yes, and you need to turn around and take a look. You're on the other side of the wall now.

She turned. His arms dropped, as he stepped away to give her a moment. She studied everything around her. *What is this?* she whispered.

It's the wall that you put up to save yourself, Maddy explained, as she stepped forward. *It's the wall we were trying to get you to open up so that we could help you.*

Jewel looked around and frowned, shaking her head. *Are you saying that my mother contacted me? From the dead, … from wherever the hell she is?*

Yes, she contacted you, Maddy explained, *and you recognized the energy. You didn't know quite what had happened or how to protect yourself, so you did the best thing you could. You hid.*

You created this whole new persona, and you hid, Stefan added.

I don't understand.

I know, Hurricane spoke for them all. *It's pretty amazing actually, and what you've just managed to do is phenomenal.*

She stared at him, looked around, and shook her head. *You're standing here in front of me in my living room. That's phenomenal, but I don't understand. Could I learn to do this?*

You're already three-quarters of the way there, Stefan declared, gently searching her. *How do you feel?*

Empty, yet alive and whole in some weird way.

Not quite yet. Hurricane looked around at the living room and at the safe and asked Jewel, *And the necklace. How is it to you?*

She shrugged. *It's just a necklace now.*

Yes. Exactly. It has no power. It has no strength now.

She hesitated, staring at Hurricane, her gaze searching as she whispered, *What about my mother?*

First, do you see this loft, your studio?

She nodded. *Yes, of course I do.*

It's not real.

Her shock was audible.

Stefan reached out a hand and whispered, *Hurricane means it. This room is another creation of yours, Jewel.*

CHAPTER 26

J EWEL STARED AT the three of them and shook her head. Then she turned to Hurricane. *What do you mean?*

All this that has happened over the last few days, everything that's happened, it's all been in your mind. Created by you in this gray space of your own, where you get to design everything, all in order to make a world that's easier than what you had before. And that maze I was caught in? After meeting Rhea, I wondered if it was her trap. But now I know better. It was your security perimeter, guarding your gray space. I got that far. I think I earned your trust that day.

She looked at him in disbelief.

Now I need you to be really brave. I need you to wake up.

When Hurricane held out his hand, she looked at it, looked at the others, and asked, *What do you mean?*

Try it, grab my hand, and wake up.

She swallowed, slowly put her hand in his, her mind in tumult, as she absorbed some of what he just said.

Almost immediately everything changed.

The smell was different; the feel of her body was different. She opened her eyes and sat upright, and there in front of her was Hurricane, their hands still joined. But, as she looked around, she realized she was in a hospital, lying in a hospital bed. Two glowing orbs were beside him, but they weren't people.

She stared at them and whispered out loud, "Maddy?" The first orb, almost a white mint green, twinkled.

And then to the golden one, she whispered, "Stefan?" He twinkled back at her.

"Oh my God." Jewel looked around again at the hospital room. She stared at the sheet covering her and whispered, "What happened?"

"This is where you really are. All the rest, everything— the loft apartment, you being taken out to the highway the second time—are all just creations of your mind," Hurricane stated, sitting down beside her.

She shook her head. "That's not possible," she cried out. "None of that is possible." She stared at the three energy workers. "How would I have even known who you were or what you were, Hurricane, not to mention how to contact you or what you look like."

Hurricane smiled. "Because of Stefan. He sent you an image of who I was and that I would be there to help, and then, somewhere along the line"—he gazed toward Stefan— "you ended up attacked and out on the highway and then came to be here in the hospital."

"That attack," she asked, "I made that up too?"

So much bitterness filled her voice that he leaned over, picked up her hand, kissed it gently, and said, "No, you didn't. That first attack was brought about by the pearls, physically by the owner of the pearls being induced by the energy of the pearls, making him do it. He's in a psych ward right now, trying to figure out what happened to him. They have him on tape, stripping you down and taking you out to the highway, leaving you and taking off. Believe me. He's already more than traumatized by the effects of the pearls, just as you were."

"And me?"

"You knew what was happening. You knew who was coming for you. You knew it was your mother, and you knew that she already had a way into your energy, simply by birth, by being the person who brought you into this world. It's a bond that is almost impossible to separate, so you did what you had to do to protect yourself. You built a wall that she couldn't penetrate. You built a wall that she couldn't get over or come around in any way. She couldn't blast through it because you were too strong. Yet, at the same time, you couldn't figure out how to get back to the world you had left. It was too hard, too confusing. You were in a maze, one spiraling out of control. A maze that you couldn't find your way through, but you knew that Stefan was sending somebody to help. So when I arrived you knew who I was."

Her headshake of denial was automatic. Yet his words resonated deep inside. That didn't stop the confusion roiling through her. "Stefan …" She remembered her call for help to him before all this. "He did more than just tell me that he was sending someone, didn't he? And when you say that you arrived," she cried out, "how did you know? How did you find me? Did they help? How? I don't understand."

"Stefan and Dr. Maddy have special abilities. They can merge with the aura of an injured person to move through their system to help them. They've been here, watching over you the entire time. They also have the ability to travel with another's energy, … like mine. Like when I went into your maze to find you. That connection allowed us to stay in contact as well."

He hesitated, looked down at her hand, then back up to stare into Jewel's bewildered gaze. "It's what I do. When the storms take over a person," he explained, "I'm the one who walks through the storm to keep the soul within safe. But, when I arrived, you were in this make-believe world that you had created—for your own safety, mind you. You even made huge orders of Chinese food that you had to overeat. All because you were burning through so much energy in order to keep up the facade and to protect yourself from that world still terrorizing you on the other side of the wall in front of you.

"Still a few of your mother's nudges, a few spirit pokes, you might say, slipped through, but you were always strong enough to reinforce those blurring edges and to keep the facade going. Although those pokes, those telepathic suggestions were enough to make you move things around, like the necklace. That was your mother's doing, by the way." He smiled at Jewel. "But this, where you are right now, this is the real world."

She felt the shock, … followed by never-ending smaller shocks rippling through her. "Stefan and Dr. Maddy knew?"

He nodded. "And were there nudging you in the direction of reality, as needed. Not that you might see it that way. But Dr. Maddy worked on you constantly to help you return to reality. After all, it was up to you. It had to be your decision, your choice. … And you made it."

He looked down at her, smiled. "Welcome back."

CHAPTER 27

J EWEL SLOWLY GOT up from the hospital bed and almost collapsed. Hurricane immediately reached for her. She looked over at him. "It seems so strange. It's as if I've known you forever."

He just smiled and didn't say anything but assisted her to the bathroom. "Are you okay from here?"

She nodded. "I will be, I just … It's been a hell of a morning."

"It's been a hell of a few days. Expect your muscles to be weak, and that sense of weakness will take a couple days to wear off."

She straightened, nodded, and said, "It'll be fine. Just give me a few minutes."

She went to the washroom, surprised when she realized that she was functioning on her own, but the nurse had departed and had left her alone in Hurricane's care. When she stepped back out again, he assessed her carefully.

"So?"

"I feel better. A lot better." She looked at him and frowned. "I have so many questions."

"I know, and we can answer them, but it'll take a bit of time. I'd like to get you home as soon as we can, but I'm not sure when that'll be."

"I don't think the doctor has any cure for me," she

quipped, with a lopsided smile.

"No, he definitely doesn't, but, at the same time, we still need clearance, so I can take you home."

"Where is home anyway? If that studio isn't really my home …"

"It's not," he confirmed, "but your house is though."

She nodded. "I wonder why I never liked that house?"

"You tell me," he said, with a chuckle.

"It never felt like home really. It was, I don't know, I don't—"

"The one you shared with that boyfriend you broke up with a while back? You stayed because you couldn't afford to go anywhere else, maybe?"

"Ah. Yeah, that makes sense. It also explains why I spend a lot of time in studios downtown, and working my whole life away in order to heal from it."

"Your show is coming up in a couple days, and the good news is that you'll be able to attend."

She stopped and asked, "Charles and Lucas? Are they real?" As Hurricane stared at her steadily, her shoulders sagged. "They were part of my imagination then?"

"Yes, … and no," he shared gently. "They were your stepbrothers, and, as it turns out, you were very close to them."

"*Were* very close to them?" she asked.

"No, you still are, but, when you created this world," he explained, "you needed to bring somebody along who cared for you and cared about you, so you brought them."

She stared at him for a long moment. "The human brain is amazing," she noted absentmindedly.

Just then a knock came on her hospital room door, and the doctor stepped in. He studied her from the doorway.

"Awfully good to see you like this. Honestly I thought you were a goner."

"Honestly I thought I was too," she said, with a half smile.

He laughed at the joke and quickly checked her over. "You need to take it easy, maybe see a doctor if you get any weird symptoms or anything. But otherwise you're good to go."

"Thank you," she replied warmly.

"We'll need to come up with some clothes. You came in without a stitch on." He looked over at Hurricane. "Will you look after her for the next few days?"

"I will," he stated. "Don't worry. She won't be alone, and I've got the clothes covered."

"Good." He shook his head. "I've seen some pretty weird things in my time, but this one was way too far out there for me. Anyway I'll go sign the forms, and you'll be good to go home." Then, just like that, he was gone.

She smiled after him. "I guess we continuously confound medical science, don't we?"

"Every time," Hurricane confirmed, with feeling. "However, they have their place in this world too."

"If you say so." She hopped up to her feet, stretched, and noted, "I feel okay."

He nodded. "You'll start to feel better and better, as every hour comes along and you get stronger."

"You mentioned clothes?"

He smiled and pointed to the bag on the floor. "We were hoping we could get you back out again, so I came prepared."

"In that case, I'll get dressed right now, so we can get out of here."

"I'll go take care of the paperwork," he offered, then hesitated at the doorway.

"I'm not going anywhere," she stated.

"Good. Nobody'll understand if you do."

"No, I know, and I'm not even sure I understand."

He nodded. "Exactly. We can deal with more questions when we get home, but let's get out of here first."

By the time she was dressed, Hurricane had the paperwork taken care of, and they were outside. She asked, "What do you have for a vehicle?"

"I have a Jeep."

She laughed. "Did I create that on my own?"

"Maybe, but most guys in my world drive Jeeps."

As she got up to it, she noted it was black too. She shook her head. "Some of this is a little too uncanny."

"I know. Don't worry about it though. This is your real life."

He led the way to her house, and, as they got out, she looked at it, frowning. "I think it's time to move."

"I think so too," he agreed. "I'm not sure what the connection was for you to be here, but I'd say that connection is dead."

She walked inside, looked around, and noted, "It's sparse, bare even."

"Yes. Apparently your boyfriend took most of his furniture when he left, and you never replaced it because you were so busy with your show."

"Great, well, at least I knew what the priority was," she said lightly.

"Absolutely."

"Besides, the good news is there won't be that much to move."

He burst out laughing at that. "Do you want to stay

here? Even for tonight? That's the next question. The whole world is your oyster, really, so you can move wherever you want to be."

She turned, then looked at him. "One of the things that you're not saying is where you live."

"I travel all over the place," he replied. "However, I live in Maine, most recently."

"I'm partial to Seattle, I think," she mentioned.

"Okay, any particular reason?"

"No, I'm not sure. Maybe I just want to travel for a bit?"

"We can do that too."

She hesitated and looked up at him. "*We?* We haven't really spoken about us."

"We haven't had a chance."

"You were always that mainstay in my world, telling me that I would get through this."

Hurricane nodded. "Yep, I had no idea that you were actually real or that your world wasn't real."

She laughed. "Yeah, that is definitely a mind-bender, even for me. What about the police?"

"Nothing left to be done at this point. As far as they're concerned, it's a closed case, and, yes, we will work at giving the man who kidnapped you some proper help."

"What about the pearls?"

Hesitating, he added, "In exchange for getting him the help, we've taken possession of the pearls, and they will be safely contained. Although they're broken, I presume they can't be revitalized with energy again. However, I don't want to take a chance, so they've gone into the museum, with the other artifacts of dark energy."

She let out a slow breath. "I'm really happy to hear that." She looked around, smiled, and shook her head. "I don't even want to stay here for another minute. I don't feel that I live here at all."

"You don't," he confirmed, "but some clothing is here and a few personal items. If you want, we can pack it up and put it in storage, then go wherever you want."

She nodded. "What about the other women? The women trapped in the pearls?"

"The connection is gone, but I would suggest that maybe, if you were up for it at some point, I could get the pearls back out again, then we could take the necklace and bracelet to this woman in New Orleans and see if she has a way of freeing the women."

"Yes, please," she agreed, spinning on a dime. "I would really like that."

"Okay. I already mentioned it to Stefan, and he thinks it's a good idea. I just don't know when would be a good time."

"No time like the present," she said immediately.

He nodded. "I could get behind that."

She looked around and shook her head. "I really don't want to stay here. Are you okay to go to a hotel for the night?"

"Absolutely."

They quickly packed up what little bit she wanted, then she looked back at the residence and murmured, "It feels to me that I only lived here halfway before."

"Maybe you only lived halfway period, looking for whatever was missing in your life," he suggested. "The good news is, you found it."

"Yeah." She smiled, reaching out a hand. "I found you."

"Absolutely," he agreed. "But also your artwork, and knowing it was all there, this sense of waiting, … that feeling should be gone."

"It is gone," she muttered. "It's a weird sensation. I feel almost too calm."

When they checked into a hotel, she looked around and smiled. "This honestly feels far more comfortable than that house."

He nodded and didn't say anything.

She walked over closer and said, "But one thing I do want to make sure of, no matter what."

"What's that?"

She looped her arms around his neck and asked, "Remember when we were in that storm and when you kissed me?" He nodded, his arms coming around her. "That felt like a blending, in a way that sex has never felt like."

He burst out laughing at that. "So true, but, at the same time, I'm pretty sure we can recreate it while making love."

"Yeah?" she asked, her eyes twinkling. "In that case, I'm all for trying."

He hesitated.

She tapped his lips and immediately argued with his silence. "Nope, I'm fine. I wouldn't mention it if you'll continue to worry about me," she declared in a scolding voice.

"What? What if I just wanted to say that you should have a couple days bed rest?"

"Oh, I like that idea very much," she said, taking him toward the bed. "Bed rest sounds perfect."

He burst out laughing and quickly reached for the buttons on his shirt. "In that case, I didn't even need to bring you any clothes to the hospital."

"I still had to get out of there wearing something," she noted. "Let's get settled, and then we'll have to order in some food later. Maybe a lot of food."

"Oh, don't tell me. Chinese?"

"Yep, absolutely., I love the stuff." She grinned at him. "Unless you want pizza."

"Maybe pizza, or we could do Chinese food for real this time."

She stopped and looked at him in wonder. "It felt so real."

Hurricane nodded. "Believe me. For me too. I was constantly amazed at the abilities you had."

"All that doubt in your eyes, what was that?"

"That was you," he replied, with a chuckle. "Knowing that something was fake about everything going on, but not having the wherewithal to understand how and why."

"So even then I was trying to figure it out?" Jewel asked him.

"Absolutely," he murmured. He walked up behind her, his chest bare. "You want to finish undressing, or shall I take over?"

She turned and found him standing there in just his boxers. She quickly shucked her clothing, until she was standing in front of him, wearing nothing.

His eyebrows shot up. "Some bruising," he noted, gently touching her ribs.

She stopped, looked at him, and nodded. "That's right. I had all this bruising show up."

"Yes, in the other realm, you had all this bruising show up. But, in this one, not so much. More of it was lividity from lying on your side."

She winced at that term. "It would have been lividity, if I had actually died."

"Exactly," he agreed.

"Talk about a mind bender."

"I know, and we'll probably still be bringing up things

years from now, trying to find an explanation for them."

"Will we find one for everything?" she asked.

"Not likely," he murmured, as he stepped up and wrapped his arms around her. "Some things are just mysteries that need to stay mysteries."

"Like the power my mother wielded?"

"Yes, though I don't know if you realize your mother worked as a prostitute, forced to the streets because she didn't have enough money to keep you in food and diapers. That type of work was something she could do, but she became very twisted, angry, hateful. She ended up with some very difficult clients—johns, if you will—who hurt her badly. That hurt and pain is what sent her on this pathway."

"Do we think she killed everybody in that necklace?"

"I think she came upon a killer who was murdering other friends of hers, other prostitutes, and during the process of him trying to kill her," he guessed cautiously, "I think she killed him instead. At that point she snapped, but I don't know any of that for sure."

She nodded thoughtfully. "I guess that is a part of the mystery that we may never know."

"Unfortunately, yes," he stated, "and sometimes we just have to be okay with that."

She looped her arms around him, kissed him gently, and said, "As long as you're there to help me get through some of this when it gets rough, I'm totally okay with it."

"I wasn't planning on going anywhere."

"Except that apparently your job takes you all over the place." And then she frowned. "Or was that all made up too?"

"No, it wasn't made up," he stated. "I do travel all around, and you can come with me, or you can stay wherever it is that we choose to call home."

"And there really is an *us*, right? I'm not just in this all alone?" She hated the weakness in her voice and the insecurity it revealed.

He pulled her tight and whispered, "No, this is definitely an *us*. Open your mind, and you can see for yourself whether it is for real."

She crinkled her brows, then heard a little knock on a mental door. Instinctively she opened it, and there he was, standing without clothes, without physical form, but only in energy. She gasped in joy and kissed him in both forms. "It really is real, isn't it?"

"It really is," he murmured. "Now remember that bed rest thing."

"Oh, I do." She giggled. "Can we really do it in this form too?"

"Let's find out," he whispered. As he lowered his head and kissed Jewel, he swung her up in his arms, carried her over to the very physical bed and proceeded to make love to her until she was crying out in joy.

Just as he was ready to take the last plunge, he whispered, "Link."

She opened the door and whispered, "I'm already here."
"So am I."

As he plunged one more time deep into the soft folds of her body, he felt his world coalesce around him. It didn't explode, but instead it united all the pieces of her that he had experienced as shattered, still pulling herself together again into one semblance of wholeness, and then, surrounded with his own energy, she whispered, "I love you."

This concludes Book 22 of Psychic Visions: String of Tears.

Read a sneak peek from Inked Forever: Psychic Visions, Book 23

Inked Forever: Psychic Visions (Book #23)

Tasmin's business isn't for everyone. Yet she recognizes the value she offers for grieving families. Still, the subject isn't something most people are willing to talk about. However, over time, her business has grown through word of mouth—much to the horror of her family.

Until a detective walks in, inquiring about a piece that had been stolen overnight. This is the first inkling she has that someone is out to destroy her business. Unfortunately it won't be the last …

Detective Hanson MacGyver isn't sure what to make of Tasmin, yet he understands the need for licensed morticians. However, how she got into the process of preserving tattoos for grieving family and friends is something he has never seen before and isn't comfortable with. Live and let live works for him as a motto, but, when her works in progress start showing up in public locations and not in a good way, he knows they have someone who hates what she is doing … or hates the owners of the tattoos.

Something's *off* about the whole mess. And that's just on the surface. When both Tasmin and Hanson dig deeper, a whole lot more is going on underneath. And none of it is normal or nice …

TASMIN OPENED UP the shop door, twisting the sign to Open. Then she propped the door wide open to let out some of the formaldehyde fumes, turned on the lights, and headed to the back room, where she put on the coffeepot. With that dripping she rinsed a cup and waited for the pot to fill before she filled her cup. When she turned back again, a man, a huge presence, filled the room. Yet she felt no fear.

He stared at her and asked, "Tasmin Rhone?"

"Yes, that's me." She walked toward him with a cup in her hand. "What can I do for you?"

"I understand you run a very unique business."

She snorted at that. "Yeah, something I fell into."

He hesitated and then asked, "I don't suppose you'd care to tell me how?"

"No, not really. What are you, a reporter?" Such disgust filled her voice that she immediately tried to change her tone. "Sorry, I didn't mean it quite that way."

"I'm not a reporter. I'm a cop."

At that, she froze, looked up at him, and frowned. "I have a business license, and everything is in order. Even my taxes are paid."

He held up a hand. "That's not why I'm here."

"*Sure,*" she quipped. "In my experience, cops don't usually come by for any good reasons."

He relaxed slightly. "That may be, but I'm not trying to make your life more difficult. However, I do have a few questions for you."

"Yeah, about what?"

He hesitated and then added, "One of the pieces that you're preserving."

She groaned. "Look. A licensed doctor did the cuttings. I have all the paperwork, including the legal stuff," she stated. "Man, I have more paperwork than you can shake a stick at," she declared, her tone somewhere between mildly irritated and pissed. "It's all legal, I assure you. Who is it you're talking about?" She looked around. "I have quite a few cuttings here. As I told you, I keep a lawyer on tap to help me with this."

"I get that," he replied, then looked at one of the framed pieces. "That's your uncle, isn't it?"

"I hate the way you say that," she admitted. "That is a piece of my uncle's artwork, yes," she stated cautiously.

"Right." The cop turned and looked at a couple others on the wall. "Have you ever had any bad press over this?"

"Lots," she answered succinctly. "People don't want to see tattoo preservation as an art form."

"It is very personal," he noted, looking at her, "and it crosses all kinds of boundaries that make people uneasy."

"Yes, I get that, but what does that have to do with you?" He hesitated. She crossed her arms, then took a sip of her coffee, her eyes watchful.

"Has anybody tried to stop you from doing this?"

She shrugged. "Not really. Most people don't know all the details, except for those interested in having their ink preserved."

He nodded. "So there have been no attacks on your shop or anything like that?"

"No. Why?" she asked curiously. She looked around and frowned. "I mean, everything seemed normal when I opened this morning, but I haven't really had a chance to get started. This is my first cup of coffee since I was a little late coming in, but now you've got me worried."

"Could you take a look around, please?"

She stared at him for a moment, then slowly nodded. "I gather you won't tell me anything until we get that far."

"No, it would be nice if I could clear something up first."

She put down her coffee cup and glared at him but walked around, checking to make sure everything was as it should be. Then she headed to the backroom, to her workshop.

When she got into the workshop, she flicked on all the lights, looked around, and said, "It looks okay in here."

"What about artwork?" he asked.

"I've got four pieces in progress right now," she stated, as she turned to look at the pieces she had saved.

"I've got two that are here." She pointed them out. "Then I've got another one in the drying room."

She walked into the drying room, frowned, and look back at him. "That one's missing."

"Missing?"

"Yes," she cried out as the realization really hit her. "Oh my God, it's missing-missing." She frantically went through the shop. Then she turned slowly, looked at him and asked, "You knew it wouldn't be here, didn't you?"

He hesitated.

"Stop," she cried out. "I don't know what's going on, and I don't know what this has to do with you. I don't know anything about it, but I'm missing a piece that matters a lot to somebody, and I will wind up in a shitstorm if I don't find it."

"I think I can help you with finding it," he said, "but it might have been damaged."

She stared at him, then he pulled out his phone and showed her an image of a beautiful tattoo.

She nodded. "Yes, that's it," she cried out in relief. Then she looked at him in shock. "What do you mean, damaged? How did you get it?"

"It was found in one of the fountains downtown," he explained, "stretched out and nailed into the bottom of the fountain."

She stared across the room, her bottom lip trembling, her gut twisting at the image. Ever-so-slowly afraid she'd break and rage at him, she whispered, "What?"

He nodded slowly. "Somebody decided that preserving the art was the right thing to do, but private it was not," he noted, "and he put it out for public display. Do you want to tell me who this artwork belongs to?"

She swallowed hard. "A model, a beautiful model who ended up with cancer and died twelve days ago. I got the legalities taken care of on behalf of her family, with all the paperwork, and the surgeon cut the tattoo off her back, and it was sent to me to preserve for her family."

He nodded. "So, do you have any explanation as to how it went from your shop to a fountain where this model's tattoo is now on display for the rest of the world to see?"

Find Book 23 here!

To find out more visit Dale Mayer's website.

https://geni.us/DMInkedUniversal

Simon Says... Hide: Kate Morgan (Book #1)

Welcome to a new thriller series from *USA Today* Best-Selling Author Dale Mayer. Set in Vancouver, BC, the team of Detective Kate Morgan and Simon St. Laurant, an unwilling psychic, marries all the elements of Dale's work that you've come to love, plus so much more.

Detective Kate Morgan, newly promoted to the Vancouver PD Homicide Department, stands for the victims in her world. She was once a victim herself, just as her mother had been a victim, and then her brother—an unsolved missing child's case—was yet another victim. She can't stand those who take advantage of others, and the worst ones are those who prey on the hopes of desperate people to line their own pockets.

So, when she finds a connection between more than a half-dozen cold cases to a current case, where a child's life hangs in the balance, Kate would make a deal with the devil himself to find the culprit and to save the child.

Simon St. Laurant's grandmother had the Sight and had warned him that, once he used it, he could never walk away. Until now, her caution had made it easy to avoid that first step. But, when nightmares of his own past are triggered, Simon can't stand back and watch child after child be abused. Not without offering his help to those chasing the monsters.

Even if it means dealing with the cranky and critical Detective Kate Morgan …

Find Simon Says… Hide here!
To find out more visit Dale Mayer's website.
https://geni.us/DMSSHideUniversal

Author's Note

Thank you for reading String of Tears: Psychic Visions, Book 22! If you enjoyed the book, please take a moment and leave a short review.

Dear reader,

I love to hear from readers, and you can contact me at my website: www.dalemayer.com or at my Facebook author page. To be informed of new releases and special offers, sign up for my newsletter or follow me on BookBub. And if you are interested in joining Dale Mayer's Reader Group, here is the Facebook sign up page.
http://geni.us/DaleMayerFBGroup

Cheers,
Dale Mayer

About the Author

Dale Mayer is a *USA Today* best-selling author, best known for her SEALs military romances, her Psychic Visions series, and her Lovely Lethal Garden cozy series. Her contemporary romances are raw and full of passion and emotion (Broken But … Mending, Hathaway House series). Her thrillers will keep you guessing (Kate Morgan, By Death series), and her romantic comedies will keep you giggling (*It's a Dog's Life*, a stand-alone novella; and the Broken Protocols series, starring Charming Marvin, the cat).

Dale honors the stories that come to her—and some of them are crazy, break all the rules and cross multiple genres!

To go with her fiction, she also writes nonfiction in many different fields, with books available on résumé writing, companion gardening, and the US mortgage system. All her books are available in print and ebook format.

Connect with Dale Mayer Online

Dale's Website – www.dalemayer.com
Twitter – @DaleMayer
Facebook Page – geni.us/DaleMayerFBFanPage
Facebook Group – geni.us/DaleMayerFBGroup
BookBub – geni.us/DaleMayerBookbub
Instagram – geni.us/DaleMayerInstagram
Goodreads – geni.us/DaleMayerGoodreads
Newsletter – geni.us/DaleNews

Also by Dale Mayer

Published Adult Books:

Shadow Recon
Magnus, Book 1

Bullard's Battle
Ryland's Reach, Book 1
Cain's Cross, Book 2
Eton's Escape, Book 3
Garret's Gambit, Book 4
Kano's Keep, Book 5
Fallon's Flaw, Book 6
Quinn's Quest, Book 7
Bullard's Beauty, Book 8
Bullard's Best, Book 9
Bullard's Battle, Books 1–2
Bullard's Battle, Books 3–4
Bullard's Battle, Books 5–6
Bullard's Battle, Books 7–8

Terkel's Team
Damon's Deal, Book 1
Wade's War, Book 2
Gage's Goal, Book 3

Calum's Contact, Book 4

Rick's Road, Book 5

Scott's Summit, Book 6

Brody's Beast, Book 7

Terkel's Twist, Book 8

Terkel's Triumph, Book 9

Terkel's Guardian

Radar, Book 1

Kate Morgan

Simon Says… Hide, Book 1

Simon Says… Jump, Book 2

Simon Says… Ride, Book 3

Simon Says… Scream, Book 4

Simon Says… Run, Book 5

Simon Says… Walk, Book 6

Hathaway House

Aaron, Book 1

Brock, Book 2

Cole, Book 3

Denton, Book 4

Elliot, Book 5

Finn, Book 6

Gregory, Book 7

Heath, Book 8

Iain, Book 9

Jaden, Book 10

Keith, Book 11

Lance, Book 12

Melissa, Book 13

Nash, Book 14

Owen, Book 15

Percy, Book 16

Quinton, Book 17

Ryatt, Book 18

Spencer, Book 19

Hathaway House, Books 1–3

Hathaway House, Books 4–6

Hathaway House, Books 7–9

The K9 Files

Ethan, Book 1

Pierce, Book 2

Zane, Book 3

Blaze, Book 4

Lucas, Book 5

Parker, Book 6

Carter, Book 7

Weston, Book 8

Greyson, Book 9

Rowan, Book 10

Caleb, Book 11

Kurt, Book 12

Tucker, Book 13

Harley, Book 14

Kyron, Book 15

Jenner, Book 16

Rhys, Book 17

Landon, Book 18

Harper, Book 19

The K9 Files, Books 1–2

The K9 Files, Books 3–4

The K9 Files, Books 5–6

The K9 Files, Books 7–8

The K9 Files, Books 9–10

The K9 Files, Books 11–12

Lovely Lethal Gardens

Arsenic in the Azaleas, Book 1

Bones in the Begonias, Book 2

Corpse in the Carnations, Book 3

Daggers in the Dahlias, Book 4

Evidence in the Echinacea, Book 5

Footprints in the Ferns, Book 6

Gun in the Gardenias, Book 7

Handcuffs in the Heather, Book 8

Ice Pick in the Ivy, Book 9

Jewels in the Juniper, Book 10

Killer in the Kiwis, Book 11

Lifeless in the Lilies, Book 12

Murder in the Marigolds, Book 13

Nabbed in the Nasturtiums, Book 14

Offed in the Orchids, Book 15

Poison in the Pansies, Book 16

Quarry in the Quince, Book 17

Revenge in the Roses, Book 18

Silenced in the Sunflowers, Book 19

Toes in the Tulips, Book 20

Lovely Lethal Gardens, Books 1–2

Lovely Lethal Gardens, Books 3–4

Lovely Lethal Gardens, Books 5–6

Lovely Lethal Gardens, Books 7–8

Lovely Lethal Gardens, Books 9–10

Psychic Vision Series

Tuesday's Child

Hide 'n Go Seek

Maddy's Floor

Garden of Sorrow

Knock Knock…

Rare Find

Eyes to the Soul

Now You See Her

Shattered

Into the Abyss

Seeds of Malice

Eye of the Falcon

Itsy-Bitsy Spider

Unmasked

Deep Beneath

From the Ashes

Stroke of Death

Ice Maiden

Snap, Crackle…

What If…

Talking Bones

String of Tears

Inked Forever

Psychic Visions Books 1–3

Psychic Visions Books 4–6

Psychic Visions Books 7–9

By Death Series

Touched by Death

Haunted by Death

Chilled by Death

By Death Books 1–3

Broken Protocols – Romantic Comedy Series

Cat's Meow

Cat's Pajamas

Cat's Cradle

Cat's Claus

Broken Protocols 1-4

Broken and… Mending

Skin

Scars

Scales (of Justice)

Broken but… Mending 1-3

Glory

Genesis

Tori

Celeste

Glory Trilogy

Biker Blues

Morgan: Biker Blues, Volume 1

Cash: Biker Blues, Volume 2

SEALs of Honor

Mason: SEALs of Honor, Book 1

Hawk: SEALs of Honor, Book 2

Dane: SEALs of Honor, Book 3

Swede: SEALs of Honor, Book 4

Shadow: SEALs of Honor, Book 5

Cooper: SEALs of Honor, Book 6

Markus: SEALs of Honor, Book 7

Evan: SEALs of Honor, Book 8

Mason's Wish: SEALs of Honor, Book 9

Chase: SEALs of Honor, Book 10

Brett: SEALs of Honor, Book 11

Devlin: SEALs of Honor, Book 12

Easton: SEALs of Honor, Book 13

Ryder: SEALs of Honor, Book 14

Macklin: SEALs of Honor, Book 15

Corey: SEALs of Honor, Book 16

Warrick: SEALs of Honor, Book 17

Tanner: SEALs of Honor, Book 18

Jackson: SEALs of Honor, Book 19

Kanen: SEALs of Honor, Book 20

Nelson: SEALs of Honor, Book 21

Heroes for Hire

SEALs of Steel

Badger: SEALs of Steel, Book 1

Erick: SEALs of Steel, Book 2

Cade: SEALs of Steel, Book 3

Talon: SEALs of Steel, Book 4

Laszlo: SEALs of Steel, Book 5

Geir: SEALs of Steel, Book 6

Jager: SEALs of Steel, Book 7

The Final Reveal: SEALs of Steel, Book 8

SEALs of Steel, Books 1–4

SEALs of Steel, Books 5–8

SEALs of Steel, Books 1–8

The Mavericks

Kerrick, Book 1

Griffin, Book 2

Jax, Book 3

Beau, Book 4

Asher, Book 5

Ryker, Book 6

Miles, Book 7

Nico, Book 8

Keane, Book 9

Lennox, Book 10

Gavin, Book 11

Shane, Book 12

Diesel, Book 13

Jerricho, Book 14

Killian, Book 15

Hatch, Book 16

Corbin, Book 17

Aiden, Book 18

The Mavericks, Books 1–2

The Mavericks, Books 3–4

The Mavericks, Books 5–6

The Mavericks, Books 7–8

The Mavericks, Books 9–10

The Mavericks, Books 11–12

Standalone Novellas

It's a Dog's Life

Riana's Revenge

Second Chances

Published Young Adult Books:

Family Blood Ties Series

Vampire in Denial

Vampire in Distress

Vampire in Design

Vampire in Deceit

Vampire in Defiance

Vampire in Conflict

Vampire in Chaos

Vampire in Crisis

Vampire in Control

Vampire in Charge

Family Blood Ties Set 1–3

Family Blood Ties Set 1–5

Family Blood Ties Set 4–6

Family Blood Ties Set 7–9

Sian's Solution, A Family Blood Ties Series Prequel
Novelette

Design series

Dangerous Designs

Deadly Designs

Darkest Designs

Design Series Trilogy

Standalone

In Cassie's Corner

Gem Stone (a Gemma Stone Mystery)

Time Thieves

Published Non-Fiction Books:

Career Essentials

Career Essentials: The Résumé

Career Essentials: The Cover Letter

Career Essentials: The Interview

Career Essentials: 3 in 1